TO FACE A SAVAGE WINTER

SAVAGE LAND
BOOK 2

JOHN LEGG

WOLFPACK
PUBLISHING
— EST 2013 —

To Face a Savage Winter
Paperback Edition
Copyright © 2023 John Legg

Wolfpack Publishing
9850 S. Maryland Parkway, Suite A-5 #323
Las Vegas, Nevada 89183

wolfpackpublishing.com

Paperback ISBN 978-1-63977-445-6
eBook ISBN 978-1-63977-444-9

TO FACE A SAVAGE WINTER

ONE

"IT'S OVER NOW, HAWWY," Black Moon Woman said.

Hawley Cooper almost smiled. Even after more than half a year together, she still managed to mangle his name. He sighed inwardly. He did the same with her name when he spoke it in Shoshoni. "I ain't so sure."

"There is no more. That evil man is dead. Damn good. No one will miss him."

Cooper said nothing. They had come back to their lodge after Cooper had killed Josiah Weeks and then gathered up what few things the old reprobate had left behind—at least the plunder Cooper wasn't afraid to touch. But he was still morose.

"Rendezvous should be fun. You wanted to..."

She stopped when someone called for entrance. "You mind lettin' a fellow mountaineer visit your lodge?" a voice said from outside.

Cooper looked at Black Moon Woman and nodded. She slipped into the shadows at the rear of the tipi, a pistol in her hand. Cooper rose and kept his hand on one of his own pistols. He was certain old Josiah Weeks, being the ill-tempered degenerate he had been, didn't have any friends here, but he could not be totally sure. It was better, he figured, to be cautious—and prepared. "Come on ahead," he called out.

A broad-shouldered man entered through the flap and stopped just inside, letting his eyes adjust to the gloom. Then he looked around. His teeth gleamed in the firelight when he smiled. "I expect she knows how to use that piece."

"She does," Cooper responded.

The man held out a hand for a moment, indicating he was not going to do anything that would make Cooper and Black Moon nervous. Slowly he slid the clips holding his two pistols off his belt and set them down to the side. They were followed by his knife and tomahawk. "Name's Elson Brooks," he said, holding out a hand.

"Hawley Cooper." They shook. "C'mon then, sit," Cooper said jovially.

The man took a seat across the fire from Cooper.

"Bring some food for our guest, woman," Cooper ordered.

Black Moon set the pistol down and came to the fire. She was not upset at the command. It was a woman's place to serve guests. Besides, a man had to feel important in his own lodge, not belittled in front of visitors. And she knew that was why Cooper had made it a command instead of a request.

Black Moon got a wood bowl and filled it with seasoned broth in which chunks of buffalo meat bobbed. Brooks slurped some down, nodding. He looked up. "You speak English, ma'am?" he asked.

"Damn good."

Brooks broke into a laugh. "Reckon you do." He gulped some more meat and broth down. "This here stew shines with this ol' chil'. Plumb shines."

Black Moon Woman beamed, though she tried to hide it. Cooper did the same. The woman poured two cups of coffee. She handed one to her husband and set the other in front of their visitor.

Brooks nodded, still shoveling food into his face. Finally he set the empty bowl down and wiped a hand across his mouth to remove the residue. He picked up the coffee and sipped.

"Sorry, we got nothin' to rest your back against," Cooper apologized. "Something like that ain't something for packin' along to rendezvous."

"That's a fact, Mr. Cooper. Wouldn't expect anything else. 'Twould be foolish to drag such things along at such a time." He pulled his small clay pipe out from the leather heart around his neck. "Mind?"

"Nope. Sounds like a right good idea." Black Moon handed him his own, which looked exactly like Brooks's.

Brooks tore a bit off a twist of tobacco and stuffed it into the pipe's bowl. Then he tossed the twist to Cooper. "Small payment for the fine meal."

Cooper nodded and within moments had filled the pipe and got it going. He blew out some smoke. "Well, Mr. Brooks," he said, "what brings you to this ol' chil's lodge? It can't be for Black Moon's cookin', as shinin' as it might be."

"Ye'd be right about that, ol' hoss." He paused,

puffing a bit. "I ain't ever saw ye before 'til just the other day."

"Never been here before."

"Reckoned. But I heard what ye done in that wee fracas with Bug's Boys. You sure made those red devils come now or I wouldn't say so. Ye for certain shined there, hoss. Plumb shined."

Pleasure rushed through Cooper, but he did not show it.

"Then that fandango ye had with that festerin' ol' reprobate Weeks, now that was some doins, boy. Damn if it weren't. Waugh! Son of a bitch got better'n he deserved, I'm sayin'."

Cooper smiled just a bit. "Now, I don't mean to be rude, Mr. Brooks, but..."

"Elson."

Cooper nodded. "Like I was sayin', Elson, I don't mean to be rude, and like most boys out here, I enjoy havin' my bravery and such extolled by the likes of an old hand in the mountains like you, but I reckon you need to come to the point of why you're here before rendezvous is over."

Brooks laughed. "Reckon I should. Like many of the boys, I like to ease into such things. But I've taken up a heap of your time and your hospitality, so I'll get to it." He absentmindedly scratched the stubble on one cheek. "Ye belong to any company, Mr. Cooper?"

"Nope," Cooper responded with a shake of the head. "I aim to be a free trapper. Don't think I could be beholden to no one else. Not after bein' saddled with that mean-tempered bastard Weeks."

"Makes god-awful good sense to me, boy. Me and

my *compañeros're* free trappers ourselves. Like ye, we ain't beholden to nobody."

"How many of you are there?"

"Eight, countin' me."

"Sounds like you got a company, Elson."

"Naw, sir. Just a bunch of free trappers. We band together for protection and to share the work. Ye ever been trappin' up in Blackfoot country?"

"Can't say as I have."

"As ye saw the other day, those are the meanest, nastiest bastards God ever put on this here earth. Live for war. Hell, they live for raisin' hair on us mountain boys." He grinned a little. "Reckon we feel about the same of them, leastways when it comes to raisin' hair. We only pay back in kind."

"Reckon I'll just avoid Blackfoot country."

"That's where the best trappin' is, boy. Streams just burstin' with beaver. So many ye cain't help but catch 'em just by wavin' your traps near the water. They'll climb onto the bank lookin' to jump right in 'em."

"If I didn't know you to be an honorable man, I'd say you were stretchin' the truth some."

"Well," Brooks said with a grin, "mayhap just the tiniest bit."

"So what's all this have to do with me?"

"We'd sure like to have ye join our little group, Mr. Cooper."

"Sounds like you want me to be in your debt, you and your friends."

"Naw, sir. Ain't like that a'tall. Like I said, we ain't a company, just a band of free trappers join together for protection and to share the chores. What we each trap is our own. We sell our plews to whosoever we choose.

What you do with the cash is your own account. Be wise to get supplies for the fall hunt." He laughed. "But most of us take what we got after that and have us one hell of a spree. Some of the boys spend heaps of specie on foofaraw for the ladies."

"Sounds like an interestin' proposal, Elson. I ain't sure, though, that I'd be on my own hook with you boys. Still uncertain as to whether I'd be in your debt."

"Hell, Hawley, we're free trappers. Found out a couple years ago it ain't a good idea to be out trappin' alone with warlike damn Injins roamin' all over the mountains. Not to say that we don't ever deal with each other. That'd be plumb foolish. But none of us has any real supplies to sell, so ye won't get in debt to anyone unless it's to an individual. Ain't happened but once, and Two-Faces paid back what he owed soon as he sold his plews."

Cooper was certain he was about to be told some fanciful tale that he would find to be a lie when he went out into the wilds with them—should he choose to do so.

"We lend a hand doin' whatever needs doin'. Help each other 'round camp, tendin' to the horses and such. Gather up firewood and such. Most of the boys have women along, and they take care of most of the things need doin'. And care for the plews of course. And the cookin'. Like they're supposed to do."

Cooper sat, mulling it over. It sounded good. He had heard trapping in Blackfoot country was the best. It was also the most dangerous. He was certain he wouldn't be going up that way, so it seemed to him that he would not need much protecting.

"Why me?" he suddenly asked. "Reckon there's lots of boys here'd take a shine to ridin' with you."

"A few maybe. Most is either bound to some company or they're freemen like us and either go it alone or hunt in small groups, like us," Brooks allowed. "We saw what ye can do, and it's always a shinin' thing to have such a man ride with us. All the boys are tough ol' critters, used to the ways of the mountains. And the Injins."

Cooper gave it some more thought. And he glanced surreptitiously at Black Moon. She shook her head ever so little, but he caught it. "I reckon not, Mr. Brooks...um, Elson. I ain't been in the mountains long, and the time I have, have been starvin' times. But I found me good people in Cheyenne Killer's band, and with Black Moon. I also figure I need to test myself in a different way, trappin', maybe tradin' some. And I reckon I need to do it on my own hook."

"Well, this ol' chil' thinks that's damn foolish. Yep, plumb foolish. But if that's where your stick floats, then that's the way it'll be."

Brooks rose, as did Cooper. They shook hands. The older trapper turned to look at Black Moon. "I'm obliged for that fine meal, ma'am. Best eatin' this ol' chil's had since George Washington was a pup." He grinned at the confusion that crossed her face. He turned back to Cooper.

"I wish ye well, ol' hoss, in whatever endeavors you try your hand at."

Cooper nodded.

"Just watch your hair if you ever get up in Blackfoot land. 'Course, I never said, but those red devils range far and wide. Never can tell where they'll show up. Like here yesterday."

"I'll do so." He started to reconsider, then decided he had made the right decision.

Brooks began gathering up his weapons and storing them in their proper positions about his body. Then he turned and grinned. "Course, just 'cause ye don't plan to ride with us don't mean ye can't join us in our spree. Share a mouthful or two of awardenty or lightnin'. We'll show you how real mountaineers fandango. Waugh!" Laughing, he pushed through the tipi flap.

Cooper turned to face Black Moon. He shook his head in wonder.

"Damn strange that fella," the woman said. "Damn strange."

Both laughed.

TWO

RENDEZVOUS WAS a revel like Cooper had never seen—fights, food, drunkenness, horse races, 'hawk and knife throwing, shooting, gambling, and whoring. He did not take part in the last, but he did get seriously drunk for the first time. Black Moon found him staggering around, bellowing what he thought was a song but she heard as a cat wailing, and dragged him back to their lodge. He refused to get up in the morning, preferring to lie there in his robes and moan when he wasn't vomiting the vileness from his system.

Black Moon said nothing, though once Cooper recovered from his hangover, he was aware that she was not pleased with him. He was contrite, and she eventually forgave him, though at a cost to him of more than twenty dollars in foofaraw, which he gladly paid.

But too soon for Cooper—and too long for Black Moon— the parties began drifting away from the rendezvous site at Bear Lake. As Cooper and Black Moon were preparing to leave, Elson Brooks pulled his horse to a stop nearby.

"You're still welcome to join us, hoss," he said.

"Reckon not, but thanks all the same."

Brooks nodded and followed by his seven companions, their women, and their pack animals, rode out. Cooper and Black Moon did the same a few minutes later. Despite figuring that going west from the south end of the lake where the rendezvous had been held was the best way to start on their way to where they were going, based on information Cooper had gotten, Cooper decided to travel with Cheyenne Killer's band north up the east side of Bear Lake. Black Moon wanted to spend as much time as she could with her best friend, Pony Woman. Cooper didn't mind, as he got to spend more time with his best friend, a Shoshoni of about the same age named Cuts Throat.

Cooper chafed at the slowness of the travel, but Black Moon kept him from getting too upset. "There's no trappin' now, anyway, Hawwy," she said one night as they lay on their sleeping robes, it being too hot to put up a lodge. "We're safe with the people."

"Hell, ain't no enemies in these parts anyway," Cooper grumbled.

"Hush," she said, placing a finger gently on his lips. "We leave them soon. Damn right." She shifted until she was on her side, head resting in her hand. She stroked his stubbled cheek, then moved her hand lower, until she reached the buttons on the front of his trousers.

He grabbed her wrist, stopping her. "No, Moon. Not with all these people around," he said, using the words he had done every night since they had left rendezvous.

"You don't want me no more," she accused, rolling

onto her back. "You don't treat me like your woman in long time."

"I want you, but it ain't right we do something like that out in the open like this."

"No one will notice."

"But..."

"If you don't want me, I go. I'll come back when you want me. Maybe." She rose and began to walk away but didn't get far.

"Get back here, woman," Cooper ordered, though not very forcefully.

Black Moon turned and stood, arms akimbo. She said nothing.

"I said get back here, woman." His voice was stronger, with less of a pleading note and more of a desirous one.

"You want?" Black Moon asked, smiling a little in victory.

Cooper noticed. "Well, maybe, maybe not. Could be I'll just find me another woman to share my robes. One more willin' to treat her man like her husband."

The smile did not leave Black Moon's face. "I try to treat you like husband, but you don't act like damn husband. You act like damn mouse, afraid people might think you are not big man when they hear us do what husband and wife do."

Cooper felt heat rising, both from a sudden burst of lust and from a growing anger that was based at least in part on the fact that she was right, which galled him. But he was not willing to plead. Not yet anyway. "You best get back over here right this damn minute."

"You treat me like wife?"

It was his turn to grin a little, the anger subsiding.

"I'll cogitate on it. There's always Red Sky to consider. She'd make a fine wife, I'm thinkin'. She won't give her man troubles like you do."

It was Black Moon's turn to feel the anger rise. She wanted him, and the thought of him being with another woman enraged her. She wanted to call his bluff but was afraid that he would let her go. Still, she did not want to give in.

"Come here, woman," Cooper said softly. It was a plea and a command at the same time. He smiled and began sliding his trousers off. His desire was evident.

Black Moon grinned. She quickly slipped out of her buckskin dress and lay down beside him. Within minutes, Cooper no longer cared who heard them.

NEAR THE NORTHERN end of Bear Lake, Cooper and Black Moon said their farewells to Cheyenne Killer and his band. The Shoshonis turned east. They would move north and east through the mountains, up toward the Snake River, then east across a great pass toward their home in the Wind River Mountains.

Cooper and Black Moon turned west, making their way slowly though mountain passes, meadows, barren valleys, and more, hoping to find a broad creek that led to the Snake River near a pair of falls. He wasn't sure where he was going, but he had heard the area was a good one for trapping. There were plenty of beaver and the Indians were friendly enough, he had been told. Free of the ponderous band of men, women, and children, the pair made good time. It was still too warm for the beaver to have their winter coats, so Cooper didn't spend much time in trapping. He stopped a day or two here and there to set his traps. But mostly for the first couple of weeks, he hunted, and they stopped every couple of days to make jerky and pemmican to tide them over the winter.

By late August as he figured it, they reached the place he had been seeking along the Snake River, then decided to backtrack a day or so, thinking the smaller streams would be better for trapping. Though the elevation was not that high, the weather was beginning to turn already, with hints of winter in the night air. Cooper figured it was time to start setting his traps in the creek and the smaller ones that fed into it. At first, his take was all right. He pulled some animals, though not as many as he had expected, and this early the fur was not as plush as it would be soon. But he had some plews, and that was good enough for now. His take soon dwindled, though, which worried him considerably.

"I don't know what's wrong, Moon," he said one day after giving her the one pelt he had garnered from his traps that day. "I don't reckon I'm the best trapper in the mountains maybe, but I can't believe I'm that bad a one either."

"You make beaver come soon, Hawwy." Black Moon sounded positive. "Damn right."

"Maybe. But it just don't seem right that pickins are so slim." He plopped down and sat quietly, thinking. Suddenly he said, "I think I've been made a fool of. Again."

"How?"

"I think some fellers named Bledsoe and his partner, Manning, told me there was plenty of beaver here knowing there wasn't. Then they could go to where the pickins are better. We best be movin' on, find us a better place to set my traps."

"Where we go?"

Cooper shrugged. "Ain't sure. The Snake's only a day or so, of course. I ain't sure trapping the big river'll be any better, but I'll try it if I see beaver sign. If not, I'll decide where to go then. Can you be ready to leave day after tomorrow?"

Seeing how worried he was, Black Moon said, "We leave tomorrow. No reason to stay longer."

They pushed slowly up Rock Creek until they came to the Snake. He prowled around for a day or so but found little beaver sign nearby. Shaking his head in frustration one night as they sat at their fire after a supper of fresh elk, he said, "I ain't sure which way to go now, Moon."

"My people say Hudson Bay Company controls land west along the Snake. No damned good to go that way, maybe. Huntin' would not be good."

Cooper thought that over. "Maybe that's why pickins are so slim hereabout. Maybe those boys've been through here and plucked the area clean." He sighed. "Well, then, looks like we head east."

They followed the course of the Snake eastward as much as they could. But there were plenty of times, and for long distances, they had to move well away from the river as cliffs and rugged land formed the banks of the river. They moved slowly, with Cooper setting his traps in whatever creek on which they found beaver sign. But the pickings remained slim. A month later, they were crossing the Blackfoot River.

At their camp that night, Black Moon said, "I been here before. Many years ago, visiting others of my people. Snake River goes north here for a spell, some miles away it makes a big damn turn to southeast. We go east and a little north, over Caribou Mountains, meet up with river soon. Save travelin'."

"You sure, Moon?"

"Yes. Maybe we find many damn beaver there. If not, we go farther east to big mountains and valley. Find many beaver there. Damn sure."

"Think there will be?"

"Damn right. Plenty damn beaver."

Cooper grinned. Even after all their time together, he could not stamp out her profane use of the English language, learned from trappers and traders who had visited her village. "If that's where your stick floats, woman, then so does mine." He grinned. "Now, come here." He reached out for her, and she willingly slid into his embrace.

———

THE TRAVELING WAS FAIRLY easy for the two, being hardened to moving through such country. They were fortunate in that they encountered few problems —a near run-in with a grizzly sow and her cubs, an early snowstorm, two thunderous rainstorms and a couple days' stretch without water.

They stopped for a few days at every stream and creek they came across, and Cooper set his traps. The take was better here, more plentiful though not overly so. Nor were they yet not prime, but good.

"Reckon you were right about comin' this way, Moon," Cooper said, as he handed Black Moon a bloody beaver pelt.

"I told you so," she said with a grin. "Damn certain I did."

"Where away now?"

"Will reach Snake again soon. Follow it south to find place to cross. Head through big valley. Cross another river. Smaller. Head into a pass that goes northeast. Come to another valley, then southeast to another pass. Come out on nice plain. Should be many buffler, elk. Plenty of beaver too. Damn good. We take time goin' that way, trappin' will be good. Then go northeast maybe three, four days, turn southeast through another pass. Keep goin' southeast." She hesitated. "Toward Wind River."

"Shoshoni country? Your father's village?"

"Yes." It was said softly.

Cooper thought that over. "Many beaver streams along the way?"

"Like I say, many. Damn so."

"Well, I reckon that seems a good place to head. I can catch me a plenty of beaver—unless you're fibbin' to me." He grinned crookedly.

"I don't lie."

Cooper grinned. "Reckon we'll do that then. Bring us to my father's village. We can winter there, and head out to new trappin' grounds nearby when spring comes. Won't be far from rendezvous either."

THREE

THE SNOWSTORM CAUGHT them somewhere in the flats of Swan Valley a couple hours after they crossed the Snake River. There was no trail, just a wide swath of open ground stretching in all directions. Cooper had known it was coming, but he knew they had nowhere to go for protection. He could not risk recrossing the river even though he was not at all certain how much farther they had to go before reaching any kind of shelter. So they could do nothing but push ahead as best they could as the wind howled, and snow dropped down on them in thick, heavy, gust-blown sheets.

The storm's violent wind, hurtling with a roar from the north, shoved them sideways, making their progress difficult at best.

The wind whipped the snow hard enough that it did not pile up much, but the gusts and the snow blowing across their faces slowed their travel all the more. The fur- and supply-laden mules bucked and brayed their discomfort and annoyance. Black Moon strained to keep control of the string of mules.

Cooper looked behind him and saw Black Moon's struggle. "Damn!" he spat into the gale. "Let 'em go!" he bellowed.

The woman hesitated.

"Do it!"

Black Moon dropped the rope and the animals disappeared into the white tempest.

"You all right, Moon?" he shouted into the raging tempest.

Freed of the resisting mules, Black Moon nodded, though unhappily. The means of their wealth and their survival had just vanished into the depths of the snow.

Still they plowed on, unable to do anything else. Black Moon moved up to ride beside Cooper. The horses began to strain as the wind pounded them, making it demanding to move forward. Cooper was glad that the wind kept the snow from piling up too much. He hoped they would find some shelter of any kind soon. The biting temperatures and the continued hammering of the powerful gale was draining both humans and animals. Cooper was no longer sure they were going in the right direction. They couldn't see much beyond each horse's nose.

After what could have been days or just hours, they stumbled into a long copse of cottonwoods and willows along the South Fork of the Snake. "Damn," Cooper muttered. "I didn't know there was another damn river here." He sighed. "Well, at least we have some protection from the weather."

The trees cut the wind down some, and lightened the snow a little, though it began to deepen as the leafless trees prevented the wind from shoving the snow aside.

"This'll do, Moon," Cooper said unnecessarily, still breathing heavily from the exertion of trying to control the horse and fighting off the screaming wind. He was glad each of them wore a heavy capote. The garments, and their sleeping robes tied behind their saddles, were almost the only good thing about their situation.

They stopped and dismounted. "How're your hands?" Cooper asked.

"Rough, but I'll be fine."

Cooper looked at her palms. They were red and raw from having been roughed up by the rope to the mules. "You sure?"

"Yes. You take care of horses. I'll make fire."

Cooper unsaddled both horses and quickly but thoroughly curried them. He hobbled them and let them loose to feed on cottonwood bark. Finally, he turned and sank down by the fire that Black Moon had struggled to make in the slight protection of a large boulder. It provided scant but welcome warmth even as the storm continued to rage around them.

"These here are some poor doins, Moon," Cooper said quietly.

"We'll be all right. Storm will end soon. We move on."

"Without all our supplies and," he added bitterly, "without all our plews. We don't get those back, rendezvous will be poor doins, too, and I'll not be able to supply myself for next season."

"We figure out when time comes. Yes."

"You're too damn hopeful, woman," Cooper groused.

She smiled a little and rested her head on his shoulder for a moment. She rose and walked to where Cooper had set her Indian-style saddle with the high saddle horn and tall cantle. It was almost covered with snow already. She returned to the fire with a small buckskin-enclosed package. She unwrapped it to show a frozen block of pemmican.

"Damn, if you ain't some, woman," Cooper said with a shake of the head as Black Moon set it near the edge of the fire to let it warm a little. He did not see her smile of pleasure at the compliment.

They ate a few minutes later, enjoying the fat-rich food as the wind continued to howl around them and the snow continued to fall heavily.

When he had finished the small repast, Cooper rose and went about building a small lean-to as near to the fire as he could manage, constructing it of willow branches and leaves.

"It ain't much, Moon," he said when he had finished, "but it'll have to do."

"It's damn good."

They soon turned in, cold, hungry, and exhausted from battling the tempest.

THE STORM finally ended three days later. While Cooper and Black Moon waited it out, they struggled to survive. Cooper managed to bring down a stringy old elk, which kept them fed. But the Shoshoni had no end of trouble trying to keep the fire going as the snow fell steadily, piling up deeper and deeper, constantly threatening to douse the flames. Cooper was kept busy peeling cottonwood bark for the animals to feed on and walking the horses around to keep them active and at least a little warm against the freezing temperatures.

They took another two days after the storm subsided to regain a little of their strength. Then they saddled their horses and pushed on, crossing the frozen river heading for Pine Creek and the pass that bore its name. Neither was sure how far it was, and because they were still on the flat before heading into the western edge of the pass, Cooper worried that they would be caught up in another storm, with the sky gray and heavy, holding an ever-present threat.

The traveling was hard going, with the horses having to fight their way through snow that was three feet deep in many places. At times Cooper had to lead the way, tramping down the snow himself, making a trail for the horses. It was exhausting work, and slow. The second day went a little slower as the fatigue grew, worsened by the biting wind and freezing temperatures. The lack of food only intensified the trouble. While they still had some of the elk Cooper had killed, it was mostly frozen and they had no way to thaw it, let alone cook it. With no feed, the horses quickly weakened, struggling even more in the snow.

They straggled into a forest in the foothills of the Big Hole Mountains, not far from the creek. Cooper and Black Moon collapsed.

Cooper did not know how long he lay there, but he knew he had to move soon, or he would freeze to death. Visions of his last trek through a frozen wilderness began to incapacitate him, and he knew he could not let those thoughts engulf him. He had beat the weather that time and he vowed to do it again. But he could not move—he was too tired, too weak, and too drained of energy. Then he heard Black Moon gasp. He glanced at her. She had tried to rise but had fallen back, unequal to the task.

The sight of his woman in such dreadful straits gave him a small burst of energy. He weakly shoved himself up, gathered a bit of wood and tinder and managed to get a fire going. He built it up little by little. Then he staggered over to where Black Moon still lie.

"C'mon, woman," he gasped, grabbing her under her arms. With what little strength he could muster, he hauled her up and helped her to the fire. He loosened her heavy capote some to let the heat flow straight into her body. He slumped down beside her and opened his own capote.

The warmth gave him a little vigor, and he finally pushed himself up and teetered to his horse. He got one of the two last hunks of elk meat from a sack hanging from the saddle horn and brought it to the fire, where he simply dumped it on a rock close to the flames. Before long, the aroma of the thawing meat was almost overwhelming for both of them. Greedily they hacked off pieces and shoved them in their mouths, heedless of the fact that it was basically raw. It was meat.

But after a dozen or so bites, Cooper stopped Black Moon from eating more. "It ain't good to have too much too fast," he said. "Will make you sick."

Black Moon thought to argue, then nodded. Cooper turned the hunk of meat over, letting it thaw throughout and begin cooking. They cupped snow to their mouths to slake their thirst as they waited for the meat. Finally, Cooper decided it had cooked enough, and they again began eating, this time more slowly.

The meat revived their strength and spirits a little. Cooper went to tend the horses, and Black Moon gathered up what forage for the horses she could. The two worked together to construct another rudimentary lean-to. Then they spread out the thick buffalo hides they used for sleeping and were soon slumbering.

Morning came cold and gray with more than a hint of a renewed snowfall. They ate the last of the elk, and were ready to face the day, though without their usual enthusiasm. Coiling a horsehair rope over his shoulder, Cooper headed out to hunt—on foot, not wanting to burden the worn-out horses—while Black Moon collected more forage for the animals, fortifying the lean-to, and keeping the fire going.

Late in the afternoon, Cooper returned to their camp, hauling a deer carcass on the end of the rope he had brought. It had started to snow again, but not very heavily. Cooper let go of the rope, leaving the deer near the fire. He looked about ready to collapse.

"Come, husband," Black Moon said, taking his hand. She led hm to the lean-to. "You rest."

"Deer needs butcherin'," he said through the fog of fatigue.

"I do. You rest."

"You sure?"

"You think I can't butcher damn deer?" she asked in mock severity.

He managed a small smile. "I don't doubt it at all, Moon. Just worried you ain't got the strength. I purely don't." He practically fell on the bed of robes.

Black Moon smiled as she covered him and then went to butcher the deer.

Cooper slept through the rest of the afternoon and

into the next morning. When he woke, Black Moon had meat cooked and kept warm near the fire. "You shine, Moon, plumb shine," he said as he dug into the strength-giving meat.

"Where's the rest of the meat?" Cooper asked when he had finished his meal.

Black Moon waved a hand at the deerskin hanging from a tree.

Cooper nodded. It would keep the wolves and bears, if any were not hibernating, away since they could not get at it. "All of it there?"

"Yep. I make small packages, wrap 'em in hide. Each make a meal."

"Good. How long will it last?"

"Four days. Maybe five."

"That shines. I ain't fond of the idea of havin' to go out and hunt again just yet. And the horses still need time to recruit themselves."

"We be all right. You see. Damn yes."

"Hope you're right, Moon."

FOUR

IT SNOWED ONLY TWICE, neither time heavily, in the week they stayed at their camp, recuperating. They finally pulled out, riding much rested and strengthened horses. Cooper had shot another deer and they carried with them a fair amount of frozen meat. Despite having lost their supplies and all their plews, they were somewhat buoyed to be on the move again, especially with the sun shining in a clear sky and the temperature nudging above freezing.

Despite the time that had passed, Cooper had decided the day before to backtrack their trail in hopes of finding the mules. Black Moon thought the idea foolish, but she said nothing and followed her husband across the valley. They made excellent time, and it took little more than a day before they reached the band of trees along the frozen South Fork of the Snake River. The next morning, they crossed it and turned northwest up the valley.

Later that day, they found the carcass of the mule that had carried their supplies. The animal had been well picked over by wolves, coyotes, and vultures, as were the supplies, the little that was left were scattered about. Cooper and Black Moon managed to scavenge up a coffeepot, three mugs, a couple of tin plates and, quite to their joy, some coffee, sugar, and salt. Cooper also recovered two flasks of powder and two small, thin bars of lead. Cooper decided not to take things such as extra blankets, cooking pots, frypans, and more, not wanting to overburden the horses.

As Black Moon packed the recovered supplies on the horses, Cooper stood there staring into the distance, contemplating a further search for the other mules. It would be a great relief to find even some of the pelts he had taken. Then he sighed. There was little chance of finding the animals at all, and they likely would be in the same condition as this one. Even if the plews were salvageable, they would have no way to carry them.

Black Moon came to stand beside him. "We go. We find 'em. Damn right."

Cooper smiled. He explained his thoughts, his voice wistful and resigned.

"If we find, and mule is dead, we make travois. Horses drag 'em."

Cooper considered that for a minute, then shook his head. "You see any trees around here, Moon?" When she responded in the negative, he added, "Then we can't make travois."

"Trees less than three hours' ride. We go there, make travois, come back."

"They might be another couple days' ride from here."

"Still worth it to find plews."

After a few more moments of consideration, he nodded. "We'll give it a day or two. No more."

They mounted up and rode off, heading north. They found another mule less than a mile farther on. It, too, was dead and had been well scavenged. The two packs of plews were torn open and scattered about. Many had been gnawed into uselessness, but some were in good enough shape to be sold at rendezvous.

"I'll ride back and make a travois," Cooper said. "Will you stay here and gather up any good plews?"

"Yep."

"You'll be all right?"

"Yep."

Cooper nodded and left. Before long he was at the stretch of trees along the river. He quickly hacked down two decent-sized poles and lashed them together as an X at the one end and tied it to the saddle. He used some buckskin strips to hold a blanket in place as the poles widened to a wide V at the other end. He hurried back across the valley on foot, towing the horse, the travois bouncing along behind him on the snow. It was almost dark when he arrived.

Black Moon had gathered about thirty still-prime plews into a neat pile.

"Good work, Moon," Cooper said, pleased that there were that many furs.

The woman nodded and helped Cooper load the furs on the travois and tie them down.

"I don't reckon we'll find the other mule with more plews," Cooper said with a sigh when they had finished.

"We look, maybe find."

Cooper shook his head after a few moments. "Nah. Ain't worth the time and effort, I reckon. We need to get across the pass soon, and we're likely to face more snow before long. 'Sides, my horse can't carry much more weight, and your mare won't pull much either bein' some smaller than mine. Nope. Time to move on."

"All right, we go."

"Tomorrow's time enough."

They hunkered down in the open, wrapped in their capotes and robes, hoping the snow didn't come or the wind start to blow.

In the morning, hungry and still tired, they again crossed the river and headed across the valley. It snowed off and on as they made their way toward Pine Creek, following it for two days before they reached the pass. Traveling across the valley was easier than before, but not much, and their camp the second night was a cold one without wood or water, other than snow. The going got tougher when they entered the pass, with the wind more of a hindrance, at times howling up the pass behind them, giving them an impetus they did not desire.

The horses often struggled on the steep incline, especially Cooper's gelding, which was pulling the travois. Cooper found himself walking almost as much as riding, the latter of which was difficult with the ends of the travois sticking up.

Another storm slammed into them in a small valley a couple of miles from the top of the pass. They struggled on, heading east, they thought, but out in the open with no real trail to follow, they had lost their bearings in the blowing snow and icy wind. After a couple of hours, they were not sure just where they were. The wind and freezing temperatures sapped their strength and left them lost in the maelstrom.

Once again, they could do nothing but move on. A few times, Cooper considered backtracking, but he didn't know if he could find the trail down the west side of the pass again, if they were even still in the pass, and there was nowhere for them to really shelter back that way. He just hoped that this valley was not too large. The horses began to falter, and Cooper was beginning to think the end was near for him and Black Moon. Again, he began having flashbacks of the previous winter, when he was alone, with no weapons and no idea of where he was. At least this time, he thought, I have weapons, a horse, and a wonderful companion.

About the time that Cooper really began to second-guess his decision to go forward instead of turning back, they staggered into the trees. Cooper's hopes rose, as did the land a little. Then they were in a forest of pines and aspens. The woods lessened the wind and snow enough that Cooper and Black Moon almost thought for a few moments that the storm had slowed.

They started working their way deeper into the trees and they felt that the effects of the storm faded a little more. But they were stopped when the travois began to catch on trees. "Damn," Cooper muttered. He unhooked the travois and led his horse farther into the forest, while Black Moon did the same with her mare.

A short way in, Cooper said, "This is good enough. Get a fire goin' while I tend to the horses."

He first hobbled the animals. By the time he finished caring for the horses and peeled off some bark for the ponies to feed on, Black Moon had a fire going and meat that had been frozen cooking over the fire. He plopped down next to the fire and nodded thanks to his wife.

"How much coffee we got left?" he asked.

"Enough for one or two times. Maybe good to have some now."

Cooper looked up through the trees to the snow coming down. "After the day we had, that idea shines with this chil'."

The Shoshoni rose and got the small sack of coffee beans and the coffeepot from her saddlebags and returned to the fire. She mashed up a handful of beans, put them in the pot with some snow and set the pot on the fire.

After he ate and drank a small cup of coffee, Cooper rose and, despite his exhaustion, managed to build a small lean-to. Before long, they turned in, snuggling together under a thick, heavy buffalo robe.

The storm had weakened by morning, though snow continued to fall in thick, large flakes. Despite that, Cooper decided to hunt, as they were almost out of meat. He was back before long, walking his horse on which was draped a half-butchered elk.

Cooper skinned it and handed the hide to Black Moon, who began cutting it into pieces. While she was occupied with that, Cooper finished butchering the animal, cutting the meat up in manageable chunks. Those were wrapped in the sections of hide Black Moon had cut except for one hunk, which they began roasting on a makeshift spit of green twigs, though it was still somewhat early in the day.

They spent the next two days eating heartily and making sure the horses had feed. Then Cooper decided it was time to resume their journey. He hooked up the travois and they moved out onto what passed for a trail. The land rose steadily, and with the accumulated snow, the going was hard and slow. All the way, they hoped that there would be an end to the pass and maybe get their bearings so they could make their way toward the next pass.

They were happy that no new snow fell for five slow-moving days, but then it started again with a vengeance. Big, wet flakes came down and accumulated quickly and deeply. They began to struggle even more as the snow piled up. The horses strained trying to make their way through the whiteness that grew steadily. It wasn't quite deep enough that Cooper had to make a trail for the gelding, but he did dismount and started leading his horse. Black Moon did the same with her mare.

With the trees packed so tightly, there was no place to settle down for the night, so they pressed on until just before dark and quickly made a fire to cook some meat. Cooper unsaddled the animals and cut down some shoots to feed them.

After eating and resting for an hour sitting with their backs against trunks it was time to leave again. About noon the next day, they came to a small flat where the trees had thinned out. They found a spot there where they could be among the pines and have the horses with them. As Black Moon made a fire, Cooper took care of the horses and hobbled them so they could feed on whatever forage they could find. Despite the snow that was still falling, they did not bother with a lean-to. After eating the next to last hunk of elk, they spread one buffalo robe on the ground, stretched out on it and pulled another over them.

As they were eating the last of the elk in the morning, Cooper said, "I best go make meat."

Black Moon nodded. It was necessary, and she would not complain even if she had thought to do so.

He arrived back in their camp carrying a very small deer. "Best I could find, Moon," he said in disgust with himself.

"We make do."

"Reckon so." He set to work butchering the deer.

Two days later, Cooper decided they would leave. The snow, which had sputtered intermittently, had finally stopped, and the animals were rested. Cooper saddled the horses and hooked the travois onto his horse while Black Moon packed what few supplies they had. They left an hour or so after daylight. Cooper was grateful that the sun was out and the temperature, he estimated, had edged just above freezing.

They moved slowly, not wanting to tax the animals, or themselves. They made only four or five miles, Cooper figured, with the snow still a foot or more deep and they were finally beginning to work their way down the mountain. Their relatively benevolent weather did not last long. They had camped on a hillside, not the most comfortable camp but was the best they could do under the circumstances. When they awoke in the morning, snow was falling again, and the temperature had dropped.

It only grew worse as they traveled that day, with the snow piling up to two feet, making the horses struggle once more trying to make their way through the growing depth.

They found a relatively flat place with plenty of trees, though not so closely packed. They made camp quickly, took care of the animals, then sat to eat some deer meat. They had only enough to last another day or two, so they ate sparingly.

They left in the morning, hoping that nicer weather would return, but it was not to be. Before noon, the horses were barely able to make it through the two and a half feet of snow on what the travelers were trying to use as a trail.

Cooper's horse, trailing the travois, began to stagger. "Damn," Cooper muttered. He stopped and unhooked the travois and then walked, towing the gelding behind him. It soon became apparent, though, that the animal was in bad shape. He stopped and walked back to where Black Moon was sitting on her horse. "This here's poor bull, Moon," he said. "But I reckon we best backtrack to yesterday's camp. I don't know what's ahead, and neither horse looks to be able to go much farther. At least a trail is tamped that way."

Black Moon looked uncertain. It would take a few hours to get back to that campsite, but it was true they didn't know what lie ahead. "Maybe you go ahead on foot, see if better place not far. I wait here."

Cooper thought that over for a minute, then nodded. He turned and shuffled off, laboring through the snow. He went about a mile, he guessed, and saw no other likely spot. And he was exhausted from his efforts. He headed back to where Black Moon waited. As he neared, he shook his head.

She nodded. "I hook up travois again."

"No. We'll leave it here. If the horses recruit enough, we'll get it when we're on the move again."

"Is damn good."

They turned, the woman still riding, the man still towing his horse. It took several hours but they finally arrived. Cooper managed to gather a little forage for the animals, then collapsed near the fire Black Moon had started. She sliced off a small chunk of meat and handed it to him on a tin plate.

"Thankee, Moon." He bit off a hunk.

With a smile, Black Moon handed him a cup of coffee.

"You been hidin' this?"

"Not really. Just savin' it. For right time. It's the last."

Cooper nodded in pleasure, then grew serious. "There enough for you?"

"Maybe a little, but I save for you in mornin'."

"No, you have it."

"You need more." Before he could say anything, she added, "Don't argue with me. No, dammit."

He nodded gratefully and drank the coffee with pleasure. When he finished, he said, "We best stay here for a few days. The horses need rest, and maybe this damn snow will stop and melt some so our travelin' won't be so troublesome."

"Is damn good."

FIVE

IT WAS ALMOST a week before they left. The horses had recovered sufficiently, and Cooper had been lucky enough to bring down an elk twice, so they had plenty of meat. They slung an elk hide wrapped around the large amount of meat they had left and tied it over Cooper's saddle. Walking his horse they pushed on. The depth of snow had lessened considerably, much having been blown away by strong winds the past two days.

A few hours later, they came upon the travois. Cooper took the hide-wrapped meat from his saddle and put it on the travois, then hooked the contraption to his horse. He mounted up, feeling better now that he was not walking, despite the discomfort of riding with the travois poles, they moved ahead.

Things went fine for two days, there was an abundance of meat for them, though no coffee, and plenty of pine needles and bark for the horses when they stopped for the night.

Then another screaming, howling storm swept over

them, the wind raging at them as if all the souls in hell were screeching their eternal despair at the travelers. It caught them on the narrow, rocky trail. They fought on through the rapidly accumulating snow, and the steady battering of the wind. Cooper was beginning to despair of ever finding a spot offering even a bit of succor from the storm, when he found a place. They burrowed in among the trees, once again having to leave the travois behind because they could not work it through the heavy stands of dark pines.

As usual, Cooper tended to the horses while Black Moon started a fire and got meat cooking. They finally sat to eat. "You think these damned storms'll ever stop plaguin' us, Moon?"

She smiled a little. "Yes. When spring comes. Damn right."

"You're no help, dammit, Moon." Then he, too, grinned a little. "But you're right. I just wish it'd be a lot sooner." He sighed. "Well, nothin' can be done about it now."

Cooper was too exhausted to make a lean-to, so as they had done the past few days, he and Black Moon just crawled into the robes.

The thick, heavy pines kept out some of the snow but they were still covered with a few inches of blanket of the whiteness. And the wind, while cut some by the trees, still shrieked between them, continuously seeking their flesh.

After breaking their fast in the morning, Cooper set about building a small but rather substantial lean-to. Then he went and gathered whatever forage he could for the animals. When he finished that, he paced around the camp. The storm was showing no sign of abating, and he wondered how long they were stuck here.

"Sit, husband," Black Moon said.

"I can't. These doins don't shine with this chil' at all, and there's no sayin' no to it."

"True. But prowlin' around won't change things."

"I know, dammit, but sittin' here not bein' able to do anything don't shine either."

Black Moon didn't argue. She knew her man and what he was feeling, and nothing she could say would ease his mind, at least for now.

The snow eventually stopped, but the temperature plunged to well below zero. Cooper began stripping bark from trees and gathering what needles he could find under the snow and spreading it out for the horses to feed on. Here and there close to the tree trunks, some tiny patches of grass remained, but they would barely last an hour, if that.

"We're getting low on meat," Black Moon said as they huddled before the fire, trying to eat.

"What'n hell do you want me to do about it, woman?" Cooper growled.

Black Moon looked as if she had been slapped. She said nothing but turned her face back to the fire.

As she did so, Cooper thought he caught the glint of tears on her cheek. "Ah, hell, Moon, you know I'm just bein' a horse's ass." He reached over and pulled her to him. She resisted a little. "I'll try to make meat tomorrow."

"Good," Black Moon said stiffly, not melting the tiniest bit.

"I'm sorry, Moon. You know I ain't afraid of no man, red or white, nor any beast, but winter spooks me.

I can fight Bug's Boys or a man like Josiah Weeks, or a griz, but I can't fight winter. You know what I went through last year. Damn winter near put me under. Wasn't for Cheyenne Killer and some of the others of your people, I would've filled some critter's meatbag."

"Is all right."

"No it ain't. It ain't just me no more. And if you was to go under because I couldn't fight these storms that've been plaguin' us..."

Black Moon snuggled a little closer to Cooper. "We'll be fine. I'll not go under. You will make sure. Damn right."

"You got a lot of faith in me, woman."

"Yes." She paused, then said, "We go to robes?" she asked with a touch of lust in her eyes.

"That'd plumb shine with this ol' hoss most times, but I'll have to be sayin' no to you."

Black Moon stared at him, a hurt look on her face. "I make you angry?"

"Hell no." He offered a rueful grin. "But with it a far sight under zero, I reckon, we try doin' that and my pizzle and stones'd squeeze up into my belly, or else freeze and fall off."

Black Moon giggled a little.

"It ain't funny, woman."

"You are big man, and no freezin' could hurt you."

"You think so?"

"Damn yes."

"Hmmm. Reckon if we was to bring them robes over here near the fire, things might shine as long's we take care."

"Is damn good."

She was right.

COOPER WENT HUNTING the next morning and returned in the afternoon empty-handed and angry.

Black Moon let him stew a little, before she said, "Sit, husband." It was an order.

When he reluctantly did so, Black Moon handed him some elk. "You'll make meat tomorrow. Or next day. Damn right. We have enough for two, three days."

Cooper nodded, a bit relieved.

"Maybe more days if you didn't eat so much."

He looked at her in outrage, then saw her grin. "You're a damned irritatin' woman, Moon." But he grinned too.

THE NEXT MORNING, he headed out again, and was lucky enough to bring down a deer. It wasn't a big one, but it would keep them in meat for a few more days. He hoped they could be back on the trail by then.

As he was nearing the camp, he sensed an odd movement to his left, fairly high on a branch. The mountain lion looked to be ready to pounce on Black Moon Woman's mare. The cat turned its face toward the noise made by Cooper and his horse.

"Damn," Cooper muttered. He slowly raised his rifle, checked the priming, and brought the rifle to his shoulder. "Think you can take one of our horses, do you? Well this might disabuse you of that notion." He fired.

The cat fell, crashing through the trees, a bullet hole in its forehead.

Black Moon jumped up at the sound, worried for a moment before she saw what had happened. She breathed a sigh of relief as Cooper entered the camp.

"You invite that catamount to sup with us, Moon?" Cooper said with a chuckle. "Looks like he was thinkin' of nappin' whilst you readied the food."

"Nope. He just said he was waitin' to see if you made meat that he could have some of." She smiled.

"Bah," Cooper said with mock annoyance. "You can see I got a deer. It ain't much though, it's pretty small."

"It's fine. Last a few days."

"Reckon so. If *you* stop eatin' so much. You're startin' to plump up a bit, woman," he said with a laugh. Truth was, though, both had lost some weight, and were beginning to look a little gaunt.

She threw a hastily made snowball at him and giggled when it knocked his hat off.

Then the two of them set to butchering the deer. Once that was done, Cooper gathered up what feed he could for the horses, then collected a bunch of firewood and dumped it on the small pile next to the fire.

As they sat for a meal, Cooper gazed up at the sky that peeked out from the tops of the pine. "Damn, I wish we had some coffee. Or even tea. And damn if I don't wish this weather to ease up so we could move on. We're still a heap of miles from your village, but if we could move on, maybe we'd find a better place than this for winterin'."

"We'll be all right."

Cooper looked at Black Moon, wondering if she felt that sure of him and herself or if she was trying to build up his confidence. Either way, he decided, it wouldn't make any difference to the weather, and they were at the mercy of its whims.

It didn't snow for several days, but the temperature never got high enough to get even close to zero. It was worse at night, when temperatures were dangerously low. They built another fire closer to the front of the lean-to and placed some large rocks behind it to reflect the heat into the shelter. It was still bitter, but Cooper and Black Moon were almost comfortable under their two buffalo robes. It allowed Cooper to tie their two blankets on the horses, trying to save the animals from freezing.

It did no good. They awoke in the morning to find Cooper's horse frozen dead, the blanket over it an icy shroud.

"Damn. Damn. Damn!" Cooper shouted into the forest. "Damn it all to hell and back. Twice!" He raged around the camp for a while, cursing the mountains, the weather, dead animals, snow, God, fractious, runaway mules, and anyone or anything he could think of. He stomped up to Black Moon who had been standing out of his way and snapped. "Pack up whatever we got that we can use. Load it on the travois. We're leavin'."

"No," Black Moon said quietly, shocking Cooper.

"Don't you cross me now, dammit. I said we're leavin', so we're leavin'. Now!"

"No," she repeated, a bit more firmly.

"You want to stay here by yourself, that shines with this chil'. Pack my things."

"No."

"That the only word you know in English now?" Cooper growled.

"No." She was worried but had to suppress a giggle as he fumed.

"I'll do it myself, then. Can you at least cook some meat?"

"No."

Cooper's anger was rapidly turning to consternation. The Shoshoni could be truculent on occasion, but he had never seen her quite like this. "What's gotten into you, woman?" he asked, puzzlement written on his face.

"Common sense, as I hear Americans say. Look. Think. One damn horse is dead, and the mare is in poor condition. She can't pull travois. We can't ride her. This damn camp not the best, but it'll do, 'til things get better."

"You're sayin' we should stay for the winter?"

"Yes, unless weather gets good so we can travel without gettin' caught again. Maybe with no place to go."

Cooper pondered that.

As he did so, Black Moon said, "We're not sure where we are. Through next pass, I think, we come to place with plenty wood, water, buffler. It would be good if we were there. Good place to stay, maybe. But we ain't sure how to get there and wanderin' the mountains in this weather is dangerous. Damn right."

Cooper knew she was right, but it galled him to be in such a dangerous plight and could do nothing about it. "I'm short on powder and ball. Might be hard to fill our meatbags."

"We find way. We butcher damn horse. That'll feed us a week, maybe more. Things get worse, we kill mare.

Horse meat not good like buffler or elk, but better than nothin'. Damn right."

"And if we stay, you'll stop annoyin' me?"

"No. When I ever stopped annoyin' you?" She grinned.

"Never, dammit. But that way I know you still care for me."

"Dammit, yes."

SIX

WITH THE DECISION TO stay here, Cooper resigned himself to its necessity. Using his tomahawk, he and Black Moon chopped up the frozen horse and wrapped the chunks in pieces of hide and hung them from trees in a large hide. It would keep the meat handy but out of the reach of any animals who might smell it even though it was frozen. It would be enough, along with the small amount of deer left, for several days.

Over the next week, the temperatures rose some but never even inched above freezing. The snow began again, sometimes hard and thick, other times gently, with soft flakes that still piled up. And when the snow stopped, the temperature plunged again. Ice formed on the trees, sometimes snapping off branches with a loud crack.

Cooper went about shoring up and enlarging the lean-to, building up the sides and lengthening the top.

Cooper gathered up armload after armload of firewood, while Black Moon stoked the original fire. They brought up the mare and tied her to a tree as near to the fire as they could without spooking the animal. They placed both blankets over the horse, hoping the blaze and the covering would be enough to keep her from freezing to death like the gelding had. Cooper also gathered armloads of whatever forage he could find.

A few days later Cooper went out to try to take meat, taking the horse with him. He returned with nothing.

"Not find meat?" Black Moon asked.

"I found some but never couldn't get a clear shot, and I wasn't about to waste powder and ball, not when we got a heap of time before we can move on."

"Damn smart."

"Thanks," Cooper said as he tied the horse to a tree and covered it. He sat at the fire and took the chunk of horsemeat Black Moon handed him on a tin plate. He stared into the flames for a while, the plate held unthinkingly in his hand.

"You are bothered, Hawwy," the Shoshoni said more than asked.

"Yep. Nothin' to be done about it. I'm concerned that we won't make it through the winter, and if we do, I worry we won't get back to the village in time for us to join 'em on the trail to rendezvous."

"We make out fine."

"You got a lot more confidence in me than I do."

"Yep." She smiled. She had just stated a fact, nothing more, nothing less.

"You're *loco*."

"Nope."

Cooper shook his head, wondering at the Shoshoni and how he had come across such a woman as this one.

She clearly loved him—and he her—but she seemed so calm and unconcerned about their situation.

THE DAYS DRAGGED ON, each seemingly longer than the previous one. Cooper hunted every few days and was lucky in being successful more often than not, while carefully preserving his ammunition. The weather alternated among snow, wind and frigidity, or sometimes all three. It made existence precarious and tiresome. They had to keep making meat and keep finding forage for the mare, as well as making her as warm as they could by keeping a store of firewood. Fighting off the harsh, hostile weather was taxing on their systems and wearing them down. Even Black Moon was beginning to wear down and losing a little of her usual cheeriness. That saddened Cooper more than did the downheartedness of dealing with these circumstances.

After two or three eternities, the weather began to change. Cooper rolled out of the lean-to and stood for a few moments, delighting in the sun's meager warmth. The temperature wasn't much above freezing but compared with what they had endured for the past three months, it was a delight.

"I figure to be leavin' the next day or two, if that shines with you, Moon."

"Yep. Damn good. You need to make meat again before we go."

"You're naggin' me again, woman," Cooper said with a laugh. He felt better than he had in a long time.

"Yep." She laughed too.

"I need to see to the mare too. I think she's come through all right, but I best be sure."

"I do while you hunt."

"You sure you can do that?" he said, a small smile playing across his lips.

"I am Shoshoni," she said proudly.

"Yes, ma'am, you certainly are."

TWO DAYS later they pulled out, the travois containing their few supplies, Cooper's saddle, as well as all the meat. Cooper and Black Moon walked, the latter holding the reins.

Though much of the snow had melted, often leaving behind a deep coating of mud, there were still places where the snow was a couple of feet deep. Moving through the spots taxed the horse considerably, and more than once Cooper moved ahead, flattening the snow with his body, making it easier for the animal to make its way along but quickly wearing him down.

The temperatures during the day were somewhat reasonable but dropped below freezing each night, so the traveling was still difficult, but they endured.

They took a day or two at one spot occasionally to give the horse some rest and so Cooper could hunt. Then they would struggle ahead again.

Almost a month after leaving their wintering place, they were nearly through Teton Pass and looked out over a huge meadow. There was little snow and patches of grass were beginning to show. The pass rose again across the glade, though it looked considerably less forbidding than the stretch they had just crossed.

They were a few yards into the meadow when Cooper suddenly stopped. "Back in the trees, Moon. Now!"

The woman got the horse turned around and within moments, they were back among the pines. "What'd you see?" she asked.

"Warriors. Not sure how many."

"Our people?" the Shoshoni asked.

"Don't know for sure, but from the glimpse I got, they might be Crows, or worse, maybe Blackfeet."

"That's not good."

"No it ain't. This here's damp powder and no way to dry it."

"What we do?"

"Wait. Maybe they'll not come this way but move up or down the meadow instead of across it right at us."

"You're not afraid of damn Crows or Blackfeet," Black Moon said. "Why you seem troubled?"

"I ain't got but about ten lead balls left and just about enough powder to send 'em on their way. We have to fight them red devils, we could be ass deep in those fractious bastards. Crows don't usually try to raise hair on a mountaineer, I've heard, but they'll rob you of everything you got. And right now, that means our only horse, the plews, my here rifle, what little supplies we got." He paused. "And you."

"That's damn worse." She was only a little sarcastic.

"Yep, it sure is. I ain't losin' you to those red devils."

Across the meadow, seven warriors came toward where Cooper and Black Moon waited, three of them ahead of the others.

Despite the still-cold temperature, Cooper was sweating. He didn't like the odds if he had to battle them; being so short on ammunition made the situation more dangerous. He couldn't let them find him and his woman. He figured he could drop the first three from here before they got close, but the gunfire would bring the other four, and he wasn't sure he could take them down before they reached him. More perilous, they could—and likely would—take to the trees and come up behind him and Black Moon. At that point he would have almost no hope of holding them off, though he vowed he would try his damnedest to do so.

He'd have to decide soon, as the Crows, he was certain now, were moving slowly but steadily toward them. The other four were a fair distance away and moving to the north.

Suddenly he made his decision. He brought his rifle up to his shoulder, sighted on the Crow in the lead, and fired. By the time the warrior had hit the ground, Cooper was halfway reloading his Dickert. Moments later, another Indian was down. The third warrior swung away, heading northeast. A few seconds later, he, too, tumbled from his horse, dead.

"Damn good," Black Moon said.

"Maybe, maybe not. Looks like those other critters are headin' this way." He hesitated only a moment, then said, "I want you to take the mare back up the trail to that spot where it opens up a little, half a mile or so back. Pull into the trees as far as you can just past there."

Black Moon nodded. She took the reins.

"Wait, Moon." He pulled one of his pistols and handed it to her.

"I fight damn good," she said with determination.

"No, Moon. If I can't take down all them bastards,

and I go under, I don't want you fallin' into their hands."

"I stay and fight. If you go under, I do too."

Cooper shook his head. "I'd have to worry about you too much. I don't plan to go under, but if I do, you'll be on your own and do what you feel the need to."

Black Moon began to quarrel with that, but Cooper held up his hand to cut her off. "This ain't no time to be arguin' with me, woman. Now git."

With some reluctance, Black Moon moved off, casting a last glance at him before disappearing deeper into the trees along the trail.

Cooper moved off among the pines. He was not about to sit here and wait for them to come to him, seeing as how they, too, were leaving the meadow, into the cover of the spruce and pines. "Think you'll surprise me, do you, boys?" Cooper muttered. "Well, that don't shine with this ol' hoss, and you're facin' one angry ol' critter, a mountaineer who's had a heap too much of hard times of late and so is lackin' in good humor."

Cooper headed toward where he had seen the Crows had left the meadow into the trees, but instead of going straight, he moved up the hill a little way, then turned north. He moved stealthily, stopping every few feet to scan the area and listen. He didn't think he would hear anything, as the Crows could move far more silently through the forest than he could, but he did so anyway. There was always a chance a twig might snap under the foot of one of the Indians. Besides, by him stopping so often, there was a smaller chance of making some noise that would give him away.

Suddenly he spotted a movement and dropped to

the ground just as an arrow thudded into the tree where Cooper had been standing an instant ago. Another followed, then a third, the last skipped across his neck where it joined the shoulder. "Damned snake-humpin' son of a bitch," Cooper mumbled.

He scooted backward on his rump and came up around another tree. He peered out. The Blackfoot, with arrow nocked, was warily approaching where Cooper had been a minute ago. Cooper grinned a grim grin. He slid the rifle around the trunk. A second later, the warrior was dead in a crumbled heap.

Cooper ran uphill, loading his rifle as he did. He saw another movement, and he dropped to a knee, Dickert raised and cocked. The Crow was headed to where his fellow tribesman was when Cooper shot him.

Before long, the warrior came into the open, moving parallel to the meadow. A second later, his head burst when a .54-caliber lead ball plowed into it just above the temple.

Cooper paused a moment, checking how many rifle balls he had left, and realized there were only five. He slung the rifle over his shoulder. "Reckon it's time to do this close up, ol' hoss," he hissed. He pulled his toma-hawk and glided through the forest.

Again he thought he caught a movement. He headed that way, when he was clubbed in the back of the head. He fell hard but managed to roll out of the way of the warrior's descending war club.

"You son of a bitch," Cooper spat. "You ain't about to make wolf bait out of this chil'." As the Crow reared back for another strike, Cooper grabbed a handful of pine needles and some dirt and tossed it in the Indian's face. It distracted him for only a couple of seconds, but it was time enough for Cooper to grab his tomahawk from where he dropped it when he was clubbed. He swung it as hard as he could while still on his back. The blade sliced into the Crow's leg, nearly severing it. The warrior collapsed. Cooper was on him in an eyeblink and finished the job of ridding the world of this Indian.

He stood there, realizing just how much his head hurt. He closed his eyes and took a few deep breaths. It calmed the pain only fractionally, but he could manage it. He heard a horse racing away, and he charged down the hill. When he hit the edge of the forest, he saw the last Crow galloping to the north.

Cooper unslung his rifle and knelt, ready to take a shot. Then he remembered he had only five lead balls and a long way to travel yet. He rose, slinging the Dickert over his shoulder again. Watching the Black-foot rushing away. "You're one mighty lucky bastard, boy."

He turned up the hill again. He scalped all three men in the forest and checked their possible sacks. He found some tobacco. He then did the same with the three he had shot in the meadow. He cursed a little when he realized none of the Crow had been carrying rifles, so they had no powder and lead on them. With joy though, he found a couple small sacks of coffee beans. He quietly tried to coax one of the ponies to him, but they were skittish. He finally did manage to get one, which he tied to a bush. With a smile, he headed toward the trail carrying his prizes, some grisly, some welcome.

As he neared the place where Black Moon should be, he called out, "Moon, it's me comin' in."

"About damn time," her voice came from behind a tree.

He grinned and moved toward her. She gasped when she saw the blood on his shoulder. "You hurt."

"It ain't bad. My head hurts like hell, though. One of those bastards clubbed me on it. My hat and hair cushioned the blow some."

She looked at him skeptically but said nothing. She saw the plunder he carried. "Scalps good. What's in those sacks?"

His grin grew. "Coffee!"

"That shines, Hawwy. Damn shines."

SEVEN

THEY CROSSED THE MEADOW, headed up the last hill of the pass and stopped for a few moments. Ahead of them was a vast plain teeming with buffalo and some elk grazing among the herd.

"Now *this* shines," Cooper exclaimed.

"Yep," Black Moon said with equal enthusiasm.

They hurried down the end of the pass onto the valley. "We'll make camp here," Cooper said almost as soon as they hit the valley floor.

"No. There." Black Moon pointed to where a rivulet wandered into the trees. "Have water, plenty wood."

"You're an infuriatin' woman when you're right. Maybe I should've let those Crow take you off. 'Course, they likely would've killed you before long 'cause you're such a troublesome woman."

"Damn yes. You're stuck with me."

Cooper gave an exaggerated sigh, then grinned. "Let's go."

They found a nice spot where there was some new

grass, though yet sparse, near to hand, right near the stream's edge. Cooper tended the horses, hobbled them, and left them free to graze. He wasn't worried much about the mare, but the Blackfoot pony had been more than a little frisky at times, so he made sure the hobbles were tight to prevent flight but not enough to make foraging hard. Black Moon gathered firewood and started a blaze and set the last of their dried meat in a pot of boiling water.

"We make last coffee?" Black Moon asked.

Cooper sighed. He wanted it now but decided it would be best to wait. "Let's save it till mornin'."

Cooper sat, ready to relax for the rest of the day, but Black Moon began to make some meat racks.

"Why're you doin' that, Moon?"

"You'll make meat tomorrow. Since it's warm now, meat won't last unless we dry it."

"Good thinkin'. I should've known that since we did that not so long ago." He cursed himself silently at being so addlebrained to not realize that.

"Not your job to worry about such things. You catch meat, I care for it."

Cooper nodded. Exhausted from the past few weeks of toil, he lay his head back on his saddle and snoozed.

Sometime later—he didn't know how long it was— Black Moon woke him. "You eat again now."

"Thank you, Moon." He sat up and rubbed his face to try to remove some of the tiredness, then gratefully took the tin plate holding a healthy number of strips of hydrated jerky. "This the last of it?" he asked.

"Almost. Enough for early meal."

Cooper wasn't sure she was truthful, but he figured

he'd know in the morning. He hungrily began chewing the jerky, made from an elk he had found just downed by a pack of wolves. He managed to drive them off, cut out as much meat as he could carry, then left the carcass to the canines. Black Moon had taken it from there, but there hadn't been much.

When he had finished, Black Moon said, "You sleep more now. You're tired."

Cooper looked over her face and saw the lines and drawn look brought on by exhaustion and too much work. "You're just as tired as I am, woman. You need your rest too. Come on over here and sleep."

"I must make meat racks."

"You got 'em started. You can finish 'em while I'm out huntin' tomorrow. Now come on over here."

Grateful, she stretched out next to Cooper and lay her head on his chest. She sighed partly in relief and partly because she liked being close to her man this way.

They watched the day fade into dusk, then darkness. Before they knew it, they were asleep. When Cooper awoke, the sun was up, and Black Moon was at work on the small meat racks. A pot was boiling and, he was glad to notice, the coffeepot was just outside the flames. He stood and stretched. It didn't help much. He felt as if he hadn't really slept or eaten decently in years. He was tired of the traveling, the constant worry about having enough meat, the dearth of all manner of supplies, and the worry about having so little ammunition. He sighed. There was nothing he could do about what they had endured; what he could do is provide enough to keep him and Black Moon alive. And then there was the loss of his plews. They should be in

Cheyenne Killer's village before too much longer. He hoped.

Black Moon saw he was awake and rushed to pour him coffee and pull a few strips of jerky from the boiling water and handed them to him on a tin plate.

"There enough for you, Moon?"

She hesitated a moment before saying, "I ate before you wake."

"You're full of buffler muffins. Now come on here and share this meat and coffee with me."

"But..."

"Don't you argue with me, Moon. You need your strength every bit as much as I need mine, dammit."

Black Moon looked to be ready to argue anyway, until Cooper shot her a look that warned her not to do so. She smiled almost shyly and came over to sit next to him.

"That's better. Now eat."

When they had finished their sparse meal, Cooper went and saddled and bridled the Shoshoni's horse. He gathered up what pieces of rope and leather thongs they had, then mounted the mare. "With all those buffler so close, I shouldn't be gone long." He sounded much more confident than he was. He was a good hunter, he knew that. But with the strains of the past several months he wasn't sure he had the strength to shoot straight. He rode off, pushing such melancholy thoughts from his head.

In ten or fifteen minutes, he was nearing the herd. He stopped in a wash, pounded a picket stake in the ground, and tied the horse to it. He stood leaning against the slanted wall of the wash, able to see over the top of it. He surveyed the herd. He spotted a cow that looked like it would provide a good supply of delicious meat. He fired. The cow didn't move. He knew his lead ball had punctured it somewhere but obviously not in a vital spot.

"Damn, Hawley Cooper, you are the most god-awful critter these Stony Mountains have ever seen. Can't drop a buffler at less than ninety yards. Useless. Damned useless."

He muttered more curses at himself as he reloaded his rifle. "You ain't exactly plumb stocked with shootin' supplies. Best make this one count. If it don't, maybe you can use one of the lead pills on yourself." He took a deep breath and let it out slowly. He lay the rifle along the rim of the wash for stability. He hesitated.

"Oh, for chrissakes, Hawley, put the damn cow down and stop your frettin'." He steadied himself, sighted on his target, and fired. The buffalo dropped where she stood.

"That's better, you damned wretched critter." He climbed out of the wash and began yelling and waving his arms. It took a couple of minutes, but the herd finally began to rumble off.

He got his horse and picketed it near the dead buffalo. Then he set to butchering. He cut a large piece of the hide and spread it out. Next came the choicest cuts like the tongue, fleece, ribs, and brisket. He threw them on the hide and stood, ready to leave. He figured to come back as soon as he dropped this load off. He figured with his weight and the meat's, it might be too hard on the mare.

He stood, contemplating, then noticed that scavengers were already starting to gather at some distance.

It wouldn't take long before the wolves came for a meal, followed by coyotes and vultures.

He knelt again and cut another piece of hide, then started to toss more chunks of meat on it. He finally rose again and tied up each meat-filled hide. Having judged packs of beaver, he could fairly evaluate the weight of these. He hefted each one and figured each at about seventy pounds. The mare could easily carry that, though not with him riding.

"Well Hawley, looks like you got more walkin' to do." He loaded the two hides onto the horse, then taking the reins, began walking.

It took almost an hour to reach his camp. He noticed Black Moon's look of relief. It bothered him. "You think I run off?"

"No. I heard two shots. I thought you went under."

A sour, disgusted looked crossed Cooper's face.

"What's wrong?"

"It took me two goddamn shots to drop that goddamn buffler. Leaves me with three goddamn lead balls, which ain't enough to protect us should fractious goddamn Indians or animals decide to pester us." He yanked down the two hides. "Take care of 'em." He walked off to tend to the horse.

As he worked on the animal, his mind bounced from thoughts of disgust with himself for getting them in this predicament and anger at himself for treating Black Moon so poorly. "Well, dammit, it ain't gonna soothe things over with you standin' here pinin' for what was or what could've been," he muttered.

Cooper went over and knelt on the other side of the hide on which Black Moon was slicing the meat into thin strips. He took out his knife to grab a hunk of meat.

Black Moon slapped his hand away. "Go," she ordered. "You're not needed here, dammit."

"But..."

"Go!" She waved her knife in the general direction of another spot in the camp.

With a sigh, Cooper rose and went to the other hide, cut the thongs holding it and began slicing the buffalo meat. He shook his head sadly at his stupidity and the impetuousness that often brought him trouble. A few minutes later, Black Moon came over and stood behind him. *Good, she's forgiven me,* Cooper thought.

"You cut too damn thick," she said. "Cut thin, like this." She dropped a slice of meat on the hide next to his hand and walked away.

"Damn," he muttered and went back to work, hoping he didn't slice a finger off in his agitation.

Black Moon had earlier built a fire a few feet from the trees. It was now down to embers, and she began hanging the still-bloody strips from one of the meat racks on the near side of the fire. Finished, she went to the stream and washed up. When she returned, she said, "Still too damn fat. Make thinner."

Cooper fought back the surge of anger, and contritely said, "I'm tryin', Moon. I just ain't as nimble as you with such things."

"You watch, I do." She knelt and began slicing the meat into very thin slices.

Cooper watched for a few minutes, then went to the stream to drink and clean up. He returned.

"You're walkin' bad. Your feet hurt?"

"My moccasins ain't got much left on the bottoms. They're just about plumb wore through."

"You sit. I finish soon, then fix moccasins."

"You don't have to..."

"You're annoyin' me, dammit."

Cooper couldn't stop himself from letting go a gale of laughter. "'Bout time you put me in my place, woman," he gasped around the laughter.

"Yep." Her smile was wide and bright.

Dodged another bullet, Hawley, he thought. He went and sat against a log, watching her, a small smile on his face. It always pleased him to watch her, no matter what she was doing.

Before long the rest of the buffalo was hanging on the meat rack, and she had cut two small pieces of the hide. She got a few things from her little possible sack. She sat beside him and said, "Take off moccasins."

Cooper did so and handed them to her. "Mighty poor," she mumbled. "Should make new."

"We ain't got the time or supplies for such doins."

Black Moon nodded.

She picked up a moccasin and began cutting one of the pieces of hide to fit. She placed it into the moccasin, fur side up. "Make soft to walk on." She began sewing it in place, having some difficulty with trying to weave the sinew onto what was left of the soles. She finally managed and went to work on the other.

While she labored, Cooper said quietly, "I didn't mean to act so harshly before, Moon."

"I know."

"It wasn't right."

"Quiet before you annoy me again."

He grinned. "Yes, ma'am."

She handed him the repaired footwear. He put them on and walked around a little.

"These shine, Moon. Plumb shine." He stopped. "Let me see your feet."

"No. Mine're damn good."

He suddenly knelt and grabbed her legs. She fought him, but he managed to get a look at the soles of her moccasins. "Fix yours," he ordered.

"No. Is good."

"Dammit, Moon, now you're startin' to annoy *me*. Yours are as bad as mine were. You got what you need to fix yours. Do it."

"Need to cook."

"Like hell. Just get to it." Before she could argue, he added, "You keep fussin' about this, and I'll pull off them mocs and sit on you till you finish."

"All right." She pushed herself up then bolted.

But she was not fast enough, and Cooper grabbed an ankle and pulled her down. "You ain't gettin' away from me that easy. Moon." He expected her to fight some more, but he was surprised when she giggled.

"I fix now. Yep. No lyin'."

"Best not be lyin'," he said in fake anger.

He let her up and she set to work. Not much later, she was done and pulled on the footwear.

"Ain't that better?"

"Damn good, yep." She grinned.

"Why'd you run, then?"

"Wanted you to catch me." She tumbled onto him. "Is good you did."

"Yep."

EIGHT

MORE THAN A MONTH LATER, Cooper and Black Moon Woman stumbled into Cheyenne Killer's village. They were gaunt, ragged, hungry, and exhausted. While they had rested quite a bit, it was not enough. Along the last part of the trek, Cooper had used one of his three remaining lead balls to kill another buffalo and they had some dried meat, but it was not enough. On some days it was hot, on others muggy. Some days it rained, and for the first couple weeks, it occasionally snowed. There were times when they had little water, and the ground was often rocky and covered with cactus. The Crow pony ran off shortly after leaving, so they both walked, gently leading Black Moon's mare with the travois. Within a week, the horse's ribs could easily be seen, and the animal was footsore and haggard.

Many Shoshonis ran up to them; others went to get Cheyenne Killer and Blue Bear, Black Moon Woman's father. Cuts Throat, Cooper's friend, raced toward the newly arrived, bedraggled travelers.

Cheyenne Killer, Blue Bear, and Cuts Throat arrived moments apart. "Daughter," Blue Bear exclaimed when he saw her condition. He looked at Cooper. "Why you make my daughter so poor?"

"Stop," Cheyenne Killer said. "Now is not the time. Let's get our children into my lodge. Some of you boys care for pony."

Blue Bear gently—more gently than Cooper had expected, given his volatility and the disrespect with which he had treated his daughter so often—helped Black Moon Woman into the lodge.

Cuts Throat hurried to help Cooper, but the white man stopped him, saying, "Wait. Who's the boy ready to take the horse?"

"Calling Elk."

Cooper waved the boy over. "Treat that pony well, you hear," he said. Cuts Throat translated. "She's a brave animal and got us back to the village at great expense to herself."

The youth nodded when Cuts Throat had finished translating.

"Come, friend," the Shoshoni said. He slid a broad shoulder under Cooper's arm and helped him walk into Cheyenne Killer's lodge.

Several women set food and coffee before Cooper and Black Moon, both of whom dug in hungrily.

"Take time," Cheyenne Killer admonished quietly. "Get sick if eat too fast."

The two slowed down. The lodge was quiet except for the crackling of the fire and the sounds of Cooper and Black Moon eating.

Finally the two were finished with the food, but they took more coffee.

"Tell," Blue Bear snapped.

Cooper looked at him with tired but agitated eyes. "I'll tell when I'm damned good and ready to do so, not because you order me to." He continued to stare at Blue Bear for a few seconds, then slowly sipped some coffee.

Blue Bear looked ready to explode, but he settled down a tiny bit after a few words from Cheyenne Killer.

Noticing it, Cooper said, "We were trappin' up along the Snake, well to the west. Weren't gettin' many beaver, so we decided to move on. Bad storm caught us in a flat after crossin' the South Fork of the Snake. Nothin' we could do but push on. Then the mules broke free and run off."

"Should care better of mules. Or horses." Blue Bear's statement was not said politely.

Cooper turned a baleful eye on the Shoshoni elder. "You talk to me like that again and I'll raise your..."

Cuts Throat placed an arm on one of Cooper's and shook his head. Then he turned toward Blue Bear and let out a string of angry Shoshoni.

"What'd you say to him?" Cooper asked. He could speak and understand the language, but not when it was spoken so rapidly and vehemently.

"Same as you. But it comes from another man not from a part of family."

Blue Bear still seethed but said nothing. Cheyenne Killer looked at Cuts Throat with a wisp of a smile. Then he turned to Cooper. "Tell more, please," Cheyenne Killer urged.

"We rode it out and make a little more progress, but not much. Then another storm rolled over us and another a few days after that. Finally seemed like we were gonna make progress, and we got hit one more time. The horses were strugglin'. We made it back to where we had stayed a couple miles back for a few days. Then we got wintered in. My gelding froze to death, Black Moon's mare lived but was in mighty bad shape, as you could see outside. I hunted some but had to be careful because I was low on lead and powder."

"You lie," Blue Bear said.

Cooper bit down his growing anger. He reached into his shooting bag and pulled out two lead balls. "This is what I got left."

"That all?" Cuts Throat asked.

"Yep."

"You waste powder and ball. Can't hunt good."

Cooper sucked in a breath and let it out slowly, then looked at Cheyenne Killer. "This old man is an insult to your...our people, Father. You should be ashamed of him. A true Shoshoni would not insult the son of a friend."

"You are not Shoshoni!" Blue Bear said.

Cooper ignored him and continued to address Cheyenne Killer. "Keep him away from me, Father. He comes against me, and I'll cut out his heart and let the women use it for a game of *dazigidɨ*—shinny."

Blue Bear jumped up and looked to be ready to leap over the fire to get at Cooper. But Cuts Throat stood in front of Cooper. He spoke sharply to his elder, who soon turned and stomped out.

"*Huuwihyu*—Thanks," Cooper said as his friend sat.

"Thought you needed help because you're tired and not in good health now."

Cooper nodded.

"You make enemy now," Cheyenne Killer said.

"He never liked me," Cooper said with a shrug. "But what I said was true, Father. Keep that man away from me. I may need to recruit myself for a spell, but I ain't against puttin' a lead ball in his lights."

"I'll do."

"Me too," Cuts Throat added.

Black Moon was weaving as tiredness grew in her, and Cooper was slumped, almost asleep where he sat.

"You rest now," Cheyenne Killer said. He pointed to a pile of buffalo robes at the back of the tipi. Cooper helped Black Moon, and both made it to the robes— barely—before they collapsed.

Cooper and Black Moon spent another two days in Cheyenne Killer's lodge, resting and regaining their strength. One of Cheyenne Killer's wives and Cooper's Shoshoni mother, Running Calf, and Pony Woman, Black Moon Woman's best friend and Cooper's Shoshoni sister, had quickly made clothes for the two— a buckskin shirt and trousers for him, a buckskin dress and leggings for her—and moccasins for both.

COOPER WALKED out into the glaring sunlight, letting his eyes adjust to the brightness. It was a dazzling late spring day, and Cooper felt himself refreshed. Then he began to stroll around the village. He was the recipient of a few unhospitable looks, mostly from friends of Blue Bear's, he figured. But most of the people greeted him warmly, remembering his bravery in a raid against the Crows last year.

He saw Blue Bear coming toward him, pulling a knife as he did so. Cooper turned to face him. Blue Bear moved confidently and slowly, apparently, Cooper thought, to impress Cooper, letting the mountain man know how mighty a warrior he was.

Cooper didn't know why Blue Bear didn't charge him, and was surprised, though only for a moment. It gave him time to set himself. Blue Bear rushed the last few feet, the arm holding the knife high, and swiftly swung the weapon down, aiming to put the blade in Cooper's upper chest, tearing down through the heart.

Cooper blocked the knife arm with his left and smashed Blue Bear across the face with his right forearm. Then he kicked the Shoshoni's feet out from under him. Blue Bear landed face down in the dirt with a thud, and before he could move, Cooper knelt on his back.

"I'm plumb tired of you bein' such a troublesome son of a bitch, Blue Bear. I never did anything to you that'd cause such hatred."

"You stole daughter, bring much shame on me," Blue Bear said, voice muffled with his face in the dirt.

"Like hell. I paid full bride price for her. If any chil' would think I stole her, it'd be Cuts Throat. He was the one plannin' to marry her before I got in the way. He got over it and married a girl in Pony Woman equal to Black Moon Woman. If Pony Woman wasn't my sister, I would've married her, and Cuts Throat then would've married Black Moon Woman. We're both pleased with our women. You got no say in it anymore."

"You're not Shoshoni."

Cheyenne Killer was among the many who had gathered around to watch this spectacle, and he knelt at Blue Bear's side. "He *is* Shoshoni," the leader said, speaking in his own tongue, which Cooper mostly understood. "He is my adopted son, and so he is as much one of the people as you or me."

"Thank you, Father," Cooper said. He paused, then, "You have a choice here, Blue Bear, leave me to go in peace and you go your own way, never to bother me again. Or I take your hair here and now."

A gasp went up from the Shoshonis. Most of the villagers had little liking for Blue Bear, who was irascible and taken to bullying people. But there were some, including his two sons, who were fond of him. Either way, Cooper knew, he likely would die as soon as he put Blue Bear under, though Cheyenne Killer, Cuts Throat, and some others would back him in a fight. Cooper also knew that if he did as he said, and a battle among the people started, it would cut a hole through the heart of this band.

"I have thought of another way, Father." When Cheyenne Killer nodded, Cooper continued, "I leave here and never come back. I have many friends here, but if it'll keep the peace between my Shoshoni brothers, I'll do it and keep my distance, even should your band come to rendezvous."

"You've brought shame to yourself and our people, Blue Bear," Cheyenne Killer said in Shoshoni. "And now you might cost me my son. I can't let him kill you, but I can. I ask you to leave my son in peace and become an important warrior among our people again."

Blue Bear lay there sweating and breathing in dirt, then finally said, "He is safe from me."

"It is good."

Cooper rose and walked away. Cheyenne Killer helped his old companion up, said a few words to him, and hurried to catch up to Cooper, who had been joined by Cuts Throat. The others drifted away to their own tasks.

"Think he'll keep his word, Father?" Cooper asked.

"Yes, but his sons might not. We will have a lodge for you and Black Moon soon." He pointed to a tipi being raised.

"Stay in my lodge with Pony Woman," Cuts Throat said. "There is room, and with two of us there, Gray Feather and Buffalo Tail will have to face us both if they try to kill you."

Cooper looked at Cheyenne Killer, who nodded. "That'd plumb shine with me," Cooper said.

"You ready for the hunt tomorrow?" Cuts Throat asked as they walked toward Cheyenne Killer's lodge. "Healthy? Strong?"

"Yep."

"Then why you look so sad?"

"Can't do much huntin' without powder and lead."

"We have plenty. You'll get all you need."

"Didn't the people have a spring hunt already?"

"Yes, but the elders want more meat before we leave for Popo Agie. You join us. Have plenty of lead and powder."

"You sure?"

"Yes. Many mules will carry all the powder and lead you need. Ten mules, a dozen mules. More than the eye can see."

Cooper had brightened, and both were laughing now. "You're some crazy redskin."

"And you are a crazy pale-face."

USING A BORROWED pony that was well trained in buffalo hunting, Cooper participated with elation. Running buffalo had become, in the couple hunts he had taken part in, a real pleasure.

When it was over, the village had plenty of meat. The women bustled about slicing meat and getting it onto racks to dry. Others were tanning the hides, some with fur, some without.

Amid the frenzy, Cheyenne Killer and Cooper picked out four horses—two for Cooper and two for Black Moon. One each was for riding, Black Moon's second horse would pull a travois; the other was an extra, to be used if something happened to one of the others.

Cooper also picked out a mule. He had some plews, and Cheyenne Killer had given him some more. It was a small pile, but he had at least something to trade and might be able to get enough supplies for the fall hunt.

Finally the crier went around announcing that the village would be moving in the morning, heading to the annual mountain man rendezvous. Excitement buzzed though the band.

NINE

"YOU KNOW WE'RE FOLLOWED?" Cuts Throat asked.

"Yep. I reckon you've known for a spell," Cooper said.

Cuts Throat shrugged. "A little."

The two were riding several days ahead of the village. They had left the women, extra horses, pack mules, and travois back with the band. The people's caravan moved far too slowly for Cooper and Cuts Throat, so they rode on ahead, figuring they'd wait at or near the rendezvous site.

Black Moon Woman and Pony Woman were not happy with the plan but accepted it, as it was what their men wanted.

"You think it's Gray Feather and Buffalo Tail?"

"Can't be anyone else."

"Figured. What do you want to do about 'em?"

"You make choice. They after you not me." Cuts Throat grinned.

"You afraid?" Cooper said with a chuckle.

Cuts Throat laughed. "Only of Pony Woman when she gets mad."

Cooper laughed too. He quieted down, then asked seriously, "You willin' to kill a couple of your tribesmen?"

"It's strange, maybe. But when they come against my friend, they no longer Shoshonis to me."

"Then we take 'em down?"

"*Oosh*—Yes."

"Fight up close or take 'em down from a distance?"

"Fight 'em."

"You sure?"

"*Oosh*. Unless their medicine is very strong, we handle 'em, easy."

"Think they have strong medicine?"

"No. They are, how you say...vermin?"

"Couple of mouse farts."

"I don't know meaning of that, but I understand," Cuts Throat said with a laugh.

They slowed their pace a little, not enough to alert their followers but enough to let them close the gap a bit. They passed one of the numerous piles of rocks they had encountered, a little larger than some, a little smaller than others. But instead of riding on, they slipped behind the rocks, ground staked their horses and climbed up on the boulders.

Gray Feather and Buffalo Tail came into view about fifty yards away. They were in no hurry and seemed to not be paying much attention.

"Slow and inattentive as they're comin," Cooper said, "I reckon they figure to catch us sleepin' tonight or maybe tomorrow or the next night."

"Means they die."

"Yep."

They waited patiently, ignoring the hot sun beating on them. Finally, Gray Feather and Buffalo Tail were less than fifteen yards away. "Ready?" Cooper asked.

"Yes." The two quickly climbed down the rocks, mounted their horses and rode out from behind the boulders. Cooper's rifle was slung through the loop just behind his saddle horn; Cuts Throat's bow was unstrung and inside its case attached to his quiver.

They stopped with not even five yards between them and the followers. "You boys're on the wrong trail," Cooper said.

"Turn back and live," Cuts Throat said in Shoshoni. "Stay and die."

"That white-eyed devil disgraced our father. We will restore his honor," Gray Feather responded in kind.

"Your father is a worm, less than a worm," Cuts Throat said. "He had no honor before he was fool enough to dishonor my friend. And he couldn't defeat *Too-Shah-Itsup-Mah-Washay*—He Who is the White Wolf Killer. He brought shame on himself."

Buffalo Tail started to pull his bow over his shoulder. In turn, Cooper pulled one of his flintlock pistols. "Don't," he said simply.

The Shoshoni looked as if he were contemplating not obeying but thought better of it and took his hand off the bow.

Cooper clipped the pistol back onto his belt. "Well, boys," he said, figuring Cuts Throat would translate for him if he thought necessary. "You plannin' to ride off?"

Gray Feather yanked out his tomahawk and charged at him. Buffalo Tail did the same at Cuts Throat.

Cooper jerked out his own tomahawk. Though he was capable enough of a fighter on horseback, he preferred being on foot. But he had to do what was needed. He ducked as Gray Feather raced up and swung his weapon. In turn, the mountain man spun his horse and waited the two seconds as Gray Feather turned his animal and came back for another try.

The tomahawks clanged as the two men swung at each other while their horses danced and snorted.

Cooper had not regained all his strength and was tiring somewhat already. He jerked his horse a bit and it bounced into Gray Feather's pony, shaking the Shoshoni a little. Cooper was on the wrong side to just chop the warrior down, so he grabbed Gray Feather's buckskin shirt and yanked. The Shoshoni tumbled to the ground.

Cooper leaped off his own pony and sent it moving away with a slap on the rump. He turned as Gray Feather was getting up. Cooper gave him a condescending smile. He advanced, swinging his 'hawk easily in front of him, a challenge in his eyes.

Gray Feather rose slowly and watched Cooper's slow, steady approach. Suddenly he swung his weapon in a swift, vicious arc meant to separate Cooper's head from his shoulders.

Cooper barely managed to block it, the shock of the blow sending a strong tremor though his arm. Cooper tried to kick the Shoshoni, but the warrior danced out of the way. Cooper staggered back a few steps.

The two combatants faced each other, breathing heavily, sweat glistening on their faces. *This ain't gonna be as easy as I thought*, Cooper realized. He glanced over at Cuts Throat, and saw the warrior go down,

Buffalo Tail ready to pounce on him. Ignoring Gray Feather, he turned and ran the few feet, grabbed Buffalo Tail by the hair, jerked his head back and clumsily used his tomahawk blade to slice the warrior's throat.

Cuts Throat leaped up just in time to have Gray Feather run into him and bounce off. Cuts Throat, who had lost his tomahawk, whipped out his knife and drove it deep into Gray Feather's abdomen and jerked it upward.

Gray Feather stood for a moment, then collapsed.

Cooper and Cuts Throat stood there breathing heavily. Finally, Cooper said, "What'n hell were you doin' takin' a nap while I was fightin'?"

"Thought I'd rest up a bit before comin' to help you," Cuts Throat responded, not missing a beat.

"I saved you."

"I saved you."

Both grinned. "We did shine in these here doins, didn't we, my friend?"

"*Oosh.*"

"What're we gonna do with these here lice?"

"You, nothing." Cooper glanced at his friend in question. "I'll take 'em back to the band, let Cheyenne Killer and Blue Bear decide."

"Let's go, then."

"No. You stay or go on. I go back alone. Better that way."

Cooper nodded. "I'll mosey along."

"I'll catch up soon."

"*Abisha'i*—Bye."

Cuts Throat threw one of the dead Shoshonis over the man's pony, and Cooper did the same with the other dead warrior. Then Cooper and Cuts Throat rode off in different directions.

After a couple of hours, moseying along, Cooper spotted a small herd of buffalo grazing in a little meadow. He shot a fat cow, cut out a few pieces of the choicest meat, wrapped it in a piece of hide and got back on the trail. A few hours later, he decided to make camp before dark. His strength was ebbing, which angered him. "Weak-kneed ol' cuss," he mumbled as he tended to his horse. He was annoyed at his lack of strength yet and hoped he could recover his full vigor before long.

Done, he built up a fire and put on coffee and some meat. As he waited for the food, his mind drifted back over the last year or so. He had come a long way. He was not the shy, frightened boy he had been when he had met the odious Josiah Weeks in St. Louis. He had suffered horrific treatment by the despicable old man, afraid to stand up for himself. But he had become a man along the way and been hardened by surviving the frigid hell he had endured when Weeks had left him unconscious with nothing but the clothes he wore. He persevered and struggled through horrors he could only have imagined before he was thrust into that snowy, glacial nightmare. He was about an hour from death but didn't know it. He simply wanted it to end and was ready for it to come. He had fought as hard as he could but his thoughts as he faded were both regretful and peaceful. After all he had gone through, he figured he would certainly be seeing the pearly gates soon.

Then came a different kind of savior—a Shoshoni war chief named Cheyenne Killer—who had gathered him up and took him back to his village. There he awoke to a sight he never thought he would see, a beautiful Shoshoni named Pony Woman. As he gained his strength then, he wanted desperately to marry her. He was crestfallen when he learned that Cheyenne Killer had adopted him, and as Pony Woman was now his sister, he could not. But then his sister introduced him to a young woman as equally beautiful and helpful as Pony Woman. Her name was *Tuhupihten Mea Wa'ippe* —Black Moon Woman—and he was immediately smitten.

Despite Black Moon returning his feelings, his wish was not to be. At least for some time. Her father, Blue Bear, had promised his daughter to Cuts Throat. Almost frantic with desire, he had challenged the young warrior for her hand. The battle was far harder than he had imagined. Cuts Throat was a strong, accomplished warrior already, but somehow, Cooper managed to defeat Cuts Throat, and Black Moon Woman was his, much to the rage of Blue Bear. Cuts Throat, on the other hand, soon became the mountain man's best friend among the Shoshonis.

He had cemented his position as a Shoshoni when he showed his courage and resilience in a raid against the Crows. He gained more fame during a small battle with the Blackfeet at the rendezvous and, later, in avenging his travails by dispatching Josiah Weeks.

He shook his head in annoyance. He had thought then that he was in a good place—a full-fledged mountaineer, tested by enemies and the elements, married to a good woman, and ready for the fall beaver hunt. Then came the winter, and the thoughts and fears of his lone trek had returned, worsened in knowing that he now had a woman to protect. And now he wanted her to be with him.

He spit into the fire, growling at himself. He cut off some meat and began eating.

———

CUTS THROAT CAUGHT up with him three days later; Cooper had not been in any hurry. The Shoshoni called out a greeting in the dark, knowing Cooper would be on alert for enemies, and he didn't want to get shot by mistake.

"What happened?" Cooper asked, as Cuts Throat settled in next to the fire and was filling his face with buffalo.

"Blue Bear was upset."

"Upset?"

Cuts Throat chuckled a little. "Like mad buffalo. Made threats. Said he'd eat your heart."

"I don't figure he's gonna get his way."

"No. Your father said that if Blue Bear caused any more trouble, Cheyenne Killer would kill him himself."

"Will he?"

"Yes. They are old companions, longtime warriors together, not really friends. Not enemies either. Cheyenne Killer don't like him much. He has, how you say, had enough?"

Cooper nodded.

"So Cheyenne Killer won't let him do anything."

Cooper suddenly had a worrisome thought. "Black Moon? He won't hurt her, will he?" The wrong answer would have him on his horse and riding hell-bent back to the band. Then, "Wait, I hear someone out there."

Cuts Throat grinned widely and whistled.

"Not to worry, Hawwy."

Black Moon Woman and Pony Woman rode into the small camp, towing two horses with travois and Cooper's pack mule with what plews he had. Black Moon was off her horse and running toward him before the surprised mountain man barely had time to rise. They hugged each other hard and long.

"How?" Cooper asked.

"These two nagged me to come till I had to surrender." He laughed. "Besides, me and Cheyenne Killer worried Blue Bear might hurt Black Moon even if he'd die. Figured to bring her. Then Pony Woman started arguin," he added.

"Hush," Pony Woman said. "You ask me to come."

Cooper laughed. As best he could tell, Pony Woman and Black Moon Woman were the only two Shoshoni women to get away with sassing their husbands.

The men's benevolence went only so far, so as Cooper and Cuts Throat went back to feeding, the women began caring for the animals and then sat to eat.

TEN

THERE WERE few men at the supposed rendezvous site along the Popo Agie. "Don't seem right," Cooper said.

"No."

They rode into the site, followed by the women. They stopped near the first man they encountered. "We too late?" Cooper asked. "Or was I told wrong about the place?"

"Nope, neither. Mr. Sublette brought goods here and traded some. Then that ol' hoss took the rest—most of 'em fer certain—and headed on to Pierre's Hole. Heard most of the boys were meetin' there."

"Thanks."

The man wandered away.

"What now?" Cuts Throat asked.

"I'll be headin' for Pierre's Hole myself. You think Cheyenne Killer and the others would figure to do the same?"

"Might. If there's trade there he will."

As they sat there thinking, a drunken trapper

strolled up and looked over Pony Woman. "How much you take for her?" he asked.

Cuts Throat and Cooper said nothing but watched the man closely.

"Don't need her for long. Just a spell of sportin'. Give you a good price."

Cuts Throat moved up a few feet, then slammed the sole of his left foot into the man's face.

Another man wandered up, as drunk as the first. "Well, hell, boys, if you won't give us a time with that 'un, how about the other?" He leered at Black Moon Woman.

Cooper smashed the curved butt of his rifle on the side of the man's neck. The man joined his fellow on the ground.

Both men rose, wobbling, and reached for pistols.

"You want to keep your hair, boys, best mosey on," Cooper said. "Though if we were to let you skunk farts have a go at these women, you'd be sorry. They'd like as not cut off your stones and stick the tiny things up your nose. Now move on."

The two seemed to be considering the odds, then stumbled off.

"All white-eyes so foolish?"

"Nope. Just some, especially when they got a snootful of firewater."

"What we do now?" Cuts Throat asked.

"Like I said, I aim to move on to Pierre's Hole. If you think Cheyenne Killer and the others'll want to do so, maybe you best ride on back and let 'em know."

Cuts Throat considered that for a few moments. "I go faster alone."

Cooper nodded. "I'll take Pony Woman along with me and Black Moon. We'll be all right."

Cuts Throat chucked his head toward the two recent offenders, who had passed out a few yards away. "What about them?"

"They'll be so ailin' from all that awardenty they had that they'll be lucky to find their pizzles to water the grass, let alone come chasin' after me and the women."

The two women giggled, and Cuts Throat grinned.

"You're not spendin' the night here?"

"Reckon not. I ain't worried about them two, or any of the others here, but it don't pay to test my medicine for the hell of it. 'Sides, there's still plenty of daylight left. We'll wait near the rendezvous site, less'n it looks like we'll be unwelcome."

With a nod, Cuts Throat turned his pony and galloped off.

"All right, ladies, let's move. Time's a-wastin'."

THEY MOVED NORTHWEST, heading for Togwotee Pass and the Tetons beyond. They did not rush, but they did not dawdle. For the first few days, Cooper kept an eye on their back trail, but finally decided that no one was following them.

The travel was uneventful except for two grizzly scares and crossing a few snowpack-swollen rivers. In just under two weeks, they were nearing Pierre's Hole, and Cooper began to grow a little apprehensive. This was too near where their winter ordeal had brought them. He wasn't afraid exactly, but the still-fresh memory of the past winter left him a bit uneasy.

Black Moon could sense it, and one night while resting in their robes, she said, "Put bad damn thoughts out of head."

Cooper just grunted in response.

"We alive. Those mountains not defeat us. We're strong. You strong. Damn so."

"Not strong enough or I would've gotten us through the mountains without half killin' us." Cooper's voice was full of shame and disgust with himself.

"But we live. You made meat, you killed damn Crows, walked many miles. You damn good man, Hawwy Cooper."

Cooper just grunted again and turned away from her, trying to fall asleep. It was a long time in coming, and he was in no better humor in the morning. He knew Black Moon was worried about him and wanted to help, but there was nothing she could do. He would have to live with his self-loathing until he could find a way to wrestle it into submission. He wasn't sure he could ever succeed. He also knew that Black Moon and Pony Woman were discussing him at times, but he didn't care.

Two days later, Cooper sensed as much as heard someone coming up on them. "Quick, get behind those rocks there," he ordered the women, pointing. They did not hesitate. Cooper took up post behind a thick spruce, rifle ready. As he heard the rider approaching the curve he and the women had just come around, he said sharply, "Best turn back, hoss, 'less you want a lead pill in your lights."

"You ain't gonna shoot me, Hawwy," Cuts Throat said as he rounded the curve.

Cooper uncocked his rifle. "I just might since you're such a bother."

Cuts Throat cast a curious eye at him. "Something eatin' at you?"

"Nope. Ride on and take the women with you. I'll follow, keep an eye on our back trail."

Cuts Throat started to say something but kept silent. He waved to the women to follow him and moved slowly up the trail.

That night as they sat at the fire chewing on some elk that Cuts Throat had shot before he had reached Cooper, he said harshly to the mountain man, who had caught up not long ago, "Time you go back east, where there're houses made of wood and stone."

Cooper looked at him in surprise and some shock not only at the words but at Cuts Throat's tone.

"Weak warrior not a Shoshoni. You say you weak. I say go back to your other people. You no longer Shoshoni."

Cooper looked from Cuts Throat to Black Moon Woman. The two, and Pony Woman sat there stony faced. "That what you want, Moon?" he asked bitterly.

"No," she said quietly, head down.

"See, Cuts Throat, it's only you who wants me gone. I leave and you can take Black Moon as a wife, like you always wanted."

"No," Black Moon said more sternly, raising her head. "He don't want you to go. Your sister don't want you to go."

"Then what'n hell do you all want? Seems like you

don't want me here either. Well, to hell with all of you."
He rose.

"Sit!" Cuts Throat said loudly and sharply.

Cooper looked at him, his eyes red with anger. He
started to reach for the tomahawk resting in his belt at
the small of his back.

"You don't want to kill me. I don't want to kill you.
Sit and we talk."

Seething, Cooper sat. "What do you want, then?"

"We want *Too-Shah-Itsup-Mah-Washay* back,"
Cuts Throat said. "We want to see the warrior who
saved many Shoshoni, who took Crow and Blackfoot
scalps. The courageous Shoshoni who conquered
winter, two times. The warrior who helped beat Crows.
The man who took revenge on the worm who wronged
him." He tapped Cooper's chest. "That strong, brave,
white-eyed Shoshoni is here, not here." Cuts Throat
moved his fingers to Cooper's head.

Cooper slapped Cuts Throat's hand away and sat
there, looked at and through the fire.

"If that warrior has left your heart, my friend, go.
We don't need weak man, afraid of everything. I need
strong friend. Pony Woman needs strong brother. Black
Moon needs strong husband."

"You son of a bitch," Cooper snarled. He half rose
and tumbled into Cuts Throat, who threw him off and
to the ground. Enraged, Cooper charged at Cuts
Throat. The Shoshoni dodged him and shoved him.
Cooper almost fell into the fire. He jumped up, pulled
his knife, and moved slowly toward Cuts Throat.

The Shoshoni stood, face indifferent, waiting.

Cooper took two steps when Black Moon screamed,
"Stop, Hawwy!"

Cooper stopped. It was as if he had been dunked into the depth of an icy half-frozen winter stream. He looked down at the knife in his hand, as if he didn't know what it was and where it came from. He dropped the blade and charged into the forest.

Black Moon started to go after him, but Cuts Throat shook his head. "He must find his heart alone," he said in his language.

Cooper ran headlong into the darkness, bouncing off trees. Finally he stopped, leaning against a tree, his breath coming in short, sharp bursts. He pounded the tree several times with the sides of his fists. He suddenly threw back his head and let out a long, unintelligible bellow—a ululating wail of pain, anger, and shame.

When it had faded away, Cooper rested his back against the tree and slid down it until he was sitting. "Lord A'mighty, you are some pitiful critter, Hawley Cooper. Ain't worth a pope's pecker."

He drew in a long, deep breath and let it out slowly. He seemed to be over the strong melancholy that he had carried the past day or so. Now there was another problem. "Well, ol' hoss, you're in some pickle now. You can't stay out here forever, but you got a new itch that maybe you can't scratch." He was too ashamed to go back to the camp—even if he could find it in the dark, he thought—and face his family, as that was what Black Moon Woman, Cuts Throat, and Pony Woman were. He'd almost rather face another winter in the mountains, unarmed and defenseless, than go back to face them.

He stood and took another deep breath. "Time to face up to it, ol' hoss." He tried to get his bearings. He thought he could see a faint flicker of the fire between the trees. It was as good a way to go as any. He stepped off, moving carefully to avoid walking into tree trunks. He moved a little faster when he realized that it was the camp's fire.

He stopped at the edge of the forest. "I'm comin' in. You can shoot me if you want for bein' such a skunk's ass." He stepped into the camp. Black Moon ran up and threw her arms around his middle and rested her head against his chest. Cooper wasn't sure, but he thought she was crying. He couldn't blame her for that. He wanted to do so himself, but he could not—would not. He was shamed enough already.

Arms around each other, they went to the fire and sat.

"I'd be obliged if you was to forgive my foolishness," he said quietly.

"It all right," Black Moon said. "Your spirit traveled a different path for a while. Now it back."

Cooper shook his head, not sure what to say.

"My strong warrior friend White Wolf is back," Cuts Throat said.

"I ain't so certain."

"Took brave man, strong warrior to do this, my friend. Your spirit is back. All is good. Damn good."

Cooper, still embarrassed, looked at Black Moon. She nodded and smiled, her eyes still sparkling with teardrops.

ELEVEN

HAWLEY COOPER SET the butt of his rifle on the ground and stood with wrists crossed on the muzzle. A shudder slid up his spine like a small serpent. He shook it off.

"You all right?" Cuts Throat asked.

"Yeah," Cooper said with a nod. He looked out over the wide, long valley, covered with thick grass and a profusion of colorful wildflowers. The river was lined with cottonwoods and willows. The remembrance of what he and Black Moon endured on that hellacious trek was still fresh in his mind, and he did not like it. But the two of them had conquered it, and that was all that mattered, he supposed. It was just another one of the ways these mountains tried to kill anyone who dared challenge their dominance. "Sure as hell looks mighty different than it did last winter, though," he said, the wind whipping the words away.

"You miss the snow and cold?" Cuts Throat asked with a small laugh.

"Maybe I'll fix it so you can spend the winter out here. Would you like that?" But he, too, laughed.

There were maybe fifty or sixty white trappers bustling about, mostly near William Sublette's series of trading tents. Their own tents and simple campsites were scattered around without organization, the way a mountain man's rendezvous should be. There was a village of Nez Perce and one of Flatheads off to the right, and a small gathering of Crows off to the left. Hundreds of horses stretched out along the Indian encampments.

Cuts Throat pointed to the Crow camp. "You should hide those Absaroka scalps hangin' on your saddle."

"Reckon so," Cooper said with a grin. "I don't suppose those master horse thievin' bastards'll try to grab some ponies here, bein' outnumbered as they are, but I don't figure they'll take kindly to a trapper flauntin' a bunch of Crow scalps."

"You're wise, White Wolf, for a white-eye," Cuts Throat said with a chuckle.

"It's *because* I'm a white-eye," Cooper responded with a small laugh.

"So what now?"

"I reckon we can wait here 'til Cheyenne Killer and the others arrive. I'd rather go on down there and set up a camp and wait there for the others. We can find a spot for the band instead of takin' the leftovers if more trappers arrive."

"That shines, I think you say?"

Cooper nodded. He and the three Shoshonis walked their horses slowly down into the immense valley and to their right. Finding a likely spot, Cooper stopped them. "This'll do."

"Too far from river." Cuts Throat said.

"Where, then?"

Cuts Throat surveyed the area, then pointed.

"Kind of far from everything else."

"We camp there. You can go camp next to Crow if you like better."

"Reckon that place you're pointin' to shines with me."

"Wise. For a white-eye," Cuts Throat said with a laugh. Cooper joined in.

"Upriver a little way from the Flatheads?"

Cuts Throat nodded. They swung to their right and began to skirt the Nez Perce village and continued on past that of the Flatheads.

"Here," Cuts Throat finally said.

The women began putting up the lodges. Cuts Throat started unsaddling his horse, while Cooper just stood there, a faraway look in his eye, as if he were staring into the sun.

"You not gonna help?" Cuts Throat asked somewhat peevishly.

"Ain't sure, Cuts Throat."

"You're angry because I don't like where you want to camp?"

"No. No. I just..." How could he explain to his friend that he was ashamed to go to Sublette with this paltry take of plews. It ate at him that Sublette—or anyone else who saw his take—would think him unworthy of calling himself a mountain man. Two years of battling hellacious weather, barely escaping with his life, and almost nothing to show for it.

He sighed. There was no putting it off. The longer he waited, the harder it would be. Better to get it done, especially when not all the trappers were here, though they would be soon.

"No, I ain't gonna help, Cuts Throat. Not now. I got some business to tend to."

Cuts Throat waited for more. When none was forthcoming, he nodded. It was obvious to him that something was troubling Cooper, but he didn't want to talk about it.

Cooper grabbed the rope to the pack mule, then mounted his horse. A worried-looking Black Moon started to approach him, but he shook his head. Then he was gone.

WITH A GROWING SENSE OF EMBARRASSMENT, he approached William Sublette's main trade tent. A stout, fierce-looking man sat on an old barrel, writing in an account book. "Are you Mr. Sublette?" Cooper asked.

"I am, young man, I am. And who are you?"

"Name's Hawley Cooper."

"Ain't heard of you before."

"No, sir. Last rendezvous was my first."

Sublette looked at Cooper in thought for a minute. "You're that fellow who made gone beaver of that detestable Josiah Weeks, aren't you?"

"Yes, sir."

"Showed your mettle against Bug's Boys, too, if I recall."

"Yes, sir."

Sublette rose and extended his hand. Cooper shook it. "So, what can I do for you, Mr. Cooper?"

"Came to trade in my plews."

"That's what I'm here for." He looked through the open side of the tent and saw Cooper's mule. "That all you have?"

"Yes, sir." Cooper hung his head in embarrassment.

"You that poor a hunter?" Sublette seemed almost amused, though Cooper did not see it.

"I don't think so," Cooper said, lifting his head to look Sublette in the face. "But I ain't had much experience. I caught more'n this, but in a hell of a storm, the mules took off with all my plews and damn near all our supplies."

"There was more than one of you?"

"Just my woman, a Shoshoni named Black Moon Woman."

"So you got some back but not nearly all, eh?"

"Yes, sir. Got caught up in one fierce storm after another." He sighed. "Hardly made it back to Cheyenne Killer's Shoshoni village alive."

Sublette grinned a little. "You ain't the only feller lost horse and beaver, Mr. Cooper."

Cooper felt a small jolt of relief, but he was still mighty worried. "Can I bring 'em, in? I got two packs."

"Certainly, young man, certainly."

Cooper hauled in one pack, then the other.

With a practiced eye, Sublette said, "These ain't full packs, son."

"No sir. I figure maybe seventy pounds each 'stead of the usual ninety or a hundred. I thought they'd be too much for one pack, so I made two. Helps balance on the mule too."

"Smart thinkin'. I'll take your word on the weight. Looks like you recovered a good amount, though."

"Less than half that. Cheyenne Killer and my Shoshoni friend Cuts Throat tossed in the rest."

Sublette called one of his assistants to cart the bales away. "I'll give you the going price for plews—four dollars. That makes five hundred sixty dollars."

"Ain't much, is it?"

"You challenging my figuring, boy?"

"No, sir. Just lamentin' the fact that I'll not be able to get as much in the way of supplies that I think I'll need."

"That's true, son, but we'll do what we can."

Cooper nodded, then drew himself up straight. "Might's well let you keep the money and just let me pick out the supplies up to my limit."

"Be happy to," Sublette said with a smile. "What are you needing?"

"Traps, of course. Six of 'em. Medicine, powder and lead, as much as you think proper for spending most part of a year out there," he said, pointing toward the mountains. "Coffee, and plenty of it, with a mill, sugar, salt, tobacco, some bacon. Reckon if it's available, a small anvil, with a few related tools and iron." He paused to think a few moments. "Frying pan, coffeepot, couple of mugs, a pot or two. Maybe a dozen or so knives for tradin', a few one-point blankets and some four point."

He stopped, almost sweating over everything he had to take. "Damn that's a heap of stuff. And mighty dear, I reckon."

"I don't give these things away, boy."

Cooper nodded. "I suppose I ain't got enough for two, three mules, do I?"

"Hell, you're far over your limit with what you've listed."

"I was worried about that."

"If I was you, Mr. Cooper, I'd leave behind the coffee mill—mashing up those beans with your 'hawk'll do just fine. The blacksmithing paraphernalia. It might be good to have at times, but it's costly and it'll weigh heavily on your mule if you only have one. Cut out the knives. You can use the tobacco for negotiating." He stopped, accounting in his head. "I ain't figured it all out yet, but I reckon if you leave out all these things I mentioned, you have about ten dollars left."

Cooper shook his head. He wasn't sure he would have enough supplies to last a season, but it would have to do. He smiled a little ruefully. "I'll leave out what you said, Mr. Sublette." His grin grew wider. "And I reckon I'll use the last little bit for some geegaws and other foofaraw for Black Moon."

"Seems you're a true free trapper, boy. Such fellers are known for treating their squaws to heaps of foofaraw and such. Most of 'em leave here with empty pockets."

"I ain't gonna have much choice, seems like."

Sublette just nodded. As a businessman, he wanted all the trappers to leave here broke, having spent as much money as he could drag out of them for supplies.

"Can you keep all that stored here till I leave?"

"No, son. But I'll keep it here for a couple of days, then you'll have to move it elsewhere."

"Obliged, Mr. Sublette. So what've you got for foofaraw?"

Sublette rummaged around in a couple of boxes and laid some items on the table. "Glass beads, a few hawk-bells, and jingle cones. And this bracelet."

It was tin, but it gleamed when the light hit it. "Thanks, Mr. Sublette. I'll take the bracelet and whatever else I can get for my money. I'll be back in a day or two to get my supplies."

Sublette nodded and went back to his ledger.

Cooper hopped on his horse and galloped back to where Black Moon, Cuts Throat, and Pony Woman awaited him. He rode with a mixture of sadness in having been able to purchase only a relative paltry amount of supplies, but with joy, too, at his expectation of the joy Black Moon would feel.

And she was delighted at the geegaws he had brought her, making Pony Woman a little jealous.

"You not a good friend," Cuts Throat said.

"Why?" Cooper asked, startled.

"Pony Woman will nag me till she gets some foofaraw. I might lodgepole her."

"You do, and you and I will have us another fight."

"Bad choice for me—fight you or listen to her."

They both laughed.

TWELVE

WITHOUT ANY MONEY TO SPEND, having used it all on supplies for the upcoming season, Cooper had little to do but wander around the rendezvous. So that's what he did, watching the wrestling, the drunken cavorting, the brawls, the rifle and tomahawk throwing contests, and the horse races. He wished he had even a few small things to wager; he might find someone who'd take a small wager on a race. But the few possessions he had he could not dare to lose.

Then he spotted Hiram Bledsoe. He walked up to Bledsoe, and slammed a left fist into the man's cheek, knocking him down. Bledsoe started to rise, and Cooper smashed his right fist into Bledsoe's face. As Bledsoe groggily tried to get to his feet again, Cooper kicked him under the chin.

"What's this, hoss?" another man asked, drawing a knife. Like many men here, he had left his pistols in his tent or lodge.

Unlike those men, Cooper had not left his pistols behind. He snatched out one of them and said, "You keep pullin' that Green River and I'll put a lead pill in your brisket, you son of a bitch."

The man, whose name Cooper remembered as Claude Manning, stared at Cooper for a moment and apparently didn't like what he saw in Cooper's eyes, and let his hand fall away from the hilt of the knife. "I'll ask you again, hoss, what's this here all about?"

"You should know damn well, Manning."

Manning looked puzzled.

"You and that sack of skunk droppins sent me on a wild-goose chase, up toward the part of the Snake where the beaver was near trapped out by the British."

"We didn't know that."

"Like hell you didn't. Now that I think back on it, it seemed you boys were tryin' to hide smiles of connivance. That don't shine with this chil'. I did make a few plews, but lost near all of 'em, when we got caught in a hellacious bunch of storms."

"Hell, boy, we was havin' a little fun with you. Figured a trapper alone could trap hisself enough beaver to make it here and get good enough money to have a real spree."

"Like hell. I want half your plews."

"Sold 'em all already," Manning said with a smirk.

"Then I want half the money you got for 'em."

"Spent it all." The sneer grew.

"Let me see your possible sack. Bledsoe's too."

"Hell, no way I'm gonna let you see my personal plunder." Manning seemed to be enjoying himself.

Cooper stood for a minute, head down, seemingly defeated. Then he suddenly lashed out and whacked Manning hard across the side of his head with the pistol.

Manning went down. Before he could get up, Cooper knelt on his chest and placed the muzzle of his pistol on Manning's forehead. "I said, I want to see your possibles sack, and Bledsoe's too. I don't get 'em right quick, I'll put a ball through that empty noggin of yours."

Cooper heard several guns being cocked, and then a voice. "That won't do, boys. Put them pieces down. Let these boys settle it among themselves."

Pulling his knife with his other hand, Cooper cut the strap to Manning's possibles sack, slipped the knife away and yanked the sack free. He rose. "Stay right where you are, hoss." He went to Bledsoe, pulled his knife again, and cut loose that man's possibles sack, then stood. He hung the pistol back on his belt with the brass clip, then opened both sacks and dumped the contents on the ground.

"Reckon you didn't spend it all," Cooper said when he saw two good-sized batches of coins scattered around. He paused, then said, "Seein' as you two boys have been so troublesome, I figure I should take all this here cash. But bein' a kind feller, I'll only take half of each of yours." He began gathering up some of the coins, putting them in his own possibles sack, then stood.

"Now, I suggest to you two that you never come near me again. You do, I'll kill you. If you backshoot me, my Shoshoni friends'll make you pay for it."

"Them redskins ain't gonna do shit with all these coons around," Manning said, regaining much of his sense.

"Reckon that's true. But you ain't gonna be here forever. You'll soon be travelin' to whatever spot you think'll have the most beaver. And then you'll be alone."

"There's more'n one of us, hoss." Manning didn't sound as confident as he had a moment ago.

"Reckon that's true too. But my people will track you down and kill you, maybe painfully."

"Your people? Hell, you ain't a Shoshoni or any kind of Injun."

"I was adopted into the tribe, and my father, Cheyenne Killer, won't take kindly to two skunk humpers like you killin' his son. So keep your distance, boys."

"They ain't here," Bledsoe snapped.

"They will be directly, next day or two."

"Watch your back, boy."

"I will."

He turned and walked away.

He got only a few feet when he spotted Elson Brooks and some of his trapping companions. "That you and your boys backin' down those other manure-eatin' bastards?"

"It was."

"I'm obliged for certain or I wouldn't say so. But why?"

"Don't like seein' an honest, courageous hoss like you bein' took advantage of by two goat turds like them."

Cooper nodded. "Well, obliged, Mr. Brooks."

"You ain't talkin' to me, are you?" Brooks asked with a grin. When Cooper gave him a puzzled look, Brooks said, "Hell, boy, you know to call me Elson, or you can just use El."

"Glad to make your acquaintance again, El. Maybe I can be of help to you someday."

"I'll ask you again, how 'bout joinin' my little group. That's something that'd be really helpful."

"Reckon I'll have to say no again, El."

"Even after last season?"

"Because of last season."

It was Brooks's turn to look surprised.

"Need to prove myself, El. Last year didn't shine at all. Got to see if I can do better."

"Well, that does make plenty of sense. I wish you well."

"Same to you."

"If ye need some real places to find beaver, jist ask. We know some prime spots. Don't mind sharin' one of 'em with a friend. Reckon ye won't be all that much competition for us all by your lonesome."

"I'll look you up later."

———

WILLIAM SUBLETTE WAS SURPRISED to see Cooper when he came into the open front of the trade tent.

"I'm here to buy me two mules and the rest of the supplies I couldn't get the other day, 'cept maybe the blacksmithin' tools if that'll get me a third mule."

"Where's you get so much specie, boy?" Sublette asked suspiciously, though not much.

"Come across a couple fellers owed me some money. They were kind enough to pay me what they owed." As far as Cooper was concerned, it was only a small lie.

Sublette grinned. "Well, then, Mr. Cooper, I reckon we can do some business."

Even without the blacksmithing tools and such, there was not enough money for a third mule, but Cooper did come away with enough money to have himself a little spree.

Cooper was off in his estimation of when Cheyenne Killer and the others would be here. As he neared his and Cuts Throat's camp, two laden mules trailing behind him, he could see the Shoshonis riding into the long string of camps along the river. It made Cooper feel somewhat better. He figured Bledsoe and Manning were smart enough to figure his threat was true.

And that night was a time for celebration, with the fresh meat the Shoshonis had brought in. Even some of the other trappers, wandered into the camp to feast, and maybe pay a bit of foofaraw to some willing Shoshoni maidens.

With a bit of money left in his pockets, Cooper became a participant, albeit a minor one, in the rousing activities of the rendezvous. He put up a few dollars in the shooting contest, which he lost. He had no better luck betting small amounts on horse races, especially two where a Flathead in one and a Crow in the other went up against a trapper.

"You shouldn't waste money," Black Moon chastised him mildly in the robes one night.

He grinned. "After all the hell we went through last winter, I figure a little frivolity would do me some good."

"But..."

"You got more foofaraw from me, too, three times. That was your reward. Havin' a little spree was mine.

'Sides, what else am I gonna do with it in the mountains?"

Her only answer was to snuggle a little closer to him.

But after a week of spreeing, even if it was rather a tame one for him, Cooper was ready to leave. He told Black Moon to begin preparing, then went to hunt up Elson Brooks. He found him soon enough, but the trapper was full of Taos Lightning and weaving around like a wayward wind, so Cooper decided to give it another day.

Late the next morning, Cooper found Brooks in front of his tent, looking like he had battled a grizzly and smelled as if he had fallen into a buffalo wallow after a hard rain.

"Mornin'," Cooper said rather cheerfully.

Brooks simply growled what Cooper took as a greeting.

"You don't look so good, El."

"Ye don't get away from me right this damn instant, I'll shoot ye dead."

"First, you'd have to find your pistol, then decide which one of us to shoot." He grinned. Then grew a bit more serious. "Sorry, El. I was hopin' you'd be true to your word and point me to some good huntin' grounds."

Brooks nodded, then winced. "I will," he croaked. "But now ain't the time, boy. I'll come find ye later."

Cooper rose. He turned to leave, and called over his shoulder, "Best have some of the hair of the dog that bit you." He tried not to chuckle as he walked away.

It was late afternoon when Brooks called for entry into Cooper's lodge. Cooper thought Brooks looked considerably better than he had this morning.

Brooks sat and nodded gratefully as Black Moon handed him a plate of roasted meat and a mug of coffee. "I ain't much given to apologies, but I reckon I was some disagreeable to ye this mornin'."

"Reckon you had reason, El."

As Brooks ate, the two men talked of nothing important, but when he finished, said, "Well, time to give ye a geography lesson. We best go outside, though. Ain't enough light in here to see."

They went outside and squatted to the side of the lodge, where the grass had been eaten and beaten down in the time they had spent here.

Brooks drew his knife and started scratching a map in the dirt. "We're here," he said, pointing with the tip of the blade. "Up here are the three forks. Prime beaver country, but it's the heart of Blackfoot land. Dangerous place, as ye can figure. Over here to the southeast a little ways from here is the Wind River Mountains, where your Shoshoni people are from. On the east side is the river of the same name. It goes to the southeast along the mountains, and then becomes the Bighorn when it turns north. The Bighorn runs all the way up to the Yellowstone. To the east of it are the Bighorn Mountains. Rough mountains those. Runnin' north and east of 'em is the Little Bighorn, then the Tongue and then the Powder. The Little Bighorn and the Tongue reach deep into the Bighorns. Damn near all the way through it seems. It's all Crow land. Good trappin' there, down out of the mountains, a land of rollin' hills and such. Some good places for winterin' too."

"That where you suggest I go?"

"Might not be bad." He jabbed the knife in. "Toward the headwaters of the Shoshone River up in the Absarokas, there's a heap of streams up that way. Prime beaver country too. Easy to get to from here, and not more'n a few weeks from Wind River country. You'll be near enough to winter with Cheyenne Killer's band if that's where your stick floats. Popo Agie, Bighorn, and some of the others ain't that far either."

"You say there's a heap of beaver?"

"Plenty."

Cooper hesitated, then said, "After Manning's and Bledsoe's perfidy, I'm a bit uncertain if I should take your word."

"Rightfully so, considerin'. Ye got no reason to trust me. Or not trust me, other than me sayin' to ye that I ain't lyin'. If ye'll recall, just the other day me and my boys kept others from interferin' with your dealin' with those two scoundrels."

Cooper thought that over a few moments, then nodded. "I got no reason to think you're not tellin' true, El. Thanks."

"No need."

"Where're you headin'?"

"Way up here," he pointed, moving the blade far to the northwest on the dirt map. "It's the country of the Flatheads and Nez Perce. I reckon that's where me and the other boys'll go at least at first. Most of the boys' women from those tribes. We'll head east from there." Brooks rose. "Good huntin' hoss."

"You too."

THIRTEEN

HAWLEY COOPER and Black Moon Woman left the rendezvous with Cheyenne Killer's people, heading northeast.

As usual, Cooper was not much of one to plod along with the slow-moving caravan. So, for the three days it took before Cheyenne Killer's people turned east toward Togwotee Pass, Cooper left Black Moon with the band while he, Cuts Throat, and other warriors went hunting. It did nothing to relieve the heat, and was bloody and messy, but it was something to do rather than just slog along.

But Cooper soon decided where he wanted to go and that he should leave. That night he went to Cheyenne Killer's lodge. "I'll be leavin' in the mornin', Father," he said.

"You won't stay with us? Trap on the Wind maybe?"

"Reckon not. But we won't be far. I heard there's plenty of beaver up in the Absarokas."

"Will you come back?"

"Certain I will. I figure we can winter with you. Be nice to spend time with the people."

"Except for Blue Bear," Cheyenne Killer said with a sad grin.

"True enough. I didn't see him at rendezvous. He still grievin' for his sons?"

"Yes. He kept to his lodge while we were there. He's much quieter now, almost broken."

"Don't worry about him, Father."

"He's an old companion, even though we tangled at times."

"He brought his troubles on himself, and I doubt he'll cause more for you or me."

Cheyenne Killer nodded.

"Remember, too, that rendezvous next summer is nearby on the Wind River."

"It's good."

Their talk turned to nothing of importance before Cooper left.

A few hours later, Cuts Throat entered Cooper's lodge and sat. "Cheyenne Killer says you're leavin'."

"Yep. In the mornin'."

"Good thing. I'm tired of huntin' to keep you and Black Moon fed."

"Hell, Cuts Throat, you couldn't hit a buffler if you were standin' on its hump with a lance in your hand."

Both men laughed.

"I'll miss you, friend," the Shoshoni said.

"I'll miss you too. But I told Cheyenne Killer that me and Black Moon would be back to winter with you."

"Good. You're strong, and Pony Woman needs help carrying wood for my fire."

Both laughed again, and even Black Moon Woman giggled a little.

———————

COOPER AND BLACK MOON pulled out shortly after dawn, with two extra horses and four pack mules, two of them from Cheyenne Killer, who had gotten them in a raid on the Arapaho. They headed north, soon entering a land of bubbling, sulfurous mud pots and exploding geysers of boiling water. The area was unnerving to them, and they did not delay in making their way through it into land that was covered with trees and creeks that did not smoke and smell like brimstone.

Before long, they skirted the north end of Yellow-stone Lake, weaving through the Absarokas, crossing numerous creeks and small rivers. Cooper trapped a little, but the furs were nowhere near prime yet, so he spent little time at it.

Almost a week out, Cooper grew uncomfortable, and that night at their fire he said, "I got me an itch that I don't like, Moon."

"What is itch?"

"A feelin' that we're bein' followed."

"Who would follow?"

Cooper shrugged. "Ain't sure. We're in Crow country, so it could be some of them. Might even be the ones that were at rendezvous, though I doubt it. They left before us and would've been movin' faster bein' a smaller group."

"Maybe hunters left group."

"Maybe, but I don't think they'd be this far south if

they were travelin' the way I figure they were. Might be a war party, which don't shine with me at all."

"Would be damned bad."

"'Course, it could be damned Blackfeet, which'd be even worse. They went and raided near Sweet Lake last year, and that's a far piece from their homeland. We ain't that far from there now."

"Could be big trouble."

"Yep. You have your fusee with you?" Cooper had brought Black Moon a trade rifle—well, musket—and its accoutrements at rendezvous and had taught her to shoot it. He had also gotten her a pistol.

"Yep."

"Good. You'll ride out front the next few days or 'til I can figure out if there's really someone on our trail and if they mean us harm. I'll keep an eye on our back trail. Might even ride back a little way to check. You just keep goin'."

"You don't go too far," she said rather than asked.

Cooper caught the worry in her voice. "Nope."

They traveled that way for two more days, moving as quickly as they reasonably could. They kept their fires at night small and blocked as well as they could by rocks.

The next day, Cooper, who was back along their trail a mile or so, galloped up to Black Moon.

"Trouble?" she asked.

Cooper nodded. "Ain't Crows or Blackfeet, though. White men, two of 'em. I think it's the ones I whupped at rendezvous."

"They come to pay back, as you say?"

"Reckon so. Could be that they're just takin' the

same trail, but I don't think so. If they were plannin' to come this way, they'd have been well ahead of us."

"How they follow?"

"Ain't sure, of course, but I figure they followed Cheyenne Killer's people—and us—out of Pierre's Hole, waitin' for us to go our separate way. Likely it took 'em a little while to figure out we had left. Might've even rode into Cheyenne Killer's camp a day or so after we left to check on us. The people are always friendly to the trappers, so it wouldn't be unusual. If they found us there, no tellin' what they planned to do, but I expect they might've saw I wasn't with the hunters for a day or two."

"We fight?"

"Yep," Cooper said with a tight grin. "Well, I'll fight. You'll take care of the animals and supplies. Unless they put me under, then you can fight 'em."

"Damn right. But you won't go under."

"Don't think I will. Let's push on a little harder, see if we can find a place to hide you and the animals, where I can confront 'em."

Two miles on, they found a place where they were able to work the horses and mules deep into the trees and brush amid dozens of various-sized boulders a few hundred yards from the river.

Satisfied that Black Moon was as safe as could be, Cooper moved across the well-worn trail and a little bit back the way they had come. He tied his horse to a bush behind a large boulder, then waited.

Before too long a pair of mountain men rode up the trail. As Cooper had thought, it was Claude Manning and Hiram Bledsoe. He thought the men foolish, until he realized that he might've done the same thing had he been humiliated the way they had been at rendezvous.

When the two were within twenty yards of the boulder, Cooper stepped out from behind it. Bledsoe and Manning stopped, surprise in their eyes.

"Fancy meetin' you fellers here," Cooper said flatly.

"Same here," Bledsoe said, recovering his wits a little.

"Why're you followin' me?"

"We ain't doin' no such thing. We're just headin' for Clark's Fork, same as you I expect."

"That's a heapin' pile of buffler shit," Cooper snapped. "If you were headed to the Clark's Fork from rendezvous, you would've turned northeast not far from Jackson Lake, not north."

"We were headin' for the Yellowstone. Wanted to avoid that big turn west and northwest of the big lake."

"More nonsense. Since I was travelin' with the slow-moving tribe, you boys would've been far ahead of me by now even if you were headed this way toward the Yellowstone, especially since I doubt you'd dawdle through Colter's Hell." He paused. "You boys best turn yourselves around, ride on back the trail, and keep on goin'."

"We don't?" Manning asked.

"You'll be wolf bait right off."

"Think you can..." Manning began, but Bledsoe stopped him.

"Let's go, Claude. Ain't worth our while to deal with this gopher-humpin' little snot."

At a look from Bledsoe, Manning nodded. The two turned and rode off down the trail, each with his two mules plodding along behind them.

Cooper knew he should kill them now and likely save himself from grief later, but that was not his way. That would've been what Josiah Weeks would have done, but he couldn't do that. He'd kill those men in an instant if need be, even back shoot them, but not like this, when they were riding slowly away. Still, he knew they would not just ride off and not come back, so it would come to death much sooner rather than later, and he was determined to make sure it was theirs, not his.

He mounted his horse and slowly rode down the trail after them, eyes roving side to side. Half a mile away, he came to a long, straight stretch. It was empty. He stopped, scanning the trees to both sides of the trail. "Damn," he muttered.

Then he spotted the slightest movement on the right side of the trail thirty yards away. He yanked the horse's head around and darted into the forest, ducking to the side just in time to keep from being unseated by a large pine branch. The move also kept the bullet that sliced across his upper arm from hitting him full in the back. He ignored it as he slid off the horse. He peered out from behind the trees, seeing nothing but pines.

Cooper drew in a long breath and let it out slowly. The two could be anywhere by now, together, separate, or even one on each side of the trail. "Dammit, you should've cut 'em down when you had the chance, you damn fool," he muttered angrily at himself.

But he couldn't stand here forever waiting for Manning and Bledsoe to make a move. He suddenly darted across the trail into the forest and stopped to listen. He thought he heard someone moving ahead and to his left. He slung his rifle over his back and pulled a pistol, then moved warily between the trees, heading straight deeper into the woods. He figured to circle back toward where he had heard the sound and hopefully surprise whoever it was—if, indeed, there was anyone there at all.

A few sweaty minutes later, he heard the jingle of a bit and the soft snort of a horse. He smiled grimly and proceeded as stealthily as he could. He stopped when he spotted Hiram Bledsoe leaning against the tree, looking out over the trail.

"Over here, boy," he said quietly.

Bledsoe jerked at the sound, hesitated a moment, then started to turn, slowly, both hands in front of him.

"Damn fool," Cooper mumbled just before shooting Bledsoe in the chest.

Bledsoe fell, and one of the two suddenly skittish pack mules stepped on his head. Cooper figured that if the shot hadn't killed him, the mule had.

"Hiram!" Manning called from the other side of the trail. "Hiram, you all right?" His voice sounded worried.

"No, he ain't all right, Claude," Cooper responded. Moments later he heard a horse racing away.

Cooper charged out onto the trail, glad this was a spot with a long, empty, straight stretch. He quickly brought his rifle up and fired. But Manning kept riding fast, unhit.

He reloaded his rifle and pistol while considering chasing after Manning, then decided it would be foolish. He gathered up Bledsoe's horse and two mules and found Manning's pair of mules in the trees. Mounting his own horse, he led the captive animals back toward where Black Moon was waiting. She was pleased with the new stock of supplies.

FOURTEEN

HAWLEY COOPER and Black Moon continued through the Absaroka Mountains, stopping every few days. Cooper would set his traps in the streams and creeks and rivers that flowed through the area and eventually into the Shoshoni or Yellowstone. Black Moon would cure the hides. The two often took an extra couple of days at one spot even after the beaver had run out to give the plews time to tan. The camps took on a somewhat festive air with several, sometimes dozens, of willow hoops holding beaver pelts.

Cooper would also use that time to hunt, and he and Black Moon would dry the meat, laying in a supply in case winter decided to make an early arrival, though Cooper had no intention of getting caught in its vehemence. Game was plentiful, and Cooper brought down elk, deer, buffalo, and even a bighorn sheep, though getting it back to camp was an adventure.

Though it was only October, Mother Nature did, however, sprinkle warning signs amid the peaks and valleys. They endured a drenching rainstorm now and again, sometimes turning to sleet and occasionally spitting hail half the size of Black Moon's small fist. There were snow flurries and even once a real, though not very harsh, snowstorm, with a bitter wind whistling from the north, bringing with it small, sharp shards of ice and whatever else it could pick up on its journey and throw at the travelers. Nighttime temperatures edged toward freezing, leaving a thin sheen of ice on puddles and along the banks of smaller streams.

The first few weeks after the confrontation with Manning and Bledsoe the take was good, though the plews were not quite prime. Still, they were worthy of being taken and would bring a good price at rendezvous. As they worked their way along, through valleys and passes, and as the days grew steadily colder, the pelts began to thicken and soon turned to prime.

About the time they reached Clark's Fork, short of the Yellowstone, Cooper called another halt, trapped the area until it was played out, then built a crude beaver press. By the time he had finished pressing what he had taken so far, he had two full packs.

They turned south, traveling down Clark's Fork, moving toward the headwaters of the Shoshoni River. Two days after moving south, they ran into a grizzly that popped out of the brush a few feet in front of Cooper, startling him and his horse. He fought to keep the bucking, rearing horse under control while trying to pull his rifle out of the loop on his saddle. Behind him, Black Moon had even more of a struggle to keep the extra horses and the mules from bolting, but she managed, turning and moving a little distance down their back trail.

Cooper jerked his horse's head around and urged it

a few yards away from the bear. "Dammit, calm down, horse!" he snapped. The mount did quiet down enough that Cooper could spin around and place a shot in the bear's chest as the animal reared up, trying to keep track of the invader into its feeding place. It dropped down on all fours, seemingly unfazed by the lead ball in its breast.

Quickly Cooper reloaded and fired again, this time hitting the beast in its open mouth, a lucky shot, he knew. He hurriedly reloaded again, keeping a careful eye on the bruin, which seemed to be trying to decide whether to charge or not.

Cooper did not allow the beast to let its instinct take over. He fired, the lead ball catching the animal in the neck just under the chin. The grizzly charged but got only a few feet before it tumbled forward onto its face.

Cooper sat there, reloading one more time, watching the bear closely. The bruin didn't move, but Cooper still gave it a few minutes before he dismounted, tied off his horse, and warily approached the beast with one of his .54-caliber pistols ready in hand. But the animal was, indeed, dead.

"Come on up, Moon," Cooper shouted. He uncocked the pistol and hung it back on his belt, then pulled his knife, knelt, and began carving the hide off the beast. It did not take long, especially when Black Moon joined in. The hide was wrapped up and tied to a pack mule, which, like all the other animals, was still rather skittish. Then Cooper hacked out the teeth and chopped off the paws with his tomahawk.

"Want some of the meat, Moon?" he asked.

"No."

Cooper shrugged, wrapped the teeth and claws in

some hide, tied them to the same pack mule, then mounted his horse. They moved off. As they did, Cooper hoped there was not another grizzly in the vicinity.

———

COOPER CAME TO A HALT, his head swiveling around. Something had caught his attention, though he couldn't figure out what just yet.

Black Moon, who had almost ridden into his horse when he had stopped so abruptly, pulled up alongside of him. "What?" she asked.

"Don't know. Something just ain't right here."

Black Moon sat, head cocked to one side, then said, "Smell not right. Old fire, dead people. Not too old, last day maybe."

Cooper was a bit surprised. "Where?" he asked.

Black Moon pointed. With care, both moved forward warily. Then they heard the soft cry of a baby. The two jerked their horses' heads around and darted into the forest, stopping sharply when they almost rode over a couple of bodies.

They dismounted and while Black Moon ran for where the sound had come from, Cooper knelt by one of the corpses.

Moments later, Black Moon came back carrying a cradleboard with a gurgling infant looking around wide-eyed.

Cooper stood. "These two suffered some indignities, Moon. Cut up pretty bad and scalped." He shook his head. "What I can't figure out is why the child wasn't killed. Or taken."

"Maybe asleep. I found cradleboard hanging from tree."

"You think that baby slept through its family bein' slaughtered?"

"Maybe. Babies sleep deep sometimes. Maybe attack was quiet."

"That could be. Looks like these two were shot with arrows, then hacked up and their hair taken. Ain't much left around. Whoever attacked these people took whatever they could find."

Black Moon nodded, tickling the infant's lips with a forefinger. As far as Cooper could tell, the child was happy enough.

"These were Crows. I figure Blackfeet did this."

"Yes."

"Crows're mostly friendly to trappers." He grinned somewhat grimly. "And I doubt they know I put a bunch of 'em under. What is the child?"

"Boy."

"Maybe we can get him back to his people."

"Maybe." She didn't sound so certain.

"Well, we best be on our way," Cooper said. He had no intention of trying to bury this couple. A white man's burial was not their way anyway, he figured. "Those Blackfeet might still be around."

"Good."

He started for his horse, then stopped and turned back. "How're we gonna feed him?"

"I can find way," Black Moon said with some confidence.

Cooper looked at her in question. "You with child?"

"No."

"Then how...?"

"Women have ways to do such a thing." She held up a hand to keep him from asking more questions. "Some things for men, some for women. This for women."

Cooper looked skeptical but shrugged and mounted his horse. Black Moon did the same and they pulled out, back on the trail, the cradleboard hanging from the Shoshoni woman's saddle horn.

Leading the way, Cooper was wary. He and his woman had not seen the Blackfeet before this, so there was a good chance they might be ahead of them on the trail. He didn't know how many there had been in the attack, but if there were more than one, which was likely, it would be mighty perilous.

They moved slowly, and as dusk began creeping over the land, darkening the already dim trail between the thick trees. Finally, Cooper pulled them well off the trail, deep amid the pines and brush.

As usual in preparing for the night's camp, the work seemed endless—unsaddling and caring for the horses, unloading the pack mules and storing the supplies under a tarp in case of precipitation, gathering firewood, sparking up a fire, and getting a meal ready. Now there was an infant to care for, and Cooper had no idea how that could be done. And the child was getting mighty fussy. Cooper did not know what to do in such a case, so he felt helpless, which irritated him.

After all their tasks were done and they had eaten, Black Moon went behind some bushes with the baby. She was gone long enough that Cooper began to worry. Finally, he called out, "Moon? You all right, Moon?"

"Yep. Not here much longer."

Cooper thought she almost sounded happy, and

when she and the infant came back to the fire, both looked quite pleased.

"You managed to feed him?" Cooper asked, thinking it was impossible.

"Yes. Ask no more. I said this is women's business."

Cooper growled, then grinned. He was happy to be relieved of any duty involving the boy—except perhaps protecting him should some savages think to cause him harm.

Black Moon cradled the boy in her arms and began singing softly to him in her language.

Cooper listened, a strange feeling growing inside him, one that he had no experience with, and it worried him just a little. Then he decided to ignore it. He figured it would either go away or he would figure it out.

Black Moon soon stopped singing. She rose, baby in her arms and placed the infant in the cradleboard hanging from a branch of a tree nearby. She looked contented when she returned to the fire.

Cooper thought that a little odd, but he mentally shrugged. Sometimes—well, most of the time—women were a mystery to him.

"There's plenty of beaver sign," he said as he sipped some coffee. "Reckon we can spend a few days here if that'll be all right with you. Give that child a bit of time to get used to things, if he even needs to." Now that he thought about it, he realized that the baby had no concept of where he was, or even who he was.

"Damn good," Black Moon said with a nod.

"Give us time to figure out where to take him. Considerin' where we are, there might be a Crow village not far from here. Maybe they'll take the little feller in. 'Specially since they killed his parents."

"Maybe."

Cooper detected some hesitation in her voice, but he let it pass.

"'Course them damned Blackfeet might still be lurkin' around here, but I figure they've moved on. I'll keep a good watch out for 'em, though. You should too."

"I will."

"How old do you think that little feller is?"

"Three moons, maybe four. Can't be sure." She cast a look over her shoulder to where the infant slept in his cradleboard.

Cooper suspected there was something more in the way Black Moon was acting other than simply rescuing a child, and he wondered about it. He was afraid he knew what it was about, and it didn't sit well with him. If he was right, it could lead to complications he—they —did not need. He peered into the fire, not wanting to look at his wife, afraid of what he might see there. He finished his coffee and went to check on the animals.

FIFTEEN

HAWLEY COOPER HAD JUST RETURNED to the camp after setting his traps when he heard horses coming along the trail. There was no jingle of bits and bridles or any other sounds that might be coming with the approach of white trappers.

"Get back in the trees, Moon. Take the child with you."

She did so without hesitation or comment. She snatched up her fusil with the strap of shooting bag wrapped around it and swung the infant in his cradle-board onto her back as she hustled behind a thick screen of shrubbery.

Minutes later, two Crow warriors made their way through the trees into the camp from the trail. Cooper figured they had seen or smelled the smoke from the cookfire. They were dressed in finely made and deco-rated buckskins, but their heads were uncovered. Each had an unstrung bow and quiver of arrows slung on his back and trade rifles across the front of his simple saddle. They were not painted, so Cooper figured they were not on the warpath, though that did not mean they wouldn't attack if they thought they could. "*Kahée* —Hello."

One warrior responded in kind while the other looked around the camp. "You not belong here," the first one said in English with an accent so thick that it was almost unintelligible.

"I thought Crows were friends of the white man," Cooper said slowly, hoping his words would be understood.

"Good friends. Maybe you give us presents, we leave."

Cooper nodded. When both Crows went to dismount, he said, "No." His voice was sharp. "Stay on your ponies. You're bein' watched."

The warriors hesitated, and Cooper rested a hand on one of his pistols. "And keep your hands away from those fusees. There's two of you and I got two pistols, and you'll never get those weapons out before I put a lead pill in your gullet." He doubted they understood all the words, but the meaning was clear. As was the expression on Cooper's face.

The Crows stayed put.

Cooper backed away slowly, then stopped behind a canvas-covered pile of supplies, where he could watch the Indians. Without looking, he rummaged around and came up with a sack of tobacco twists. He quickly drew out two, then dropped the bag. He went back around the pile and stopped a few feet closer to the Crows than he had been when they first arrived.

"Nice horses," the other warrior said.

"Yep."

"You give one. Each. Then we go."

Cooper spit on the ground. "Go to hell, boys. I need 'em, and I wouldn't give 'em to you if I had a hundred." He tossed a twist of tobacco to each one. "Now, move on, boys."

The first held up his tobacco. "Not enough," he said harshly.

"It's all you're gonna get."

"We take," the second insisted.

"You'll have to kill me first." He knew for sure that they well understood his words when he noticed that their eyes had suddenly grown brighter in anticipation of a white man's scalp. He eased out a pistol.

"You do that, and if the other mountaineers learn you did so, you'll not be welcome in any trapper's camp or trade room again." He knew that was a load of manure, but he hoped the Crows didn't.

"We come back," one warned.

"You do and I'll raise your hair. Now, move on before you really piss me off."

The two looked blank. "Make me angry," Cooper informed them.

Each Crow jerked the head of his pony hard, and they rode slowly off.

When they were gone, Black Moon came out from behind the tall brush. "They come back," she said.

"I know."

"What we do?"

"Don't know yet. I need to think on it for a bit."

"Not too long."

When Cooper turned toward her to retort, Black Moon smiled.

His return smile was small but obvious.

He gave the situation some thought but knew he

could not delay. "Reckon we best move out. How fast can you get ready to leave?"

"I have little to gather—cooking things, other small things. And baby." The last was said almost shyly.

Cooper nodded. "Get to it, then. I got plenty to do."

"I help packing animals. It makes us ready damn quicker."

Cooper nodded again. "Get your stuff done, then throw in with me. We best be fast about it. I reckon those Crows won't be back 'til after dark, but I can't be sure."

"Yep."

"Oh," Cooper said as Black Moon started to head off to start her work, "and build up the fire a little."

"Make Crows think we still here?"

"Yep. Might slow 'em for a bit." He hurried over to start putting pack saddles on the mules.

It took longer than Cooper had hoped, but within two hours he had the mules all packed and the horses saddled. They headed out, moving as quickly as they could. There was even less of a trail the way they went than there had been when they had reached the camp they were leaving. They simply moved south taking whatever path of least resistance though the pines, spruce, and various small foliage.

They headed toward the stream, where Cooper would pull up a trap, not caring if it was empty or not, then move on to the next trap and the next, until he had all six. He tossed the three beaver that had been snared in them into the water. That done, they pushed a little harder, though they could not go too fast in the close confines of the forest.

Cooper hoped they were not leaving much of a

trail, but he and Black Moon could not keep the animals from crushing pine needles or breaking twigs off of bushes, which likely would allow expert trackers like the Crows to follow. And since the two warriors were unencumbered by pack animals and extra horses, they could move rapidly.

A mile or so from the camp, Cooper led them into the stream, rode down a little way, and came out of the water on the bank on the other side. Over the next hour or so, they continued that pattern, until finally leaving the stream on the opposite side from where they started. Cooper hoped that would be enough to slow the Crows down, perhaps giving him and Black Moon a chance to find some kind of haven.

They stopped a few hours later to give the animals a chance to breathe, forage, and drink a little from the even smaller stream—little more than a rivulet—they had come across. Black Moon took the time to feed the child, whom they had named Left Behind, though in the few days the infant had been part of their camp Cooper was wont to call him Caleb, after his brother, and then they were off again.

As dusk arrived, Cooper wondered what to do. Even now it was mighty difficult to see this deep into the trees and night had not yet fallen. He was wary about just stopping where they were, but it was becoming clear to him that they had no choice. They were still following the rivulet, and Cooper called to halt in an area that was at least a little open. They did not unload the mules, though they did unsaddle the horses. There would be no fire, and thus no cooked meat or any coffee. They had to be satisfied with jerky, a little pemmican, and water from the tiny creek.

They pushed hard the next day and had another meager camp. Cooper thought Black Moon looked tired, but the baby seemed happy and healthy. Cooper, too, was tired—tired of the hardships, though they were to be expected, tired of being chased by two Crow warriors, tired of seeing Black Moon's exhaustion, and tired of cold, miserly camps. It irritated him and made him clump around the camp muttering imprecations about everything and just about everyone, most of all himself.

Cooper had them moving early the next day, with him holding the rope leading the pack mules and extra horses, giving Black Moon an easier day. She had many duties, including now caring for an infant, and so deserved a break, Cooper figured.

Sometime in the middle of the afternoon, Cooper came to a stop. Behind all the animals, Black Moon's eyes raised in surprise and a little fear. To her, Cooper did not seem alarmed or expecting trouble. She moved up past the animals until she was next to him. "What's wrong, Hawwy?"

He was silent for a while, then said, "This is far enough."

"For what?"

"For runnin'. It doesn't shine with me to keep runnin' from a couple goddamn Crows. If I can't handle them two, I don't deserve to be in these here Stony Mountains. Fleein' from trouble ain't my way, and I'll be rolled in molasses and set on an anthill before I take another worried step to run from them bastards." He pointed to a rough circle of boulders. "We'll make our stand there."

"Maybe the damned Crows don't come."

"If they don't, we'll spend a few days here to recruit our strength, then move on."

Black Moon nodded. She too was tired of running.

It was a good place to make a stand. It would accommodate all the animals and provide plenty of protection. The rivulet ran to one side of it into the thick trees behind the natural fortress. There was some grass inside, so the horses and mules would have something to eat. It was as good a place as he figured he could find to take on the warriors with the least amount of danger to him, his woman, the baby, or the animals.

Black Moon sat with her back against one of the rocks to feed the baby, while Cooper started to unsaddle his horse.

"Good place," the woman said.

"Yep. Those damned Crows show up, I'll make wolf bait out of the sons of bitches. Or they'll put me under."

"And me," Black Moon said firmly.

"You got your pistol and rifle."

"On horse. I get after feedin' Left Behind."

Cooper nodded, wondering how she could hold the infant to her breast with success. He shook his head and went back to work. It was not his business. He kept his ears peeled as he finished caring for the horses and began unloading the mules, storing the supplies and packs of plews against the back "wall" of the boulders and covering them with canvas.

While he worked, Black Moon leaned Left Behind's cradleboard against a rock and then got her weapons. "All right to start fire?" she asked.

"Yep. Be good to have something hot to fill our meatbags."

Black Moon gathered firewood, started a fire and set

bacon—a rare departure from their usual game—to heating in a frypan. She pounded coffee beans and poured the grainy powder into the coffeepot she had filled with water from the creek.

Soon they were sitting to a meal. Sparse as it was, it was filling and tasty enough. Cooper and Black Moon wished it was buffalo, or even elk or deer, but this would do. He relaxed a little afterward with a mug of coffee, which he appreciated.

Finally Cooper rose. "'Bout time I should start keepin' watch," he said. He took his rifle and climbed onto one rough boulder, which allowed him to watch over another one, facing the "trail" they had taken to get here.

Dark crept up on them, but Cooper did not leave his post. He told Black Moon to get some sleep. She brought him coffee first, then dozed on and off, making more coffee and bringing him a mug of it whenever she thought he needed it.

SIXTEEN

IT WAS a few hours after daylight when Cooper snapped awake from his light doze when Black Moon screeched in fear. He spun and saw one of the Crows leaping off a boulder behind him. With tomahawk in hand, the Crow was barely two feet from Black Moon and Left Behind.

"No!" Cooper bellowed. He brought the rifle up and fired wildly. The ball went well wide, but it gave the Crow pause. Cooper jumped down from his rocky perch, tossed his rifle aside, and charged toward the Indian, ignoring his pistols. It was too dangerous for Black Moon in such proximity to the warrior.

Unflustered, Black Moon, who had been feeding Left Behind, squashed the baby against her chest and spit at the Crow. The spittle hit the warrior in the face, and it, too, gave him a second's pause. It was enough for Cooper to crash into the Indian, smashing him against the boulder the Crow had used to launch himself from into the enclosure.

Cooper grabbed the Indian's hatchet arm with his

left hand, pushing it up and back against the rock. The other hand went around the warrior's throat and squeezed. The warrior was not so easily subdued, and with his free hand began pounding Cooper's side, not able to reach his face.

Suddenly, two things happened simultaneously—a blast came from one side of Cooper and an arrow hit him in the calf. The Crow sagged and Cooper glanced at Black Moon, who had a smoking pistol in her hand.

Cooper let the dying Crow fall and whirled, yanking out a pistol as he did. Another arrow flew by, tearing through his shirt and leaving a thin groove in the skin. Cooper fired, but the Crow had dropped around the boulder near the "entrance" to the trapper's makeshift fort. Moments later, Cooper heard a horse galloping away.

"Damn," he muttered. He ran to his horse and attempted to leap on it, ready to take off after the fleeing Crow. But the arrow in his leg and the beating his ribs had taken made that effort unsuccessful, and he slumped against the animal.

Another explosion came from behind him, and he looked over to see Black Moon standing over the Crow, having used her fusil to make sure the warrior was dead. Cooper gave her a wan smile as he plopped down on his rump.

A few moments later, Cooper managed to get himself to his feet and hobbled to a slightly better place to sit, leaning his left shoulder and arm against a rock, keeping the wounded leg bent so the arrow would not sink deeper into his leg. He was next to the baby, who was crying. "Hush now, little feller," he said. "All the bad doins are over."

"For now," Black Moon said, coming over to squat by the two of them. She carefully loaded Cooper's rifle and her own pistol and fusil. While she did so, she said more than asked, "You're hurt."

"Not bad. I just hope that arrow didn't sink too deep. Hate to have to cut it out."

"Go on stomach. I look." Cooper did as he was told. The woman slit open a few inch stretch of his pants and examined the leg. "Not so bad," she said. "Don't move. When I come back, take whipping stick and put between teeth." She swiftly heated a knife in the fire.

"Damn," Cooper muttered as Black Moon returned. "Bite." He ground his teeth into the wood. Moments later, there was a searing pain as Black Moon pulled out the arrowhead and slapped the hot knife blade against the wound, cauterizing it.

"That didn't shine," Cooper gasped.

"Better than havin' too much blood come out."

"Reckon so." He turned onto his back and inched his way up the boulder until he was sitting, his left leg bent at the knee, keeping the wound away from the dirt. He smiled a little. "What you did was shinin', though. Sure made that Crow run, woman, sure as anything."

Black Moon beamed, though she kept her face downcast a little so he would not think she was being too immodest about her feat. "It ain't good the other got away."

"Nope," the mountain man said.

"Reckon he might bring war party back after us."

"Yep."

"What we do?" the Shoshoni asked.

"Rest up a bit. Then move on. I suppose it'll take

him a little while to get back to his village, unless it's a heap closer than I hope it is."

Black Moon nodded. "We leave tomorrow, maybe. You rest now. You got no sleep last night."

"Food first."

Black Moon served him some pemmican and coffee.

"Keep a close eye on things," he mumbled, knowing it was a stupid statement, as he crawled into his robes.

COOPER SLEPT for much of the day, and when he awoke, he felt rested and the pain in his leg had subsided enough that it wouldn't trouble him much. One side of him hurt from the punches he had absorbed, but nothing he need concern himself about. He ate hungrily of pemmican, bacon, and some stale bread dipped in the grease.

"Think that red devil who run off saw Left Behind?" Cooper asked.

"Maybe. Baby was against breast, but cradleboard was against rock on the other side of one who attacked me."

"Reckon it don't matter if either of 'em saw the child himself. Couldn't tell what kind of baby it was. But if he saw the cradleboard..."

"That might tell him baby is Crow. Or maybe just think that."

"Might be hard to take the little feller back to his people now that I've put under another Crow warrior."

"One who run might not've seen cradleboard or thinks we traded for it and baby is Shoshoni."

Cooper thought he caught something in her voice that seemed to be more than just a simple statement, but he wasn't sure. "We can hope that, but we can't count on it. Damn Crows are gettin' near as bad as the damned Blackfeet. At least to me they are." He paused a moment, then said, "Reckon we ought to be off at sunup. Maybe we can cover our tracks better this time."

"You can do."

Cooper grimaced. "Thought I did so the last time." He sighed, wondering if he would ever have a peaceful and trouble-free time for more than a couple of days at a stretch. Then he shrugged inwardly. *It could always be worse*, he thought, his mind wandering back to the past two winters. "But I reckon they'll be more than two warriors comin' for us, if they do."

"You'll cover tracks good this time."

"Hope so."

"And we will defeat them again, too, if they want damn fight."

"You're mighty optimistic, woman, now that you've counted coup on a Crow." He smiled a little. "I forgot in all the excitement and me sleepin' so long, to tell you I'm obliged to you for killin' that son of a bitch."

Again she was thrilled but reluctant to show it.

He shrugged off his newfound gloom. "Well I still need to do more trappin'. Ain't got enough plews yet to outfit myself for a new season. And to get you more foofaraw." He grinned.

"I don't need no more."

"Like hell you don't. What're all them other boys gonna say if I can't load you up with all kinds of shiny geegaws and such? Tell me that."

"They will say you are damn miser, don't put

foofaraw on his woman, spends all his money on fire-water and fancy things for self." She couldn't help but giggle.

"You're sayin' I ain't a man who can care for his woman?" Cooper asked in mock ferocity.

"Yep. I say that." Still giggling she rose and started to run away, but Cooper launched himself at her and caught her around the waist. She didn't fall, but she let herself be tugged down. "I'll show you how a man treats a woman good," he said.

Black Moon wrapped her arms around him. "Yep. You will. Damn good."

They quickly headed to the robes, happy that Left Behind was sleeping.

THEY WERE on the trail just after dawn and pushed hard throughout the day. They had a small, but mostly comfortable camp that night, and set out again shortly after daylight. It was the same for several days and nights.

Cooper did all that he was capable of in trying to make their trail hard to follow, crossing and recrossing rivulets and streams, riding on rock when he could find any, and trying to avoid low-leafed trees or bushes, not wanting to leave broken stems for others to follow. But it was difficult to hide their tracks with eight mules and five horses, especially at times when there was no trail and they had to force or hack their way through thick underbrush. Cooper cursed every time that happened, which was far too often.

A heavy rainstorm set upon them as they rode two

days after leaving, and Cooper was not sure whether that was good or bad in foiling any possible trackers. The rain would wash away much of their passage, but the resulting mud would leave at least a trace of hoofprints. But there was little he could do about any of it.

After that day and another, they reached what Cooper thought was Dry Fork of the Shoshone River, and they turned to move along it as it wound its way eastward to the Shoshone itself. A day later, Cooper decided again that they had run enough. He found a good place amid the trees to put down stakes for a short while at least. "I reckon this'll do," he said. He looked around the area, while Black Moon fed Left Behind.

When he returned, he said, "There's plenty of beaver sign and a heap of willows and cottonwoods. In addition to this here stream runnin' along the side of the small glade here, there's several other streams rollin' into this one. Only thing that worries me is that sharp, rocky slope off to that side, even if it ain't all that far down," he added, pointing. "There's another stream at the bottom."

"It's a good place," Black Moon agreed. "Damn good."

"I reckon so. It ain't winter yet, late October, maybe, but I already got two packs of prime plews. I should add to that in a big way here. We can spend maybe a month here before headin' to my father's village to winter."

They set about making their camp. The woman gathered plenty of wood, started a fire, and began cooking some of the elk Cooper had shot earlier in the day while they were on the trail.

Cooper set about unloading the mules and storing the supplies under canvas to protect them. Dark, heavy clouds were gathering, and Cooper figured they were in for more rain, probably heavy, soon. He unsaddled his and Black Moon's horses and tended to them, then tied all the animals to a picket line between two stout cottonwoods. When he went to the fire and tiredly took his seat, he smiled at Black Moon, who was tying willow branches into hoops.

"Think I'm gonna make them beaver come, do you?"

"My man is best damn trapper in mountains," she said proudly.

"Damn right I am."

They both laughed.

After eating, Cooper was just finishing up a lean-to when the rain came, in thick, blinding sheets. Thunder cracked, boomed, and rolled over the land, making the animals fidgety, and Cooper had to stay out in the pounding rain to try to keep them as calm as possible. Tongues of lightning flashed, giving everything an eerie glow and leaving behind an odd odor and a lingering tingle that raised the hair on their necks and arms.

Their fire was quickly quenched under the assault of the storm as Black Moon, with the baby, huddled in the crude, leaky lean-to.

The thunder and lightning lessened, though the rain did not ease and with a drop in temperature, it turned to sleet. Still, the animals quieted enough that Cooper could join the woman and baby in the lean-to. "Damn if this don't beat all," Cooper grumbled.

"It goes away soon."

"Maybe, but I'm worried that stream might run over and that part of this damn camp might get pushed over that slope there."

But as Black Moon had predicted, and Cooper knew despite his irritability, the storm did pass, though not until well after dark. In the morning, the two adults and the infant came out of their meager shelter. Cooper looked around. There was little damage that he could see, and the animals were all right.

Black Moon managed to get a new fire going, and soon they were eating and drying out. When Cooper finished his meal, he rose and got his traps. "Time for me to get to work." Then he was gone.

The storm was just a prelude to the coming winter, as were the other ominous signs of the coming winter.

AS THE CALENDAR inched through November Cooper's hunt was very good, the furs thick and prime. Soon the little camp was festooned with willow hoops with hides curing. Black Moon was happy, while Left Behind usually emitted happy gurgles.

SEVENTEEN

THE ARROW DIDN'T MISS by much, but it was too damn close for comfort. Hawley Cooper rolled to the side, behind a log, grabbing his rifle as four Crows on foot burst out of trees across from him. He saw with relief that Black Moon was laying flat behind their saddles, Left Behind in his cradleboard beside her. He was glad to see that she had her flintlock pistol in her hand. No fear showed on her face.

As he settled his rifle over the log, Cooper saw two Crows heading for the mountain man's horses and mules. "Dammit all," he muttered, then fired. One Crow went down, dead. He yanked out a pistol and fired again. Another fell but managed to get up.

Cooper heard Black Moon fire, and saw another Crow fall, then rise. Another shot from his left missed, as no other Crows fell. Cooper pulled his other pistol, but the three Crows, including the two wounded ones, were headed back into the trees.

Cooper could see at least one more warrior cutting

loose the picket line to which the horses and mules were tied. "Shit," he muttered.

The mountain man rose up on one knee to reload his rifle, when a warrior burst out of the trees to his right, tomahawk in his hand, heading straight for him. Cooper managed to bring his rife up horizontally in both hands to block the Indian's swing of the weapon. But the Crow's momentum drove him back to the edge of the sharp slope behind him. The last thing he saw as he toppled backward down the slope was a scar-faced Crow and a warrior with short hair grabbing a struggling Black Moon and the baby and tossing them on horses behind another Crow he could not see. He heard the warriors racing northeast up the slim trail as he rolled and tumbled down the rocky incline, the Crow falling with him.

The two bounced and rolled, knocking loose a shower of dirt and rocks, until landing a few feet apart on the edge of the frost-crusted stream at the bottom. Cooper's rifle clattered down after him. The warrior's tomahawk was lost in the rough journey.

The mountain man was a little groggy as he got to his feet, but the Indian more so. Before the Crow could do anything, Cooper ripped out his knife and sliced open the warrior's throat. He cleaned the blade off on the Crow's shirt and slid it away. Then he grabbed his rifle and checked it quickly. Though there were some scratches on the stock, it otherwise seemed to be in fine shape.

He ran down along the stream to where there was an easier place to climb up, cursing himself all the while for having chosen a spot to make camp with such an incline behind him. He thought at the time that it would help protect them from Indian attack, having to defend only a semicircle in front of them—a meadow some yards wide, ringed with trees.

He finally managed to scramble up to the top on the edge of the camp. Knowing it was foolish, but having to try, he made sure his rifle was loaded, ignoring his pistols, one of which lay near the log he had first used as shelter, the other having been jarred loose in his tumble down the slope. Then he took off running.

After a mile, he stopped leaning on his rifle as he breathed like an overworked bellows. "Dammit. Dammit. Dammit! This here's poor damn bull, and ain't no denyin' it," Cooper told the wind and trees. "And there ain't no fixin' it either."

When his breathing returned almost to normal, he continued to stand there a bit longer, debating in his mind whether he should go back to camp or keep on the trail as best he could. He finally decided to head back to camp. Following the Crows with no supplies other than what he carried with him at the moment would be foolish. He didn't expect to catch them quickly, but with some supplies he could stay on their trail, hoping that they would slow down or even stop before too long, allowing him to catch up. He also hoped that one of the animals had gotten loose and drifted back to the camp.

As he trotted back toward camp, he wondered why the Crows did not stop to plunder the site, especially since they would almost certainly think he was dead. Maybe, he thought, they knew about Left Behind and grabbing the infant was their purpose. Once they had the boy, they took Black Moon as a wet nurse. He supposed, too, that with the number of horses and mules Cooper had had, that they also might think other mountain men might be in the area.

He walked up to the warrior who Black Moon had wounded. The man had a ghastly large hole in his back where the woman's .54-caliber lead ball had blown out. The Crow was trying to rise but having little success. Cooper kicked him in the side. "Worthless damn savage," Cooper said as he kicked the man again. The words caused a flashback to Josiah Weeks cursing all Indians to flicker through his mind and gave him a shiver. He hoped he was not about to become like that old reprobate. Then he noted with relief that it was only the Crows for now that had earned his deep-seated hate.

He set the rifle down against the top saddle in the pile—the ones his woman and the baby had hidden behind—then grabbed the groaning Crow by his hair and dragged him to the edge of the sharp slope and dropped him. "Farewell, you damned devil." With a foot, Cooper shoved the Crow down the slope.

He did the same with the man he had killed, then stood in the middle of the camp looking around. Willow hoops with drying beaver plews were still hanging all around, most of the furs ready to be taken down and packed. The stack of supplies was untouched, as were the saddles, the equipment, and all the rest. Cooper growled. There were decisions to be made, ones that would be difficult. Without a horse, or even mule, to ride, there was no way he could catch the Crows. At the rate they were galloping, he figured they were already several miles away. And while he planned to chase them, there were all his plews to think about. He had almost a thousand dollars' worth already, if the price was about the same as last year's, and to leave them here like this would be foolish. On the other hand, the only thing he could think of would be to cache them, and that would take hours, ones that he could spend on the trail of the Crows. Unless...

It wasn't the best solution, but it would take the least time. He quickly carried the two packs of plews to the slope and tossed them down. They were followed by the ones on willow hoops torn from trees. He ignored the trade goods. And much of the food. The saddles were the last to join everything at the bottom of the incline.

He sat and ate the last of the meat that had been keeping warm on a rock near the fire and finished off the little bit of coffee.

Finished, he set aside the pot and mug to let them cool, while he fashioned a backpack from a piece of canvas. Then he filled it with as much as he thought he could carry—the pot and mug, coffee, jerky and pemmican, sugar, and a canteen made of a buffalo bladder. He added a few small trade goods like beads and bells, which he wrapped in a hunk of cloth so they would make no noise, an extra blanket as the winter was nigh on him, and, most importantly, lead and powder.

He tied his blanket capote atop the pack and slung that over his shoulder. With a last look around the camp, missing Black Moon and, he realized, even Left Behind, he vowed silently that he would get them back —or wreak vengeance if they had been harmed. The child might be a Crow, but he would be better off raised by the Shoshoni.

He stepped off, walking at a good pace, using the sound of the creek on his left to help guide him. Dusk was falling, but that did not deter him, though it did slow him somewhat. The real trail quickly faded until it was just a faintly marked path weaving among the trees barely seen in the dim light of the moon. He avoided what branches he could and cursed the ones he couldn't.

He tried to keep his mind off his wife and the infant, but it was difficult. With a horse, he stood a chance of catching the Crows. On foot, there was none. But he still had to try. He had a faint hope that the marauders would stop before long to eat, rest and—he thought with a sick feeling in his gut—amuse themselves with Black Moon. Even if they wanted her solely for feeding the baby, they would not hesitate in abusing her. The thought made him shiver despite the warmth provided by his strong pace. He also wondered about the boy. The Crows, he expected, would not hesitate to dash the child's brains out if the infant became an annoyance even if he was one of them, though if they had gone through all the trouble to snatch the child, the boy likely was safe. Of course, they might not know that the baby was a Crow. In addition, the baby might not've been the object of the attack. Perhaps they had found the bodies of the baby's parents and thought Cooper was responsible. Or maybe they just came across a mountain man's camp and took advantage of the opportunity. He finally growled at himself. He had no answers, would get none, and whatever they were made no difference. He did not care why they had taken Black Moon, only that they had taken her.

He stopped after several hours to take a few swigs of water from the canteen and to take out a few strips of jerky. He gnawed at the latter as he set off again.

Cooper walked through the night and all the next day. As dusk began covering the land in a grayish blanket, he found a likely spot and decided to stop. The raiders had spent a night here, probably the night that the Crows had attacked his camp. He had a splash of hope in the thought that they might have spent more than one night here, something that perhaps would let him gain ground on them. That hope was dashed as he surveyed the site. It was obvious to his trained eye that they had spent only one night here.

"Damn," he spat. Then raindrops began to splatter the trees and his head. He sighed, set down his pack, and pulled on his capote. Thunder rolled overhead, though there was no lightning, and the temperature dropped considerably, once again turning the rain to sleet.

The shuffling sound of pine needles being disturbed caught his attention, and he turned slowly, dropping to a knee as he did. Maybe I can get one of those bastards right here, he thought. Then he realized it was a deer. He felt a touch of disappointment mixed with a bit of pleasure. But, figuring there were no Crows around to hear a shot, he slowly pulled his rifle out of its buckskin covering. He primed it and fired. The deer went down.

He had a welcome meal out of the deer meat and hot coffee. Despite the rain, he found dry pine needles and stretched out on them, covering himself with his capote. It wasn't the most comfortable night he had ever spent, but it was far from the worst.

He felt better in the morning after more venison and coffee. Not more hopeful, but rested and ready to push on. The days had gotten cold enough to preserve the meat, so he butchered out some deer flesh and wrapped it in a piece of hide. With his rifle loaded and back in its protective covering, he headed out.

Two nights later, he found a camp where the Crows had spent a night. "Dammit," Cooper spat out. If they had come this far in two nights and it had taken him five, they were pulling away with every hour that passed.

"Dammit all anyway," he said with a shake of his head. He collected wood and then started a fire and put meat and coffee on. He sat listlessly and ate without enthusiasm. He considered just giving up and heading for Cheyenne Killer's village. If he could get there quickly enough, he could winter there. Then in the spring, he could borrow some horses from his adoptive father and ride to the camp and retrieve the plews. At rendezvous, he could sell those furs and any others he might trap if he had time and get enough supplies to hunt down the Crows instead of hunting beaver.

Or he could get to the village and ask Cheyenne Killer to form a war party and go against the Crows. The Shoshoni could easily whip the Crows. They had done so more than once, including the raid in which Cooper had taken part.

Then he shook his head. He didn't think he could face Cheyenne Killer without having done everything that he could to have found Black Moon. Or if she had been killed, exacted at least some reckoning on the raiders.

No, he decided, he would continue on, at least until he decided it was futile for the time being.

EIGHTEEN

HAWLEY COOPER TRUDGED ALONG, one foot in front of the other. Despair and anger fought for dominance in his mind. Even if they were moving at a slow pace, the Crows were pulling away from him, step by step, mile by mile, day by day. At his night camps, the despondency usually won out, but in the mornings, the anger would take hold and propel him forward.

He followed the trail along the North Fork of the Shoshone River easily enough for days, even after two days of rain wiped out most traces of the Crows' trail. Still he pressed on, heading in a direction they had been going.

It being near the end of November, he figured, the temperature dropped frequently, then rose only a little. Snow, sleet, hail, and rain fell fitfully, sometimes days apart, sometimes on the same day. Though it was often freezing, the walking, his beaver-felt slouch hat, and his heavy capote kept him warm and dry enough.

While the low temperatures kept meat from spoiling for days, Cooper could carry only so much. He was lucky the three times he had had to hunt. But his coffee and sugar were running low after a week and a half. Soon after, both were gone. At times, he missed the coffee, but not much.

But the weather was not the only obstacle. A few days out, he almost fell over a sheer cliff, but managed to catch himself at the last minute. It took him two days to find a way around it, only to find himself sliding down a sharp, frosted, rocky slope, rolling to a stop at the bottom just feet from an icy stream. He was battered and sore, but he didn't care about that. His main concern again was his rifle, which, to his relief, was scratched more but unbroken. His pack was ripped but he had little in it now, so he was able to refashion it and press on.

He had to take most of the next day, time he didn't think he really had, to work himself around a waterfall.

He pushed on, feeling the growing threat of winter. He was tired, and his dejection was growing. He no longer had any kind of trail to follow, so just followed his own path along the North Fork of the Shoshone River, sometimes near it, more often half a mile or more away from it where sheer walls protected the water. But after crossing several ice-crusted streams, struggling up, then down hills, and skirting two larger creeks, he was beginning to think it was time to give up the idea of finding Black Moon and Left Behind. But he did not know what to do. He figured he had two choices—winter out here by himself or try to make his way to Cheyenne Killer's village, though that was miles away, and he wasn't sure he would be able to make it on foot.

He sat at his fire one night, huddling close to it to ward off the chill, and he had visions of the past two winters. Either option was daunting. But he didn't really want to spend another winter out here just trying to survive.

However, it did not take him that long to decide. Two days later he came to the Bighorn River. "Looks like this's where my stick floats now, ol' hoss," he muttered. It was time, he decided, to head to the closest thing he had to a home—Cheyenne Killer's village. He turned south along the river's western side.

ABOUT MIDMORNING ALMOST A MONTH LATER, he saw signs of a village up a large tributary near where the Bighorn turned into the Wind River— thin plumes of smoke and circling vultures and ravens looking for an easy meal. He could faintly hear the barking of dogs.

He wasn't certain but he figured it would be a Shoshoni village even considering where he was. He was a little apprehensive because it might be a Crow village since he was still along the fringes of land that the Absaroka roamed. If it was a Shoshone village, it likely would be of a different band that might not be so friendly toward him, though to his knowledge the Shoshonis had never harmed a white trapper. Still, there was always a first time, and he was rather vulnerable. He moved on, turning up the river from the Bighorn, heading toward the village, scrambling over rocks, and up and down ragged little slopes. Finally he stopped on a small hill, reassured in seeing that it was a Shoshoni village.

He plodded along, until he was surrounded by

yapping, snapping mongrels. He stopped and stayed stock-still where he was, not wanting to be gnawed to death by a raging pack of canines. He smiled a little. If that did happen, it would somehow be a fitting end to a life that seemed to be going nowhere.

Before long, though, several warriors rode hard out of the village, scattering the dogs with quirts and shouts. One of the young men offered a greeting in sign language. Cooper answered in kind, then said in Shoshoni, "I'm *Too-Shah-Itsup-Mah-Washay,* son of Cheyenne Killer."

"I know of Cheyenne Killer," one warrior said in Shoshoni. "He has no white son."

"He adopted me into his band a couple years ago."

"So you are the one who was saved by him and married into the tribe," the warrior said. "I am Bad Eye. Come." He held out his arm.

Cooper grabbed it and with Bad Eye's help leaped onto the horse. With a holler the three warriors trotted back to the village, accompanied by the pack of mongrels.

Villagers ventured out of their lodges into the cold to see what the commotion was all about, then stepped back inside. They had seen white trappers before.

The warriors and Cooper dismounted and entered a large lodge. The men took places around the fire, where three older warriors were already seated.

"What's your name?" one of the elders, who Cooper figured was the civil chief of this band, asked in English. His voice was deep and resonant, and heavily accented.

"Hawley Cooper." He spoke in Shoshoni now. "It's a pleasure to meet an elder of the people." He figured his Shoshoni was as accented to the people here as the chief's English was to him. He wondered why there had been no ceremonial pipe smoke but shrugged inwardly. He was just as glad there was none. He was, however, grateful for the bowl of buffalo meat in broth and the cup of coffee given him by an old woman, whom he assumed was the chief's wife.

With a combination of English, Shoshoni, and sign, the men were able to converse, starting off with the old man saying, "I am Tall Dog. Where are your companions?"

"Got none. I'm alone."

"Foolish. Where is your horse? Mules? Furs?"

"Gone. Took from me by Crows. Took my wife too —a Shoshoni like you, daughter of Blue Bear, a friend of Cheyenne Killer's. Took a child that was with us too."

"You were alone then?"

"Yep." Cooper felt a deep sense of shame.

"What will you do?"

"Catch the son a bitches and raise their goddamn hair," Cooper snapped, feeling the heat of rage build in him.

"Alone? On foot?"

"Yep. Got no horse, so afoot is the best I could do. I followed 'em for a spell, then decided to go to Cheyenne Killer's village. I can get some ponies there and go out after those bastards again."

"You'll die. Winter is harsh."

"I know damn well how harsh it is. Lived through it the last two years without much in the way of supplies. 'Sides, it don't matter much if I go under. Black Moon likely is dead already, and I got no claim to the child."

"He's not yours?" Tall Dog asked, showing some surprise.

"Nope. Found him hangin' in his cradleboard from a tree. Parents was killed, by Blackfeet, who didn't know a baby was around. Black Moon took to him and mothered him. We were thinkin' maybe of returnin' him to his people, the Crows, if we could. Bein' set upon by those bastards put that idea to an end. Knowin' the Crows, they might kill him if he gives 'em any nonsense. If the boy lives, he'll be raised by his people since he is one of 'em, whether they know it or not."

"Your woman faces a hard life."

Cooper nodded. "If she lives. If not..." he shrugged.

"If she does live, and you find her, you will take her back?"

Cooper paused a minute, trying to decide whether Tall Dog was mocking him, then decided he was not. "Don't know. I'll figure that out if I find her alive."

"And if she's dead?"

Cooper shrugged again. "Then there'll be a heapin' pile of dead shit-stinkin' Crows."

"Some warriors could help him hunt down the Crows," Bad Eye interjected. "The Crow are our enemy in these times."

The elders consulted with each other for a few moments, then Tall Dog shook his head. "No," he said. "We need all our warriors here."

"Why?" Bad Eye asked angrily.

"The Blackfeet are more troublesome this year. We need all here in case they attack."

Bad Eye went to argue but stopped when Cooper placed a hand on his arm and shook his head.

"I understand," Cooper said. "You must protect

your people. But can you let me have a horse? It'd make my travelin' a heap easier."

"What have you to trade?"

"About nothin'. I need what powder and ball I got, as well as my weapons. I got a little almost-fresh meat, maybe a couple beads, that's about it."

"Not enough for a horse."

Cooper was taken aback. "You'd deny a fellow Shoshoni a horse because he's got nothin' to trade?"

"You're not a Shoshoni."

"I am the son of Cheyenne Killer," Cooper snapped.

Tall Dog shrugged. "You're a white trapper, not a real Shoshoni."

"That might be, but I thought the Shoshoni were strong friends with the white trappers."

"With most, yes."

"Well, then, piss on you, you miserly bastard. I'm obliged for the meal." He rose, hefted his rifle with one hand, and slung his pack over his back with the other. He spit into the fire, all the while keeping his eyes on Tall Dog. "You ain't fit to be a Shoshoni." He spun and roughly pushed through the flap door of the lodge. He stood for a moment outside, then turned and walked off, heading back toward the Bighorn, his stride strong.

As he walked, he looked enviously at the large horse herd a short distance from the village. *Damn, it sure would be nice*, he thought. Then he shook his head. *Dammit all, I can't do that to some Shoshonis, even if they were inhospitable.* So he pushed on.

He was maybe two miles from the village, near the tributary's confluence with the Bighorn, wandering through the thick cottonwoods and some pines rising up a slight incline when he thought he heard horses—ridden horses—not loose ones. He cached behind a cottonwood, crouching low. Through the trees several yards to his left, he saw five Blackfeet riding toward the village. He waited a few minutes, then began following.

Cooper stopped as he saw the Blackfeet pause at the edge of the trees. Then they began galloping toward the Shoshoni horse herd. Cooper swiftly dropped to one knee and fired his rifle. A Blackfoot tumbled off his pony. Cooper hastily reloaded and fired again. With the Blackfoot racing away, and at this distance, it was a difficult shot. Cooper knew he hit his target but apparently did not kill him.

By now, the Shoshoni were aware of the attack, attracted by the Blackfoot war cries and the sound of Cooper's rifle. They were boiling out of the village on foot and horseback, aiming to cut off the Blackfoot attempt to drive off the Shoshoni ponies.

Cooper reloaded again, then slowly approached the dead Blackfoot's horse. The animal was standing close to his master's corpse. Cooper gently clutched the rope rein. He talked quietly to the animal, hoping to ease any fears it might have. The pony did not seem nervous, but it didn't like when Cooper leaped into the simple saddle. It took off, ready to join its companions, but Cooper fought to control the beast, and finally managed to turn its head.

With a feeling of satisfaction, and relief, Cooper headed into the trees and up the hill.

NINETEEN

COOPER TURNED up the Little Wind River, moving fast now that he was mounted. He figured he would reach Cheyenne Killer's village—if he had no trouble finding it—the next day.

Part of him wanted to find the village straight away, but part of him hoped he might never find it. Facing Cheyenne Killer and the other warriors was something he dreaded. He expected that his father—and more so, Blue Bear—would be unhappy not only that Black Moon had been taken but also that Cooper had not been able to find and rescue her. It was a meeting he wished he did not have to attend, but also one that he could not avoid. It was simply something he would have to face and deal with the repercussions as best he could.

Just under a month after Black Moon and Left Behind had been taken, Cooper rode into the Shoshoni village. It was a few days before Christmas, he figured.

People popped out of their lodges, then ducked back in, not wanting to either be out in the cold or let the cold into their warm lodges. But soon some came out again, their colorful Hudson's Bay blankets or dark buffalo robes, worn with the fur inside, wrapped around them. Cooper knew they were wondering where Black Moon was.

As such things usually did, word of his arrival had reached Cheyenne Killer's ears, and the chief was outside his lodge waiting. With a sinking feeling, Cooper dismounted and gave the rein of the Blackfoot pony to a boy just into his teens. He followed Cheyenne Killer, who had not waited, into the lodge. Within minutes, half a dozen other warriors, including Cuts Throat and Blue Bear had arrived. With all the bodies, his heavy capote, and the fire, it was almost stifling to Cooper after days of riding through the cold.

"Where is my daughter?" Blue Bear demanded. He seemed to have found life inside him after the summer's traumas.

Cooper ignored him, instead nodding thanks for the food and drink one of Cheyenne Killer's wives provided. As he sipped his coffee, Cooper thought Blue Bear looked old beyond his years, the skin of his face sagging and wrinkled, his shoulders drooping, his hair far grayer than that of Cheyenne Killer, who was about the same age.

Everyone else was quiet as Cooper ate and Blue Bear fumed.

After a few minutes, Blue Bear again demanded, "Where is my daughter?"

"She ain't here," Cooper said, his tone contrarian.

"But..."

"Shut up," Cooper snapped. "She ain't your daughter anymore. She's my wife, and you have no claim to her. Any that you did have, you gave up last year."

Blue Bear started to protest but Cheyenne Killer cut him off. "Where is your woman?" he asked quietly.

"Don't know for sure. She was taken by the Crows more than a month ago. I ain't kept much track of time. We were in a camp on a stream near the North Fork of the Shoshoni River."

"You searched for her?"

"Yep. Couldn't make much progress, though. Crows not only took Black Moon and Left Behind, they also..."

"Left Behind?" Cheyenne Killer asked, surprised.

Cooper's head bobbed. "Of course you wouldn't know. Me and Moon found an infant hanging in a cradleboard from a tree. Blackfeet killed his ma and pa —Crows. Apparently, the war party didn't see—or hear —the child. We named him Left Behind and took him with us. We thought we might try to find his people and give him back to them."

Cooper held out his cup for a refill of coffee. After he had received it and took a sip, he added, "Soon after, a couple Crows come along fixin' to make trouble. I run 'em off, but figured they'd be back. Me and Moon skedaddled, but the two caught up to us a few days later. We killed one and sent the other packin'. We figured he'd come back with some friends, so we packed up and moved off again."

"They found you," Cuts Throat said rather than asked.

"Ain't sure it was the same feller. I was a mite busy fightin' 'em off. I put two under, but they grabbed Moon and Left Behind and run off all the horses and mules."

"You came here on horse," Blue Bear said accusingly.

Once again Cooper ignored him. "I dumped my plews and whatever else was of value into a ravine, then set off after them devils on foot."

"Ain't likely to catch 'em that way," Cuts Throat said. He was not accusatory.

"Nope. They rode off in a hurry but I figured they'd slow down some before long. Still, I figured that for every mile I went they went ten. No way was I gonna catch 'em." He shrugged fatalistically. "Had to try, though."

All the other warriors, except Blue Bear, nodded and murmured their acceptance of his effort.

"How'd you come by a horse?" Cheyenne Killer asked.

Cooper smiled, though there was little humor in it. "I was gettin' mighty weary bein' on foot all those miles, and I thought I was lucky when I come across a Shoshoni village, near where the Bighorn changes to the Wind."

"They gave you a horse," Cuts Throat said with a nod.

That turned to surprise when Cooper said, "Nope. I asked 'em to have some warriors come with me to hunt down those damn Crows. One of 'em even said he and few others'd come. But the elders said no, claimed they had to worry about Blackfeet." He gave another grim smile. "Reckon they were right in thinkin' so."

The others sat in silence, waiting for more.

"I asked for some supplies and a horse. They said they couldn't afford to lose any supplies and had no horses to spare. Also said I wasn't a real Shoshoni."

Cheyenne Killer's eyes widened in surprise and anger. "A Shoshoni not helping another. Unthinkable," he said in his own language.

Others growled their assent.

"So you went and took one of their horses," Cuts Throat said in a tone that indicated he thought that would be a reasonable—even expected—response to such an insult.

"Nope," Cooper said with a shake of the head. "I contemplated doin' such, but I ain't like them."

"So...?"

"I was a couple miles from the edge of the village, moving into the trees, when I heard, then saw, a small Blackfoot war party. It looked like they were plannin' to try to run off the Shoshoni horses. I followed. Then they—there were five of 'em—came boilin' out of the trees, headin' straight for the ponies. I made gone beaver of one for sure, and maybe a second. Took the dead one's pony and skedaddled."

The warriors sitting in a circle let out a few whoops of joy at handing the Blackfeet a small loss and perhaps saving the Shoshoni horse herd, even after their refusal to help Cooper.

"I was already headin' here, so I just kept on comin'. Not sure I can find those skunk-humpin' bastards, but I aim to go lookin' for 'em, even though winter's full on the land. I'll need your help, though."

"You seem to like this child?" Cheyenne Killer asked.

Cooper shrugged. "Don't much matter to me. He's just months old, and if the Crows don't know he's Crow and don't think he's too much of an annoyance, they'll raise him as their own, which I expect is only right and proper since he is a Crow. I expect they know, though. I think it's why they raided us and just took Moon and the baby and didn't take all the plunder. But Moon, she was beginning to have feelins about that child. I worried about that a little but figured there weren't anything I could do about it. If the two of 'em hadn't been taken, it's likely she would've wanted to raise him 'stead of sendin' him back to the Crows."

"If they're alive?" Cheyenne Killer asked.

"Then I doubt she'll be of a mind to leave the child with those bastards."

"You don't think that'll happen, do you?" Cuts Throat said.

"I don't reckon Black Moon is alive. She wasn't faint-hearted, and I don't reckon she'd put up with any nonsense from them Crows—or anyone else, like as not."

"She thought you were not man enough to come after her," Blue Bear said with a sneer.

"She might've figured I was gone under. I was down in that ravine after one of the Crows dropped me and him down there. Even if she figured I was alive, I had no horse or mule and so would have a devil of a time chasin' after them damn savages."

"So you think she's gone under?" Cuts Throat asked.

Cooper nodded glumly. "I figure that she thought I was gone under or was unable to come rescue her. She might've acted docile for a spell to try to protect the baby, but if something happened to the child, she'd be powerfully recalcitrant to bend to the Crows' ways. She knew what would happen to her if she got to a Crow village—or even before that—and would not have been willing to undergo such degradation without a fight. So she would've become a regular annoyance to 'em and they would've made swift work of her. At best, they would've taken the baby to a Crow woman for nursin', meanin' Black Moon would be of no more use to 'em."

"So you will winter with us?" Cheyenne Killer asked.

"Maybe. I'd rather rest up a little then set out with some warriors and go hunt those bastards down."

The elders shook their heads. "You know winter is not the time to make war," Cheyenne Killer said. "If you knew where those Crows were, I would lead a war party at your side. But you don't know where they are. The people can't have their men roamin' all 'round tryin' to find them while our families are unprotected and maybe starving."

"You sound like those cowardly Shoshonis that wouldn't help me. You sit around the fire all winter tellin' each other how brave you are, recountin' brave acts that are likely as not a pile of buffler droppins. Ain't got the balls to go after a few Crows. I'm ashamed of my father. I could understand Blue Bear over there bein' too scared to go to war, but you, Cheyenne Killer? I'm outraged." He started to rise, but Cuts Throat stopped him. He plopped back down.

"Your words are hurtful, my son," Cheyenne Killer said quietly. "You should know I'm no coward. Neither are these others." He swept a hand around taking in all the others, most of whom looked angry. "You should know, too, that makin' war in winter is foolish. Food is scarce, the animals have trouble travelin' through the snow or findin' forage. We aren't cowardly, but we are wise in such things."

"Blackfeet make war in winter. Crows too, as I've seen. You think they are foolish?"

"Maybe."

Cooper looked at his father in surprise. "Maybe?"

Cheyenne Killer grinned a little. "The Crows are foolish. Arrogant too. Think the snow can't stop 'em because they're Crows. The Blackfeet, well, they are touched in the head."

The others chuckled a little.

"We'll wait out the winter, then we will go find some Crows to kill." Seeing Cooper's hesitation, he added, "What would be done has been done. Challengin' winter won't change that."

Cooper sat a few minutes, thinking. Then he drew in a deep breath and let it out. He nodded.

TWENTY

"GOIN' somewhere?" Cuts Throat asked.

Cooper glanced over his shoulder as he continued saddling the horse he had taken from the Blackfoot warrior he had slain. "Huntin'."

"You wouldn't lie to your Shoshoni brother, would you?"

"Likely would if I thought it was necessary."

"Is it necessary this time?"

Cooper finished what he was doing, then half turned and rested an arm on the Indian saddle that had come with the Blackfoot pony. "Could be. Depends on why you're askin'."

"I'm askin' because I think you might be contemplatin' something foolish."

"And if I were?"

"I'd tell you that were a damn fool."

"Wouldn't try to stop me?" There was almost, though not quite, a challenge in Cooper's voice.

"Maybe. Maybe not. Depends on how serious in your foolishness you seemed."

Cooper grinned. "I ain't plannin' on nothin' foolish. Ain't plannin' to do any huntin' either really."

"Then what?"

"Just want to get away from all you folk for a little, be by myself a bit to think."

"To contemplate doin' something foolish?"

Cooper laughed. "Could be. Or maybe not. Depends on where my thinkin' goes."

"Ain't you had enough of bein' on your own? Seems you been doin' a heap of travelin' on your own, through snow and rain and damn near everything else."

"That's true," he shrugged. "Can't be helped, I reckon."

"You want some company?"

"Just said I wanted to be alone, didn't I?"

"Yes. So?"

"You're a bigger pain in my rump than Black Moon," Cooper said, then grimaced at the thought of having lost her.

"Can be."

"All right," Cooper sighed. "Go saddle your old nag, and I don't mean Pony Wo..." He clapped his mouth shut.

Ten minutes later they were riding across the prairie away from the river where the Shoshonis had their winter camp. Off to their left was the large horse herd, the ponies pawing at the snow to get at what grass they could, though mostly they fed on cottonwood bark. Beyond that, off in the distance, rose the Wind River Mountains, the towering, jagged, snow-covered sentinels watching over the Shoshoni people.

"Why'd you bring that extra horse?" Cooper asked.

"Figured if we saw something worth huntin', might as well make meat of it."

"We do, you can do the butcherin'."

They rode in silence for a while, each occupied by his own thoughts. Cuts Throat looked over at his friend and wondered what was going through his mind. He thought he knew, because he would have thoughts that Cooper likely was having now if Pony Woman had been taken by warriors from another tribe. The thought —no, desire—for revenge would be strong in his heart, he knew, as it was in Cooper's. He smiled inwardly. He would have acted the same way Cooper did the night he had arrived back in the village. Cuts Throat could understand his white friend's anger, shame, and yearning for revenge.

Cooper wasn't sure he liked having company on his ride. He liked and trusted Cuts Throat but he also really did want to be alone, to fuel the rage inside him. He wanted to formulate a plan for avenging Black Moon and Left Behind, and he did not need someone who was likely to try to argue him out of whatever he was considering. He knew deep inside that Black Moon was lost to him forever. Even if she still lived, she likely would be in no position to be his wife again. She would have been mistreated, abused, probably tortured, and more. He wasn't sure he could be her husband again either, knowing she had been so ill-treated. Death might be better should she have been abused by the Crows, he thought. She would be free of pain and suffering that way. But he would not.

"So, are you fixin' to do something foolish?" Cuts Throat asked, breaking into Cooper's thoughts.

"If I think of something, it won't be foolish," Cooper

responded, his eyes fixed on the mountains, his breath pluming in the cold air.

"Ya know, gettin' killed by the Crows won't bring Black Moon back if she's gone under. And it sure won't make her feel good if she's alive."

"That's my concern, no one else's."

"That's wrong thinkin', my friend."

"How's that?"

"You got to think of others."

"Like who?"

"Me," Cuts Throat said with a grin. "I got few friends."

Cooper gave him a baleful glance.

"Well, maybe I ain't that important to you." He grew more serious. "But there's Cheyenne Killer. Your father would feel at a loss if his son was to go under."

"He'd get over it soon enough."

"Would Pony Woman? She's your sister, and she cares for you, though I can't figure out why."

"'Cause she knows I'm a better man than her lazy, ill-tempered husband," Cooper countered but with much less joy than the words would indicate.

"She'd argue that with you." Cuts Throat knew his attempts to lighten things were failing to work, but he had to try, he decided.

"I should've shot you when you insisted on coming along here. I said I wanted to be alone to do some thinkin'. That's gotten mighty hard to do when you keep flappin' that gapin' hole in your face."

Cuts Throat decided to be quiet. He knew that if he kept up trying to talk to Cooper, to bring him out of his melancholy, they might come to blows again, something he remembered with a grimace. Cooper's chal-

lenge to Cuts Throat over Black Moon Woman had led
to the two young men whaling the tar out of each other,
with a bleeding, weaving, hard-breathing Cooper being
the last one standing. The two young men soon became
fast friends. Cooper married Black Moon Woman, and
Cuts Throat had married Pony Woman, Cooper's
Shoshoni sister and Black Moon Woman's best friend.

They rode in silence for a while, letting their horses
wander as they would mostly, just keeping a light hand
on the reins. Finally Cuts Throat said, "You inclined to
do some actual huntin'?" He pointed to a small group of
buffalo a few hundred yards away.

"Reckon I could show you how it's done."

"Hah! There'll never be a day you can beat me at
huntin'."

"We'll just see about that."

They rode forward, still slowly but with more
purpose. Cooper stopped about a hundred and fifty
yards from the herd. "You go on a little closer, Cuts
Throat." He dismounted.

"We're not gonna run 'em?"

"I ain't in no mood for runnin' buffler today."

The Shoshoni shrugged and moved on until he was
a little less than a hundred yards from the animals. He
looked back, and Cooper nodded.

"I'll take me that fat cow there to the left," Cooper
said loudly enough for Cuts Throat to hear but not loud
enough to spook the buffalo.

Cuts Throat nodded again, unlimbered his bow,
and nocked an arrow. He fired the moment he heard
Cooper's rifle shot and sent three bolts deep into a
buffalo cow to the right of the one Cooper had indicated he would take. Both beasts went down.

The two men raced up to the herd, waving blankets and shouting to drive the herd off. Both buffalo that had been shot were still breathing but were all but dead. Cooper took one pistol and put a fatal bullet into his cow, then used the other pistol to finish off the one Cuts Throat had shot.

"Looks like we both didn't do well," Cuts Throat said.

"We made meat, that's the important thing, I reckon."

The trapper and the Shoshoni set about butchering the animals and before long they were heading back to the village with the extra horse loaded with a goodly amount of ribs, tongue, fleece, and more.

Cooper took some of the choicest cuts to Black Moon Woman's father, Blue Bear, and Cuts Throat had Pony Woman take some to her father, Cheyenne Killer. The two lodges ate well that night and throughout the next day.

But Cooper was getting fidgety. The more he thought about Black Moon, the more he cursed himself for having let her be captured and not being able to rescue her or make the Crows pay for their evil deed.

"Weren't your fault," Cuts Throat said one day when Cooper voiced his concerns. "You were alone and had made a camp best as you could. Nobody could've prevented those damn Crows from takin' her or the child."

"I let my guard down, dammit. By not mindin' business the way I should've, the Crows had an easy time of it."

"Not easy. You killed at least two of 'em, and

another when you finished off the one Black Moon had shot."

Cooper shrugged, not appeased. But he thought there was little he could do now that winter had laid its heavy hand over the land.

He gave it much thought over the next two days, and finally made a decision. Surreptitiously, he began gathering supplies, pilfering a little here, a little there, and stacking them under a tree a mile or so upstream from the farther lodges. He rode out of the village just as dusk was falling, with night's arrival speeding closer.

Cooper was sure that Cuts Throat knew something was up with him and tried to follow him, but it was easy to lose the Shoshoni in the darkness, and when he returned to Cheyenne Killer's lodge, he came in from a different direction to throw off any guesswork as to where he was going and what he was doing.

And he began looking over the horses, and the few mules, that Cheyenne Killer had.

Finally, he thought he had enough—some jerky and pemmican, coffee and coffeepot, a little sugar and salt, a frying pan and little kettle, two blankets, his buffalo robe and capote, and some extra powder and lead.

Two nights later, he lay quietly in Cheyenne Killer's lodge while the chief, his wives, and two nephews slept. He had pretended to fall asleep; he didn't think he could have slept even if he wanted to. He picked up the carving of a horse he had made and in the dim light of the fading fire, he cut two notches near the carving's mane and another slightly bigger one near the rump. He picked up his sleeping robe and lay the carving down in its place. He hoped Cheyenne Killer would understand that Cooper would be taking two horses—including the one he had been riding—and a mule from his father's herd.

He slipped out of the lodge and saddled his horse, which he had staked nearby, with the white man's saddle Cheyenne Killer had given him. Then he vaulted onto the animal. He would get the other horse and the mule when he rode out and passed the clan's giant herd.

Dawn, such as it was, was barely breaking as he rode out of the village into the swirling gray screen of light snow. He did not know that Cuts Throat watched with a heavy heart.

TWENTY-ONE

HAWLEY COOPER HAD no real idea of where, exactly, he should go, only that he could not sit in Cheyenne Killer's village all winter wondering and worrying about Black Moon. He headed back the way he had come, down the Little Wind River to the Bighorn. Days later, relying on a description Cheyenne Killer had given him, Cooper crossed the river and headed east along a creek he had been told would take him across a stretch of the Bighorn Basin and into the mountains. Cheyenne Killer had said it was called Five Springs Creek. He followed that into the mountains, and into the thick trees.

———

COOPER WAS NEARLY HALFWAY across a long, narrow meadow when he stopped as a figure burst out of the scattered trees on the other side. Cooper thought he looked like an older boy—maybe young teens. He was running as best he could, slipping and sliding on the couple inches of snow on the ground like the devil himself was after him. Moments later, two warriors on horseback loped out of the same spot across the glade.

It took barely a moment to realize that the youth was a Crow, and his pursuers were Blackfoot. Cooper sat a few moments, as the warriors neared the unarmed boy, who was running hard for the trees to Cooper's left. They were in no real hurry, and it seemed to Cooper that they were laughing and almost certainly insulting the youth.

The Crow looked back over his shoulder as the Blackfeet approached and put on a bit more speed, but Cooper figured that was all the swiftness he had in him.

Cooper knew the youth would not make the forest to his left and wondered why the Crow hadn't kept to the trees lining both sides of the glade instead of darting out onto the open meadow. Cooper started turning his horse to get to cover himself before the Blackfeet saw him. But he stopped when one of the Blackfeet trotted up to the boy and with his bow, smacked him sharply across the back, just under the shoulder blades. He laughed and the other Blackfoot let out a few high-pitched yelps as the Crow fell on his face in the snow.

Cooper sat a few moments wondering what to do. He had no love for the Blackfeet, but the Crows had stolen his woman and tried to kill him. He knew he should just ride off back into the trees until the drama in front of him played out. Then he sighed, his breath billowing out in a misty cloud. He could not let a couple of Blackfeet take this boy prisoner and kill him, perhaps taking him back to their village so they could torture him. He might be a Crow, Cooper thought, but he was still a boy, and he deserved a chance to grow some, become a warrior and go against the Blackfeet on a more equal footing.

He pulled his rifle from the loop on the front of his saddle and dismounted. He knelt for a steadier stance and fired. The Blackfoot who had counted coup on the youth went spiraling, arms flailing, and then fell.

The other Blackfoot spotted Cooper instantly and quirted his horse into a run, heading for the mountain man, bringing his bow out and nocking an arrow.

Cooper reloaded swiftly, ignoring the first two arrows that came at him, which missed widely as they were caught in the wind. He stood this time and fired again.

"Damn," Cooper muttered. He was sure his lead ball had hit the Blackfoot, but not in a vital spot as the warrior did not fall or even slow his pony. Cooper ducked behind his horse and an arrow thudded into his saddle. The horse bolted across the meadow.

Cooper let out a long string of curses as he turned to face the Blackfoot. The warrior dropped his bow, and Cooper saw blood on the blanket covering the warrior's upper chest. The Blackfoot spun around on his horse and charged at Cooper, launching himself off the animal, knocking Cooper sprawling onto the ground and his rifle bouncing away on the snow.

The Blackfoot had landed mostly on a knee and slid a little on the snow but was quickly on his feet, tossing off his blanket. He tried to kick Cooper, but the mountain man grabbed the warrior's foot and twisted. The Blackfoot fell.

Cooper pushed himself up and pulled one of his pistols, but the Blackfoot was too quick and came at him with his knife hungrily seeking Cooper's flesh. The mountain man pulled the trigger, but the powder had gotten damp in the snow and misfired.

"Dammit," Cooper muttered. He shifted as the Blackfoot's blade cut through Cooper's capote and left a thin, bloody line across his side. Cooper slammed the warrior on the side of the head with the pistol, and the Blackfoot fell. Figuring that his other pistol also had damp powder, Cooper dropped the pistol and yanked out the tomahawk from where it rested in his belt at the small of his back under his capote.

Only with luck did Cooper avoid the Blackfoot's next darting attack, and the mountain man lashed out with the 'hawk, deeply slicing the warrior's knife arm. The Blackfoot dropped the blade and staggered back a few steps as pain ran up his arm.

Cooper moved in fast, and before the Blackfoot could defend himself anew, Cooper had hacked him down with two chops to his side, smashing and slicing though ribs and internal organs, followed by a final hack to the throat.

Breathing heavily, breath pluming out into the air, Cooper stood and looked around. The dead warrior's pony was nearby, and his own horse stood, pawing the ground, looking for grass near the edge of the forest. The young Crow had picked himself up and was gingerly heading the way he had before he was attacked.

Cooper wiped the blade of his tomahawk on the dead warrior's blanket and slipped it away. He reloaded his rifle as well as his two pistols, making sure the powder was dry. With a shrug, he took the fallen warrior's scalp and stuffed it in his belt. Then he took the skittish Blackfoot pony and walked, towing the animal toward his own horse. He stopped along the way to collect the second warrior's scalp and stick that in his belt too. Then he moved on again. The other Blackfoot pony was grazing as well as it could nearby. Cooper tied the rope rein of the second horse to the tail of the first and that one to a tree branch.

Still holding the Blackfoot pony's reins, Cooper mounted his own horse and rode slowly after the Crow, who had ducked into the trees. As he rode, he wondered if he should just let the youth go. There would be no point in catching him, he thought. Or was there? Maybe this young Crow could tell him where his prey was. He nodded. He would get the youth to talk, perhaps even to lead him to the men he wanted to catch —and Black Moon. He picked up the pace and headed back into the woods, knowing the Crow did not have a weapon.

He caught up to the youth within minutes as the Crow had slowed considerably. "Stop, boy. Quit your runnin'." He did not know if the Crow understood him.

Either he did, or he understood the meaning as he stopped and turned. The youth's chest moved in and out like a blacksmith's bellows.

"You speak and understand English, boy?"

The youth clamped his mouth shut, which made his breathing all the harder.

Cooper figured he'd try talking to the youth anyway in hopes he would understand. "I ain't about to hurt you, boy, but I'm lookin' for a few Crow warriors, and you bein' a Crow, I thought maybe you could maybe help me."

The new silence grew, and then the youth shook his head.

"Can you take me to your village so I can talk to others there?"

There was more hesitation on the Indian's part.

"Just what'n hell are you doin' out here alone and without a weapon?"

"Got knife."

"Well, that's better than nothin', but won't help you in a fight."

"I was huntin'."

"With a knife?" Cooper said in disbelief.

"I had bow, arrows." He looked abashed. "I lost 'em when Blackfeet find me." He almost spit out the word "Blackfeet." "Pony run away too."

Cooper shook his head, then asked, "What's your name?"

"Slow Fox."

"Well, Slow Fox, how far is it to your village?"

"An hour, maybe, as you say?"

"Grab one of these ponies and lead the way."

"I do not take you."

"Why not? The Crows and white trappers have always been friendly," Cooper said, the lie sitting hard in the pit of his stomach.

"The elders will be angry."

"Don't see why. I just want a little parley with 'em." It was less of a lie seeing that it was true unless his quarry were there.

"They will be angry with me for losing pony, bow, arrows. Not like that I bring a stranger to village."

"Well, you may've lost a pony, but now you have two Blackfoot ponies. That should make up for the lost one, plus your lost bow and arrows. I reckon you can find one of the warriors to make you new ones. Best of all, you got two Blackfoot scalps, which ought to put you in good standin' with your people."

The Crow brightened, but the joyful look soured almost immediately. "I never had gun; they know you kill him."

"How in hell're they gonna know that? It ain't like we're aimin' to take the bodies back, just the scalps. Oh, and you can tell 'em you lost your bow in fightin' the Blackfeet."

"What about you?"

"What about me?"

"Where did you come from?"

"Back that way a bit," Cooper said, pointing.

The youth looked at Cooper as if he were an idiot. "They'll ask how we joined here and came to the village."

"Hmmm, that might cause some wonder." He thought for a few moments, then shrugged. "I happened to come along just after you had made wolf bait of those two Blackfeet. I asked you to take me to the village because I wish to talk to the elders."

It didn't take long for the boy to nod. After all, this white man had saved him and killed two of the hated Blackfeet in doing so. "I take you."

"Good." Cooper tossed him the two scalps. "So, like I said, grab either of those two ponies you want and lead on."

Slow Fox hurriedly did as he was told. He rode easily through the forest, seeming to Cooper to know where he was going even though there was no trail. Cooper did have some moments of doubt, wondering if the young Crow was leading him into some kind of trap. The Crows were known to dupe trappers in a bid to steal everything of the trappers that they could get their hands on.

TWENTY-TWO

THE VILLAGE WAS in another meadow a few miles up Five Springs Creek from where Cooper had found Slow Fox. It was small for a Crow one, perhaps a dozen lodges. It seemed to have been set up recently. There was little detritus and there still was some forage for the dozens of horses. Even a small village like this would have to move every couple of weeks or so in need of fresh feed for the animals and to avoid the accumulated piles of waste and other rubbish.

The few people who were out in the cold seemed friendly enough, Cooper thought, though he vowed silently not to let down his guard. They stopped in front of a large lodge, where three men, none of them young, but not old either, waited. They had heavy wool blankets wrapped around them. Two had roundish fur hats, while the third one wore a coyote's fur hat, the head still on. The edges of their blankets flapped in the wind.

"Welcome, friend of the Crows," one of the three said in Absaroka and in signs. "Come inside, get warm, eat, we talk."

Cooper understood it and smiled to himself. *Friend, my ass*, he thought. *I reckon these critters would steal the hairs of my mustache if they thought I wasn't looking, even though they had no use for such things.*

Aloud, he said tactfully in the same fashion, "Greetings, Chief Deer Tail." He had learned the man's name from his young companion on the ride here. "I am glad to be in such a welcoming village. I know that the Crows hearts are big." He almost gagged on the words, considering what these people had done to him. "We have much to discuss." He dismounted and handed the reins of his two horses and the mule to a youth about the same age as Slow Fox. Looking at Deer Tail, he said, "My animals will be well taken care of, and my supplies well looked after?" It was not a question, really, and the three Crows looked at him with signs of annoyance in their eyes.

"Come," Deer Tail said, heading into the lodge. Cooper followed him, as did the other two warriors and Slow Fox. Cooper was thankful for the warmth in the lodge, though he figured it would be overwhelming before long, especially with all the occupants.

Inside, one of the warriors looked at Slow Fox and said in Crow, "Outside. You don't belong in here with men."

Before the youth could reply—or leave—Cooper said, "You saw these two ponies?" When the warrior nodded, Cooper added, "They belong to Slow Fox."

All three warriors looked at the youth in surprise.

"He took them from Blackfeet. We will tell of it after we eat and smoke."

Slow Fox, looking nervous, sat next to Cooper, a little away from his three elders.

A few other warriors entered and took seats around the fire. All looked askance at Slow Fox but said nothing.

"What's your name?" Deer Tail asked as two women served the men a savory soup with large chunks of elk.

"Hawley Cooper." He hadn't realized how hungry he was until he started spooning down the food.

It was not long before the men were done eating, though they still had coffee. One of the warriors picked up a long pipe, lit it with a twig from the fire and handed it to Deer Tail, who offered it to the four cardinal directions, then Mother Earth and Father Sky before passing it to the man on his right. The pipe finally made it around the circle.

"So, you captured two horses from the Blackfeet, Slow Fox?" Deer Tail asked, not believing.

"Yes. I..." He began to falter.

"I'll tell of it," Cooper swiftly jumped in. "So you will know the truth of it." He smiled inwardly at the lie. "I saw him in battle with two Blackfeet, and I rushed to help. He didn't need it, though. He counted coup on both, but his bow was broken in the fight. He grabbed an arrow and stabbed one of the enemies with it. The other knocked Slow Fox aside, but this young warrior fought like a wildcat and hacked the other down with his knife."

Cooper let the buzz of conversation from the others filter around the lodge, a little worried that one of them would ask what happened to the quiver Slow Fox had carried. He had no answer for that, and he wasn't sure he could come up with one.

But no one asked. Instead Deer Tail said, "Maybe

he doesn't tell the truth, eh, Slow Fox." His voice and visage were stern.

"Show 'em," Cooper chucked his chin to where the two scalps hung from the youth's belt at the back.

Slow Fox pulled out the bloody trophies and tossed them somewhat nonchalantly over the fire to land on Deer Tail's lap.

The chief looked at them and showed them to the warrior on each side. Then the three of them let out some joyful yips.

As the others celebrated, Cooper leaned over and whispered to Slow Fox, "If you go out on the war trail with these fellers, you best be able to fight well. If you don't know how, practice."

The pleasure dropped from the Crow's eyes, and he slumped a little. "I will," he mumbled.

The small celebration quickly wound down. Deer Tail tossed the scalps behind him, on his own sleeping robe, and Cooper figured he meant to keep them for himself.

"You have reason to come here with Slow Fox?" Deer Tail asked Cooper, switching to English.

"Lookin' for a couple of Absaroka," Cooper said in even tones.

"Why?"

"I have something to give 'em."

"You give to us; we'll give it to them."

Cooper could see the greed in Deer Tail's eyes. "You don't even know what it is."

"You'll tell us."

"Eventually. Why're you so keen on gettin' what I have for them?"

"Help fellow Absaroka."

*You really don't want to know what I have in store
for them*, Cooper thought. "Nice of you but I reckon the
person who entrusted me with it wouldn't like it. Hell,
he didn't ever tell me the names of the two I'm lookin'
for."

"Then how you find 'em?"

"One feller has a scarred face, the other has hair
that is very short among your people."

"That's..." one of the warriors started before Deer
Tail shut him off with a sharp gesture.

"I've heard of such men," the chief said. "They ain't
of our village."

"What band are they with?"

Deer Tail's skinny shoulders rose and fell. He
suddenly showed no interest in the subject.

"You sure?"

Deer Tail nodded.

"Well, then, I best be on my way." Cooper rose.

"Stay," Deer Tail said, suddenly sounding jovial.
"Night comes soon, travel dangerous."

"I been out in the dark before." Cooper didn't know
what Deer Tail was cooking up, but he did know that
whatever it was, was hazardous for him. "Now send
somebody to have your boy—the one that took our
animals—bring my horses and mule here."

Deer Tail looked like he was going to argue, but
then just nodded to one of the younger warriors, who
rose and headed for the door flap.

"Before you go," Cooper said, stopping the man,
"you need to know something. If there's one hair
missing from either animal, one grain of salt or sugar
from my packs, Deer Tail here will die."

Most of the warriors started to rise, reaching for their knives.

Cooper casually slung his rifle over his shoulder and drew both pistols. "You boys can kill me," he said harshly. "You know that, and so do I. But know that your chief here will be going to the Spirit World right alongside me, as will at least one of you others."

He met hostile stares. "I don't mean any of you harm. I purely don't. But I can't have any of my animals or any of my supplies taken."

"You call us thieves?" Deer Tail asked.

He sounded determined, but Cooper could see some fear in his eyes. "Not necessarily. But your people have been known to take advantage of white trappers when they ain't payin' as much mind to their possibles as usual." He thought he saw a tiny smile flicker on Deer Tail's face.

"Now, I been in here all this time, so I ain't had a chance to keep watch on my things. Could be that some of your folks might be thinkin' that I'm bein' neglectful in takin' care of my property and think to take advantage."

Cooper saw the fear leave Deer Tail's eyes. "Maybe you right. Maybe some think you do not pay attention."

"So...?"

"So your things will be untouched." Deer Tail nodded to the young warrior who had been heading toward the flap. He disappeared into the afternoon. Then he indicated that the rest of his men should return to their seats. "It'll take a little time to make sure everything is as it was."

The chief's tone and sly look let Cooper know he

had been right—the Crows were about to take some, maybe even all, of his property.

They sat for what Cooper felt like was a year or two before the warrior returned.

"You go now," Deer Tail said.

The words might have been said pleasantly, but Cooper was suspicious of there being something else in them. "Thanks," he said and turned toward the flap, then turned back. *You ol' bastard, sendin' me into a trap, are you?* he thought. "I think you should accompany me, Chief."

"Not necessary." A new anger was deep in his eyes.

"Oh, yes, it is, Deer Tail. I don't mean to insult you, but if I was a bettin' feller, I'd put a big wager that there are several warriors out there ready to take my plunder —and maybe my hair—if I was to resist. So you'll accompany me until we're well out of the village."

The scowl on Deer Tail's face told Cooper he was right, at least to some of it. "All right, boys, you first. I'll follow along with my pistols aimed at Deer Tail's back. Chief, you'll mount a horse, and we'll ride out of the village nice and easy." He sighed. "And I'd a heap rather you other boys didn't come after me. Like I said, I got no hankerin' to battle you. Won't anyone get hurt if you let me just ride on."

Deer Tail shrugged, with a chuck of the chin, indicated that his warriors should head out. He followed, with Cooper just behind him, pistols mere inches from the chief's back.

Cooper clipped one pistol back into place on his belt and mounted his horse. Despite the near-freezing temperature, he was sweating. The time he spent sitting in the lodge, he had been a damn fool to have tried this recklessness. But though he was in deep trouble, he had nothing else to do than keep on with what he was doing.

Deer Tail mounted one of the Blackfoot horses, and the two men rode out of the village, side by side, Cooper still keeping one pistol trained on the Crow's side. At this distance, the .54-caliber ball would blow Deer Tail's innards to pieces, and the chief knew it.

A mile outside the village, Cooper stopped. "You're free to go, Deer Tail. I'd be obliged if you didn't send any warriors against me. Neither you or any of your people have been hurt, and if any warriors come after me, like I said in the lodge, I may be made gone beaver, but I guarantee you'll be missin' a warrior or two."

Deer Tail stared hard at Cooper for a few moments, then nodded. "Don't come to village again." He turned and rode off, not looking back.

TWENTY-THREE

FIGURING the Crows would have some men try to hunt him down, as soon as he got half a mile beyond where he had released Deer Tail, Cooper pushed hard for an hour or more, then slowed to a trot, not wanting to tax the animals. But by then he knew he was being followed. He did not like it, and his ire began to rise as he wondered just how many warriors the Crows had sent after him. He knew there was at least one.

Still, he did not want to wear the horses and mule down if he didn't have to, so he was on the lookout for a place where he could make a stand.

He was beginning to think no such place existed in this part of the country, but he finally found one—a thick stand of spruce at the edge of a small meadow. He had been following a real trail for once, and the copse was just off it. Anyone following him would come out of the trees at the other side of the meadow and move straight across, right into Cooper's sights.

He did not have long to wait. A rider towing

another horse loped into the meadow. "Stop there, hoss!" Cooper shouted.

The rider stopped.

"How many warriors are with you?"

"I'm by myself."

"Horse droppins. I figure you boys plan to run me down and raise my hair. I ain't about to let that happen."

"I alone. I'm Slow Fox, who you helped."

"I reckon they sent you out ahead of them to catch me off guard. Ain't gonna work."

"I don't lie."

"Don't know as if I believe you, boy. I reckon you figure to come up nice and friendly, get me off guard, then the others come ridin' in fast, or maybe sneakin' up like you bastards are known to do, raise my hair and steal my animals."

"They want my hair too."

Cooper heard pleading in the youth's voice, and that gave him pause. Crows, or any other Indians he knew, wouldn't sound so cowardly if they had their faces painted black against someone. If they wanted to deceive an enemy, Cooper thought, they would pretend friendliness, not fear.

"How many comin' after me?"

"Don't know. I come alone. Others say they will come after you, make you pay for insultin' 'em."

"What're you doin' out here?"

"Tell you others come. Then ride with you."

"Why?"

"Others don't believe I kill Blackfeet, want to punish me."

"Hell, your people are enemies of the Blackfeet. Shouldn't matter who killed a couple of enemies."

"They say I pretend to be warrior, not real one. Threaten to hurt me. I take the two Blackfoot ponies."

Cooper found himself in a quandary. If the youth were telling the truth, he could be helpful. But if he were lying and Cooper allowed him to ride alongside him, there could be danger. Slow Fox could easily leave a trail for a Crow war party to follow, and when Cooper let his guard down in a day or a week, the Crows would attack.

"I have bow now," Slow Fox shouted, holding the unstrung weapon over his head held in the center, the bow horizontally. "I stole from Stinkin' Paw."

Cooper thought he sounded a little braver with that statement, which, again, he thought, could be a ruse. "Ah, hell," he finally muttered. *Maybe this boy really was running from his fellow tribesmen*, he thought. He sighed, making his decision. "Come on ahead, boy, slow and easy. Keep your hands where I can see 'em."

Slow Fox was in the pines and dismounted when five Crows entered the meadow from where Slow Fox had been minutes ago.

"Dammit, you little bastard," Cooper spat. "I should've known better than to let you in here. Drop your bow."

The young Crow did not seem to be paying attention. Cooper, once more sweating despite the cold, brought his rifle around. He hated to use a shot to bring down the youth. That would speed the other Crows and lessen his chances of killing one with his rifle.

He was shocked that Slow Fox had strung his bow and sent an arrow toward the five warriors across the meadow rather than fire a bolt at him. "I'll be damned," Cooper muttered, even more surprised at Slow Fox's accuracy as the arrow found its mark in one warrior's chest.

Cooper swiftly turned his attention to the suddenly charging Crows. He sighted on the one who had glowered at him in the lodge and fired. As the sound faded, the warrior fell, dead with a lead ball in his head.

In the time it took Cooper to reload, Slow Fox had fired four more arrows, killing one warrior and wounding another, Cooper sighted on another and sent him to the Spirit World.

The last two Crows, including the wounded one, spun and raced away. Slow Fox whooped and shook his bow at the sky in exultation. Cooper watched, smiling a little but still wary.

Slow Fox started to run out to the battlefield, such as it was, but Cooper shouted, "Stop! Get your ass back here, boy!"

The young Crow looked at him as if he were crazy, then stopped and moved back into the trees where he had been. He glared at Cooper.

"You maybe figured out how to use that bow, boy, but you got no sense. You ever think that those two might be hiding just into the trees like we are and waitin' for a damn fool like you to go runnin' out there to collect some scalps and kill your fool ass? Just wait some. With that one wounded, they might head back to the village straight off. But we best give it a little time."

"Not long," Slow Fox said. "They send more warriors after us maybe."

"I know. But the village is more than a couple hours away."

Cooper waited five minutes, then nervously said to Slow Fox, "Go do what you're gonna do, boy."

Slow Fox ran out from behind the trees, sliced off three scalps and jerked all his arrows loose, dropping them back in his quiver. He gathered up the reins to the three dead warriors' ponies and led them back to where Cooper waited. "Where we go?" the Crow asked Cooper as he tied the three new horses to a tree with his original two.

"I'm headin' that way," Cooper said, pointing vaguely toward the northeast. "I don't know where you're goin'."

"I go with you."

Cooper shook his head. "I don't need a Crow taggin' along with me. I'm lookin' to maybe killed some Absaroka, and I don't need you to help 'em try to stop me."

"I help you, not them."

"Nope. I plan on movin' fast," he lied.

"I move fast. Have good ponies."

Cooper stood there thinking, then said, "I don't know as if I can trust you, boy."

"I fight," Slow Fox said, sounding nervous. "Kill own men of tribe. Can't go back. They kill me."

"Reckon that's true. But you have nothing besides your bow and a couple horses."

"More than two horses now," Slow Fox said proudly.

"Reckon that's true too. But you have no food or..."

"I hunt for food. I have blankets to keep me warm." To Cooper he sounded both eager and desperate, and the youth had, indeed, killed some of his own people. He could not just abandon the youth. "All right, you can ride along. You go first so's I don't have to worry about you in back of me, and that'll allow me to keep a good eye on our back trail. Find us another Crow village that maybe don't know yours, and you can stay there. Make yourself a home. Find yourself a nice, pretty, young squaw, and settle down. You've killed men and taken scalps. You're a warrior now, and so you need a woman. If you even know what to do with one."

"No Absaroka will take me in if they hear what I do today."

"Damn," Cooper mumbled. "All right, Slow Fox, maybe we can find a Shoshoni village that'll take you in."

"Shoshonis are enemies of the Absaroka now. They'll kill me too."

"Not if I tell 'em you're a friend."

"They won't believe you, even if you know Shoshonis."

"I am a Shoshoni."

Slow Fox looked at him, skepticism writ on his face and in his eyes.

"I was adopted into the tribe, and my wife..." He clamped his mouth shut. "Gather up all the horses and push them ahead of us, boy," he said gruffly.

Slow Fox looked at his white companion, then did what he was told.

They rode on quickly, wanting to put as much distance between them and the Crow village as they could in case Deer Tail decided to send some warriors after them.

They pulled to a halt well after dark. It was cold enough that Cooper decided to take a risk in having a fire. He doubted that the Crows, if any were after him and Slow Fox, would not have stopped long ago. The mountain man and Crow youth were miles from Deer Tail's village. They ate some of the meat Cooper had carried and drank coffee. Within an hour of halting here, they were asleep.

Cooper was up before dawn, and stoked the fire, set coffee to heating back up and got meat roasting. Then he gently kicked Slow Fox awake.

The youth was not happy at being roused from sleep and grumbled as he sat to eat.

A few minutes later, Cooper snatched the hunk of meat Slow Fox was eating out of his hands. "Hey!" The young man protested in annoyance. "Give meat back. I'm hungry."

"You can fill your meatbag when you stop your bellyaching. I'm of no mood to set here and listen to you piss and moan about bein' woke."

"But I was tired."

"So was I. But a real warrior won't complain about such doins. You want to be considered a warrior, boy, you best act like one, else you'll not get far in your life." He handed Slow Fox back the chunk of meat. "Now fill your face with food, boy, and quit your damn squawkin'."

Within half an hour, they were on the move again, still heading mostly east, riding slowly along the crooked course of the creek through the bitter cold and the wind that blew in fits and starts. They stopped near noon for a small meal of jerky and water, then pushed on. They finally stopped an hour or so before dark and set about making their small, sparse camp quickly and efficiently.

"You know of another Crow village anywhere

nearby, Slow Fox?" Cooper asked that night as they sat around the fire sipping coffee after a filling meal of roasted elk.

"Not sure. Can find maybe."

"Maybe you know the fellers I been chasin'."

"You say one has very short hair, yes? Other has scar on face?"

"Yep. There's another one, but I didn't get much of a look at him."

"I think I know 'em. The one with short hair I think is Fallin' Stone. Other warrior I think is Lame Weasel."

Cooper fought back a surge of anger. "You know where I might find those bastards?"

"I think maybe in village somewhere along Little Bighorn. We keep going same way here, along creek. There's a valley there." He paused, then said, "It takes us farther from Shoshoni country."

"Reckon it does. You willin' to continue on?"

"Yes."

Cooper hesitated only a moment, then nodded, "When this is finished, I'll take you to my village." When Slow Fox nodded, Cooper asked, "You can find the village of those two sons a bitches?" Cooper felt a rush of hope.

"Yes." Slow Fox paused. "What you do when we get there?"

"I ain't sure. Reckon I'll figure something out then. Ain't much use thinkin' on it now. I need to get a look at things, see how I can take care of business."

"We figure it out."

"We?"

"You help me with Blackfeet, lie to save me. Now I help you. Maybe lie too."

TWENTY-FOUR

"SO DEER TAIL and the others didn't think you were a warrior, eh?" Cooper asked Slow Fox as he and the youth sat around the fire. It was near dark, and they decided they might as well hunker down for the night, especially as it looked like a storm might be brewing.

The youth blushed as much as was possible with his dark skin. "No. They say I not worthy."

Cooper could see that Slow Fox was humiliated. "Why ain't you worthy?"

"I not counted coup. I have not killed enemy."

"You have a chance to do so? You look like you're just comin' of warrior age."

"Is true. Until I see Blackfeet."

"You would've taken 'em even if I hadn't helped."

"You lie," Slow Fox hissed in embarrassment. "I afraid. Dropped bow."

"Ah, hell, boy, you ain't the first feller ever been scared first time he went into battle. I like to heave my innards on the ground first time I saw a man killed."

"That different. You a white-eye, always afraid of killin' first time."

"Maybe that's true, but it don't make a difference once the first time is over. It gets easier each time, though I ain't sure that's a good thing."

"Is good. Warrior lives for war. War is what makes a man."

"Good way to get put under."

"Is honor to die in battle."

"Dead is dead, boy. Don't matter how it comes about. Dyin' of old age ain't no worse than dyin' with a Blackfoot arrow in your chest."

"You a white-eye. You don't understand."

"I understand dyin'. And I'll go under if I have to from a Blackfoot arrow or a Crow lance. I maybe won't mind as much if I go under while helpin' friends or family. But to be honest, Slow Fox, I'd much rather cross the divide lyin' in a comfy bed with my dear ones, includin' a passel of grandkids, or better, with their kids, surroundin' me." He grinned.

"Growing old not good. Teeth fall out, eyes go bad, manhood not work."

Cooper laughed. "Hell, boy, you ain't ever used your pizzle, I'd wager."

"I have!" Slow Fox insisted.

"Now whose tellin' tall tales?" He laughed again.

Slow Fox blushed once more.

"No call to be embarrassed. You're about the age when most fellers get to test how manly they are with some fine, sweet-smellin' woman."

Slow Fox just glowered at him.

"Besides, you're a warrior now after you raised hair

on them fellow Crows the other day, sure as hell. The Shoshonis'll respect that."

"Hmph."

"If you were scared of them Bug's Boys when I come along, you didn't show any fear when we had that battle recent. Why's that?"

"You there," Slow Fox said, hanging his head in deepening shame.

"So? You fought as well as any warrior I've come across."

"You fight good, I know, from first time. I know you fight good this time too. It gave me courage to face enemy knowin' you help. If I am afraid again, you take care of them."

"Don't matter none that you were afraid. We're all afraid at times, 'specially when you're outnumbered. Nothin' wrong in that, like I said. You just have to learn to put that fear aside when you go into battle. Once it's over, you can celebrate, have yourself a scalp dance, let what's left of the fear go up to the sky where it'll be blown away with the wind."

After a few minutes of thought, Slow Fox said, "You know much of the ways of a warrior—for a white-eye." He offered a shy grin.

Suddenly Cooper said, "A vision. You need a vision. Havin' a spirit helper and a vision will give you strong medicine, and that'll help you keep the fear from defeatin' you."

Slow Fox's face brightened considerably. "I will do that."

Another sudden thought struck Cooper. "Ain't it kind of late in the year to be seekin' a vision? It's winter, and I thought warriors sought a vision durin' summer."

"It's true," Slow Fox said contemplatively. "But we can't wait. I know place. Several days."

Cooper thought that over, regretting that he had brought up the notion. He did not want to waste any more time. He wanted to be on the trail of Falling Stone and Lame Weasel and more importantly, find Black Moon Woman. But this youth might be able to help him, and if having a vision quest gave the boy courage and determination, it could help tracking down his foes and learning the whereabouts of his wife. Besides, it had been so long now since Black Moon was taken that a few more days here and there shouldn't matter. His wife likely was dead, and if so, revenge could wait. If she were alive, she would have been much abused, and he would have no way to remedy that. "How long will it take to do your quest?"

"Four days. And one to prepare."

"Prepare how?"

"Sweat lodge."

Cooper knew of such a thing. The Shoshoni warriors took sweat baths to cleanse themselves before a quest and for other reasons. Cooper had reluctantly tried one with Cuts Throat. He did not see the need for another.

"Damn," Cooper muttered. "You know I'm on a quest of my own, remember? Spendin' four or five days while you seek a vision is an awful long time lost in my search. And it'll take some time to get to a place where you can have this vison."

Seeing Slow Fox's sudden gloom, Cooper sighed. "I reckon I can spare the time, though we'll have to move fast when it's over with if we don't find those two snake humpers at the village nearby. And if we do find 'em, you can take your time with your quest." He grinned crookedly. "Might be you'll be doin' it alone, though."

"We find 'em and kill 'em, maybe I don't need vision. If we don't find 'em here, I'll have a vision. Make strong medicine for both of us."

"I'd be obliged for that. Where is this place?"

"Along Porcupine Creek. Before we get there, we likely to find village."

"Think it's the one we want?"

Slow Elk shrugged. "Can't know 'til we see."

Cooper just grunted acknowledgment.

They rode on the next morning, Slow Fox leading the way. They moved slowly, as they had been. Cooper chaffed at the slowness, but he kept his desperation in check. They could not afford to be surprised by running into an unknown village or a war party. And in places there was no trail, just a stretch of underbrush and trees and fallen logs that had to be gotten through, around, or over. They reached the headwaters of Five Springs Creek and crossed an unusual, barren spot, maybe half a mile wide, and picked up at Long Park Creek.

Slow Fox suddenly stopped.

"What's wrong?" Cooper asked.

The Crow pointed, and Cooper could see thin streams of smoke and a circling of carrion seekers. "A village?"

"Yes. Like I think, winterin' in canyon. Good place."

"You goin' in there to ask about Lame Weasel and Fallin' Stone?"

Slow Fox looked ready to argue but finally nodded. "I go. You wait here."

"I'll do so, but if you come back bringin' others,

you'll not live out the day. Unless, of course, you bring those two sons a bitches."

Slow Fox left and Cooper found himself a small isolated semi-cave surrounded by trees and with a small running trickle of water. He built a small fire and ate before falling into a reasonably restful night's sleep.

Slow Fox returned about midmorning the next day. "Those men ain't here. Some say they are in village on the Little Bighorn."

"How far?"

"Several days, maybe more if the snow keeps up."

"Make your sweat lodge, boy. You'll purify yourself here and seek your vision up there in those rocks." He pointed.

"Is no good here. We go north. I know place. One day's ride."

"The Little Bighorn's south and east of here, ain't it? Not north."

"Yes. But we don't go far. Day's ride, like I say. Then turn south and east soon after, go to Little Big Horn that way."

"You best not be lyin' to me, boy. I intend to be on the trail as soon as possible. I'm bein' mighty generous to even give you that much time. So get to doin' what you need to be doin'."

"My medicine will be poor," Slow Fox said sullenly.

"That's your account, not mine. I got enough bad medicine of my own, you can have yours. We'll get through all right, I reckon." Seeing the look of desperation on the Crow's face, Cooper sighed. "All right, Slow Fox. We'll move on at first light. No delayin'. We'll travel one day, then you'll do what you need to."

By dusk the next day, Cooper called a halt. "We close?" he asked.

"Yes." Slow Fox pointed. "I go there."

"Then we'll make camp here. In the morning they hastily built a sweat lodge. Slow Fox entered it, and Cooper kept it supplied with water and hot rocks. The next morning, Slow Fox drifted off to the jutting ledge just to the east of the camp.

COOPER FIDGETED over the next few days, pacing and sitting, pacing and eating, pacing and drinking coffee, pacing and hunting.

Finally, though, Slow Fox returned, exhausted and starving. After eating and then sleeping for twelve hours or so, the youth beamed and excitedly recounted his quest.

Cooper wasn't interested. "That's fine, Slow Fox," he said. "Glad to hear you had a good vision. Maybe it'll bring us both some good medicine. Now let's get on the move."

TWENTY-FIVE

THEY PUSHED AS HARD as they could, fighting for every yard. With each step, Cooper excoriated himself for having wasted so much time letting Slow Fox seek his vision. The weather had turned worse too. Snow fell frequently, sometimes piling up to a depth of three or four feet. Twice they had to wait out storms with heavy snow, biting winds, and frigid temperatures. With each day, Cooper's anger at himself increased. He kept telling himself that nothing could be done about it now, but inside the thought that he might have doomed Black Moon ate at him, a nagging, hungry beast gnawing at his innards. If she had been alive, she might've been killed in the few days he dawdled to let Slow Fox seek a vision.

It made him less than a cordial traveler. And he regretted that too. Slow Fox could not be blamed; Cooper could blame only himself. But he could not help being the way he was, and he saw no need to apologize for his lack of civility.

They made their way as rapidly as they could—

which wasn't at all speedily—along a rough trail through the Bighorn Mountains. They finally reached the Little Bighorn's headwaters and began working their way up the river.

"Village we seek is maybe at place where Little Bighorn comes out of mountains, near where it meets Elkhorn Creek."

"You ain't sure, though?"

"No, but that's what chief at other village said."

Cooper only nodded.

Snow was falling regularly as they moved, and the wind often roared, lashing them. It made for miserable camps and even more miserable traveling.

"How much longer 'til we get to the other side of the damn mountains, Slow Fox?" Cooper asked one weary afternoon. "It's been damn near a month, I reckon."

"Two more days, maybe more if snow keeps coming."

"Damn. You're just a bundle of good news," Cooper said. "This here's damp powder and no way to dry it. I thought you made good medicine in your quest."

"I did. We're alive, not dead."

"Yet," Cooper snapped. "But I reckon you're right. We ain't dead, huntin's been passable, we got coffee and sugar. Reckon we're a heap better off than many people." He could not hide the sarcasm in his voice, though he was sure Slow Fox did not get it anyway.

But Cooper had little peace. He knew in his head—though not in his heart—that Black Moon was lost to him forever, so taking a few days to let his companion go through an important ritual for a warrior would make little difference. But that did not make him feel any better. It would, though, probably make the almost impossible task of finding Black Moon even more difficult.

He also began to wonder if he would even find the village that Falling Stone and Lame Weasel supposedly called home. And if he did, how would he learn if Black Moon was there? Even more important, should he be able to do that, would be getting her out—with both of them still alive. There were times as he and Slow Fox struggled along the rugged, sometimes almost-impossible-to-traverse trail that he considered giving up his quest. But he would not—*could* not—quit. It was not in him to do so. If he were that kind of man, he would have died two years ago, freezing and alone in a mountain winter with nothing more than a pocketknife and his wits to keep him alive. He also owed it to Black Moon to keep doggedly searching for her. She had stood by him last winter when the two almost died in the savage winter they had faced together.

He also wondered if Slow Fox really knew where he was going. The youth seemed to Cooper to be guessing which way to travel.

They finally came to a large canyon some distance away from the river. Cooper sat there for a bit gazing at it. It did not look easy to pass through. Then he shrugged. Facing what he expected to be a formidable trek though the canyon, he decided that a bit of a rest would make sense. Though it was barely past noon, they decided to stop and make camp. A hot fire, hot elk, and hot coffee helped elevate their spirits considerably, though gloom still hovered just over their heads.

"You sure the village is where you said it'll be?"

"Unless they moved village, yes. You know they

move sometimes. Need new forage, clean place to put lodges."

"Will you be able to find it?"

"Yes. Might take time, though. Have to search."

"We've already taken a heap of time. I don't need to be wanderin' around deep in Crow country in the winter lookin' for a needle in a haystack," Cooper said, allowing a little of his irritation to creep into his voice.

"Lookin' for *what*?"

"Something almost impossible to find, but not quite. Takes a heap of searchin'. Like lookin' for one tiny stone inside a lodge-size pile of leaves."

"We find."

"Don't know if it'll be the right one, though. All of 'em look pretty much the same." He looked over at their small herd. "Be nice, I reckon, if we didn't have those extra horses to push through this canyon."

"Need 'em. Maybe something goes wrong with ours. Maybe use 'em to trade to learn about Fallin' Stone and Lame Weasel."

"Reckon you're right, but it is troublesome."

They pushed on the next morning through another snowfall, though it was not heavy. Still, herding the five extra horses along the rock-strewn trail was no easy task for Cooper, though the path's rockiness did not allow the animals to roam much. The snow turned to freezing rain sometime in the afternoon making their travel even more treacherous.

About an hour after the shift in the weather, Cooper yelled to Slow Fox, who was, as usual, leading the way, that they should call it a day. They found a small break in the rocks that they could make their way into with all the horses. It cut the wind considerably but did nothing to stop the precipitation. There was one stunted cedar and a juniper, offering little in the way of forage for the horses or firewood for the men. Not that making a fire or keeping it going would have been easy. They "feasted" on jerky and rainwater caught in a pot and slept as well as they could in their heavy buffalo robes.

The morning brought another sparse meal, but the weather had improved. The temperature was near freezing, but the sleet had stopped at least, and the breaking of the clouds allowed a weak sun to shine. So they pushed on, silently bearing the tough travel as they had all along. It was bothersome, though not unusual, and both men were inured to it. Didn't mean that they had to like it.

Late in the morning, the sleet started again. The rocks soon became slick, making the going even harder. The extra horses got finicky, and Cooper was having trouble keeping control of them.

Slow Fox soon moved back to ride next to Cooper. "I'll go farther ahead, look for place to camp."

Cooper nodded tiredly. He was sick of it all. The travel, the fractious horses, the tortuous trail, the foul weather. The only thing that kept him going was the thought of getting Black Moon back. Or taking vengeance on those who had taken her. And the child. He had realized somewhere on the trail days ago that she had truly come to care for the child, considered the boy her own. Even if she were alive, she would be disconsolate if her captors had harmed the infant or taken him away.

Thunder began to reverberate in ominous rolls over the mountains, and small rocks and pebbles occasionally skittered down the sides of the canyon. The sky continued to darken, making the going increasingly perilous. None of it boded well, and Cooper hoped Slow Fox could find them a haven, no matter how tenuous, soon.

The thunder made the horses even more unmanageable. Though they could not stray far, they were nervous and often stalled, not wanting to move ahead over the slick rocks, through the increasingly frost-coated mud, and squeezing past boulders. Cooper had to force them along with curses and whacking their rumps with a rope. Even his own horse was growing cantankerous. It was frustrating and tiring.

Half an hour of strained travel passed, and Cooper began to really worry about Slow Fox. The light cascade of small rocks, pebbles, and dirt was increasing a little and the freezing rain had worsened, pushed now by a wind sweeping up through the canyon.

Suddenly came a colossal rumble and crashing ahead, punctuated by short screams of man and animal. Cooper pulled up sharply, figuring he was a goner, as the landslide inched closer to him. Then it slowed and finally stopped, except for a few stones and pebbles, not far ahead of him.

"Slow Fox!" Cooper bellowed, his voice carried forward by the wind at his back. As he suspected, there was no response. "Damn, damn, damn!" he shouted in anger.

He stayed where he was for a bit, preventing the extra horses from bolting back down the trail. Finally, he decided to push on—if he could. He got the ornery animals moving and less than half a mile ahead, he saw the jumble of boulders and smaller rocks that was now

Slow Fox's tomb. Cooper sat again, thinking, as the rain mixed with sleet continued. He could either press forward, hoping he could make it through the massive pile of rock ahead, or turn and go back. The former might be impossible and there was the chance of another rockslide; the latter would be heart crushing to him as it would mean Lord knew how far around this canyon he would have to go to find another way eastward. Besides, there was no guarantee that there wouldn't be a landslide in that direction either.

"Dammit, you can't give up now," he said aloud, with the ridiculous hope that his determination would make the mountain more amenable to his passing through. "You haven't let winter make wolf bait of you or break your spirit yet, boy. Best go on or go under."

Just starting was easier said than done, though. Getting the animals to move was an endeavor, but he finally managed. He pushed them however he could over large, slick rocks, around huge boulders in spaces the animals could barely fit through, and mud almost cannon deep on the horses.

It took more than four hours, but Cooper finally made it through the landslide's devastation.

Midway along, he stopped for a few moments to say farewell to Slow Fox as he thought sadly that the young warrior's medicine was not all that strong. Cooper felt a little responsible since he had tried to hurry the Crow in his vision quest, but it could not be helped. "May your spirit rest well in the Great Beyond, my friend," he whispered. Then he moved on.

By the time he was past the destruction, he was exhausted. Yet he could not stop. There was no reasonable place to make a camp, and he was worried about another rockslide. So, on he went, still dodging rocks, riding through a wind-pushed rain and the resultant mud. Eventually, he had to stop, though. Darkness was creeping up on him, though it was hard to tell when it fell with the sky having been nearly black all day.

Like the previous two nights, there was little in the way of protection, though the rocks cut the wind and one small overhang could allow a fire if Cooper could get enough firewood from the single little pine tree. He cared for the horses hurriedly, then tied them to the tree in hopes they could find something to nibble on. He collected a little wood and set a hunk of the frozen elk meat down that he had been carrying for days, which he and Slow Fox would whittle a piece of when they could build a fire. The meat and two cups of coffee filled him. And, while he was not cheered, he was mildly less disgruntled. More elk and coffee in the morning had him thinking he might live another day, despite his lingering exhaustion, especially with the weak sun having made another rare appearance.

He saddled his horse, herded the other animals back onto the trail, and once again moved ahead with as much alacrity as he could manage.

TWENTY-SIX

AS WAS USUALLY THE CASE, he encountered signs of a village on the horizon before it actually came into sight—smoke, circling scavenger birds, and dogs barking. It was in a small, seemingly comfortable, well-watered valley at the confluence of the Little Bighorn and Elkhorn Creek. There was little snow on the ground near the lodges, having been worn down and erased by feet and hooves. Farther out was more snow but nowhere near as deep or abundant as in the mountain.

Cooper finally spotted the nearest lodges from a perch on the southern slope. Coming in from the southeast, the Little Bighorn was off to his left, Elkhorn Creek to his right.

When he had first spotted signs of the village, Cooper moved off into the trees, off the thin trail he had been following after leaving the canyon. He stopped and tied the horses and mule together with a string. Then he tied them and his own mount to a large, winter-denuded bush. He moved down the slope some and stood behind a large spruce. Through the other spaced pines, he could keep an eye on the village. He did not know what he hoped to see other than perhaps a glance at Black Moon if she were here. Even in his desire for that, he knew, really, it could not happen at this distance. Any woman who came out of even the nearest lodges would be indistinguishable from another since all would be bundled in a capote or buffalo robe. So as he watched, he tried to figure out some way to learn if she—or her two abductors—were in the camp.

No brilliant strategy—or even non-brilliant one— came to him. It would be difficult to visit the camp as a friendly trapper, given the response before in such villages. If he thought it necessary, however, he would consider risking it.

He tensed in sudden anticipation as a mounted warrior headed toward the trail not far to Cooper's right. The Crow had a bow and a quiver of arrows across his back over the capote he wore. Cooper grinned grimly and headed on foot toward the trail. Along the way, he slung his rifle over his shoulder and picked up a log perhaps four feet long and six inches around. He stood behind a tree on the edge of the trail and waited with nervous anticipation.

The pony seemed to sense something and shied a little, but the warrior calmed it. As the Crow slowly came abreast of Cooper, the mountain man stepped out from behind the tree and swung the log hard, catching the Indian across the chest and knocking him from the pinto. The animal bolted up the trail, and Cooper made no effort to stop it.

With the warrior struggling just to breathe, Cooper swiftly sliced the leather strap holding the Crow's quiver near the top and pulled it free. He used it to tie the Indians hands together behind his back. Grabbing the warrior by his very long hair, Cooper dragged him into the woods and dropped him, then knelt at his side. Seeing that the Crow's breathing was coming back to normal, he cut off a chunk of the man's coat and stuffed it in the Indian's mouth.

"You speak English?" Cooper asked. When the Crow, showing no fear, nodded, Cooper said, "I'm going to ask you some questions. For you to answer, I'll have to take the gag out of your mouth. If you try to holler for help, I'll smash you in the face. That might not scare you, but after I do that, I'll raise your hair. All of it, not just a piece. You understand?"

The warrior nodded again.

Cooper pulled the wool from the Crow's mouth. "Is there a warrior named Fallin' Stone in the village?"

"No."

"How about one named Lame Weasel?"

"No."

Cooper wasn't sure the man was telling the truth, as he showed nothing in his eyes. So he would have to take the man's word for it. "There a woman captive here? A Shoshoni."

"No." But his eyes changed.

Cooper remained where he was, knee ready to land on the Crow's stomach if he tried anything. He wondered if he should try to get more information from the warrior but soon realized that would not get him anywhere. Since the Crow had already said there was no captive woman in the village, he likely would not divulge where Black Moon was. Or worse, Cooper suddenly thought, maybe the warrior was telling the truth, though perhaps there was more to it. A Shoshoni woman captive might not be in the village because she had been killed—or died—which was the same to Cooper as it would have happened while she was a Crow captive.

Judging by the Crow's reaction to his question about Black Moon, he figured his woman was dead. That made his next decision much easier. He slapped a hard hand across the warrior's mouth, drew his knife and jammed the blade into the Crow's heart. The Indian bucked and jerked for a few moments, then fell still except for a few death shudders.

Cooper stood, only a fraction of his anger dissipated. Now he was back to where he was before he had captured the warrior. How to get into the village, find out if Black Moon was alive, and get her out if she were. Of course, if she wasn't there, it might not mean she was dead, only that she might be in another village.

Shaking his head at his quandary, he mounted up and moved through the trees farther from the trail and the dead Crow. Despite the odds against success, he would have to go into the village and try to somehow determine whether Black Moon was there. It was a fool's mission, he knew, but in this case, he was a great fool. He could live with that. Trouble was, he might very well die from that.

While Cooper pondered what he could do, he moved across the trail. Taking up a position at the tree line, he now was within seventy-five yards, he estimated, of the nearest lodges and had a good view of the river. He stood and watched, looking for he knew not what.

As dusk was just beginning to edge in, he spotted a

woman heading to the creek with a hatchet and a bucket of some kind. Without much thought as to what he could do, he slipped away from the trees, heading for a copse along the creek not far from where the woman would reach it. As she knelt to chop through the ice on the water, Cooper slipped up behind her and wacked her not too hard on the head with the flat side of his tomahawk. The woman slumped. With a look over his shoulder to make sure no one else was coming, Cooper hauled the woman up and pushed her toward the copse, where he shoved her down behind a cottonwood. He knelt next to her and hurriedly bound her hands behind her back with a thong torn from his pants and stuffed the piece of blanket he had used before into her mouth and tied that in with another buckskin whang. "You understand English?" he asked.

She nodded, fear in her eyes.

"Is there a Shoshoni woman held prisoner in the village?"

Another nod.

"Which lodge?" He reached to pull the gag free but didn't when, with wide eyes, she shook her head vigorously.

"I don't want to hurt you, but I will if you don't answer me." He pulled his knife and ran the side gently down her cheek. "Will you answer?"

Aware of the knife, she nodded gently, eyes still frightened.

"If you scream, I'll cut your throat." He turned her head to untie the thong, then eased the piece of blanket free. "What lodge?"

"Yellow Bull's. Third from here. Red painted horses go around."

"Obliged." Cooper continued kneeling there, wondering what to do. He really did not want to harm this woman, but he could not just set her free. He suddenly jammed the cloth back into her mouth and smacked her over the head with the 'hawk again, harder this time, knocking her out. Taking a chance, he grabbed her knife and cut the bond holding her hands, hoping she did not regain consciousness too soon. He stuck her knife in the back of his belt.

Dark was nearing, and Cooper decided he could not wait. With his rifle still slung over his back he moved out of the copse, walking boldly, the hood of his capote up. He figured that if anyone saw him in this low light, they would think him just another tribesman.

He stopped behind the right tipi, glad that it had no other lodges behind it so he could squat there unseen. He waited, listening with his ear practically against the buffalo skins that made the lodge, hoping that the occupants were asleep. He detected the voices of at least two men and three women. He thought he heard some children, too, but he wasn't sure.

Still he squatted there, ignoring the cold as best he could, waiting for signs that the inhabitants were sleeping. As the minutes passed, Cooper began to worry that the woman he had captured would regain consciousness and raise an alarm. Finally he could delay no longer. He jabbed his knife into the side of the tipi and as quietly as he could, cut down through the thick, tough hide. He gingerly stuck his head through the slit he had cut, hoping no one was going to bash his brains in with a war club, and looked around. In the dim light thrown off by the embers and still flickering of the few remaining small flames, he spotted Black Moon. She was near the flap of the lodge, as far away from Cooper as she could be.

He began to step in, then stopped, realizing he was about to step on someone. "Dammit," he whispered. He pulled his foot back out and reassessed the situation. There was only one way to do this he finally decided. He sidled around the tipi, stopping just to the side of the flap opening to make sure no one was around. Then he slid quickly inside the lodge and knelt at Black Moon's side. He slapped a hand over her mouth and whispered, "Moon. Wake up, Moon."

She started, seeming ready to fight, then settled down as if browbeaten. "It's me, Moon. It's Hawley. I come to take you out of here."

The woman's eyes widened in fear for a moment, then in quiet joy.

"Come, then. Grab your blanket and let's go. Quietly." He backed out of the opening, pushing the flap out of the way with his rump. Black Moon rolled onto her knees, wrapped the thin blanket around her shoulders and edged out.

They swept around the side of the lodge away from the interior of the village. Both began walking quickly toward the hill where Cooper had left his horses. As they neared the last one, the squaw whom Cooper had knocked unconscious came staggering along toward the inner part of the village. She spotted Cooper and Black Moon Woman and screeched out a warning in her own language.

"Dammit! Can you run, Moon?"

"Only a little."

"Well, come on, as best you can." Hand in hand they trotted toward the hill, though Cooper soon veered toward the copse, since it would provide some protection, though it might slow them even more. Some shouts came from behind them, but Cooper thought they were safe in the dark although the full moon and a sky full of stars provided some light.

Just before reaching the trees, Black Moon suddenly grunted, stumbled, then fell, slipping out of Cooper's grasp. He stopped, turned and saw the arrow sticking out of her back through her blanket.

"Shit," he muttered. He helped her up and, with a shoulder under her arm helped her hobble into the trees. Before the Crows could really mount any kind of attack, if they even cared enough about someone spiriting away a female captive, Cooper and Black Moon were on the hill. Minutes later, Cooper heaved his woman onto one of the extra horses and mounted his own. Riding next to her, helping to hold her on the animals, with the others strung behind, he raced through the forest, onto the trail, then a minute later, dodging into the trees, heading west.

Two miles later, he crossed the Little Bighorn, hoping the ice was thick enough to hold him and all the animals. It was. He figured he had put any likely pursuit off, so he pulled into a spot amid some boulders. He eased Black Moon off the horse and laid her gently down on her side.

TWENTY-SEVEN

"I NEED to get that arrow out of you, Moon," Cooper said urgently.

"Can't. Too deep. Hurt inside."

Fearing what he would see, he took a closer look. Her thin blanket and buckskin dress had done little to stop the arrow. Nor had the distance the bolt had flown lessened the damage. It had been a mighty lucky shot for the Crow who fired it considering the only light was the moon and stars.

"Well, let me get a better look." Though it was a risk, Cooper gathered wood and started a fire. In its light he was shocked to see that Black Moon's face was also bruised. "They hurt you?" he asked.

"Yes. Men sometimes, women always. I expected."

Cooper nodded. It was, indeed, to be expected. The Shoshonis would do the same to a captive Crow woman. He pulled off his capote, folded it, and lay it down near her head. Then he rolled Black Moon onto her stomach, with his folded garment as a pillow for her head. He cut a small slit in the blanket covering her back, not enough to really damage it but enough so he could get a look at the arrow embedded in Black Moon's back a few inches below the shoulder bone. He wiggled the arrow a bit to see how tightly it was enclosed by flesh.

Black Moon screeched in pain.

"It's bad, Moon. Trouble is I don't think I can get it out of you without hurtin' you even more or doin' some real damage. I can try to cut the arrowhead out." Cooper's voice was full of doubt.

"No. I said it's too deep. Hurt things inside."

"Well, I can't just let you lie here with it in you." Cooper was filled with worry, anger, and a deep-seated fear.

"Nothing you can do. I go under soon."

"Dammit, I ain't lettin' you die," Cooper snapped in his helplessness.

"You can't stop it. Me neither, dammit. I die soon."

"But I..."

"It's all right. I die with you here." Tears of agony dripped unbidden from her pain-clouded eyes. She coughed a little and groaned. "You catch enemies," she whispered, clutching one of his hands. "Kill them. Take hair so they can't go to see Great Spirit."

"Is one of them a son of a bitch named Fallin' Stone?"

"Yes."

"And another is Lame Weasel?"

"Yes. One more. Black Dog."

"One has a scar on his face. Which one?"

"Lame Weasel."

"Does Fallin' Stone have very short hair for damned Crow?"

"Yes." Her voice was weakening. "Black Dog always wears a leather piece around his neck. Some say to hide scar there."

Cooper snapped off the arrow shaft, eliciting a sharp hiss of pain from Black Moon. But this way he could roll her partly on her side so he could hold her. She looked up at him and managed a smile. "Is damn good," she said.

Cooper nodded, sick inside in knowing that she was going to die and there was not a damn thing he could do about it.

"Are all three in the village?"

"No. They give me to an old warrior named Yellow Bull."

"His lodge is the one where I found you?"

"Yes."

"What about the others?"

"Said they would visit friends in another village. Where Bighorn meets Yellowstone."

"How do I find it?"

"Little Bighorn and Bighorn meet, maybe four suns. Follow Bighorn then, another couple suns."

"What's Yellow Bull look like?"

"Old. Very tall. Always has two eagle feathers in hair."

Cooper nodded, though Black Moon could not see it. He was silent for a while, just holding her, mind blank and numb with his wife's imminent death. Suddenly he had a thought. "What about Left Behind?"

"Gone. Don't know where. Given away, I think."

Cooper nodded again as he quietly stroked her hair a little. He didn't worry too much about the infant.

Because Left Behind was a baby, he would be raised by his own people. If he were still alive, he would be all right. Finally he said, "You know I love you, don't you, Moon?"

But she was no longer alive.

Cooper continued to sit there, ignoring the cold, heedless of whether Crows were hunting for him. He didn't know how long he remained that way, but he finally laid her down and stood, his legs shaky after sitting so long. He wondered what to do. With the ground frozen, he could not dig a grave, and he did not want to do that in Crow territory anyway. That would be an insult to her spirit. But, he realized, he had no choice but to inter her in Crow land. If he were closer, he would consider returning her to Cheyenne Killer's village, but that was impractical and would deter him from his renewed desire for vengeance.

Indecisive, he pulled out the large hunk of frozen deer meat he had and hacked off a small piece. He tossed it on a rock just outside the flames. When it had thawed, he jammed a green stick through it and hung it over the fire to cook. He had decided that the Crows were not hunting him. If they were, either they would have caught up to him by now or he likely would have heard them because at the distance he had traveled they would have been on horseback. And since he had not killed anyone, they probably would not care that a captive woman was taken from them.

Cooper ate without tasting the food but did so because he needed the fuel in his body. Finally he rolled into his buffalo robe and fell asleep. He awoke before dawn and finished the last of the meat. Then he kicked the fire out. He gently lifted Black Moon's body and placed it facedown across one horse. Cooper hated to subject the corpse to such an indignity, as he saw it, but it had to be done. He tied it down, then mounted his own horse. Towing the mule and extra horses, he headed south following the river's path though well away from the bank.

Along the way, he stopped and chopped down two stout trees, maybe six feet long and eight inches around. By midafternoon he was in the canyon where Slow Fox had died and was buried. He hobbled the animals. They might wander but they wouldn't get far. Then he set to work even as snow began falling. Using the two logs as levers, he moved a number of boulders and smaller rocks. Finally he decided he had space enough.

He wrapped Black Moon's body in his buffalo robe, then gently laid her in the space he created.

He stood there looking down at the body of his wife, not knowing what to do or say. He had never felt this sense of despair, and he was bereft over the loss of his wife. He didn't know what he was going to do without her. Other than the thirst for revenge, he had no idea of what his future held for him. He said a couple of prayers he remembered from his youthful days in church, let fall some tears, and then allowed them to be washed away in a cascade of anger. At last, he levered the rocks and boulders back where they were, covering Black Moon's body. It was a grave that would not be disturbed. He shook his head at the sense of loss but in knowing that two people important to him —one the light of his life, the other a new, trusted friend —were buried near each other.

Reluctant to leave, he stood by Black Moon's makeshift grave, thinking of the times they had had together. There had been plenty of good—the laughter and the making love. And there had been bad—the fights with Crows and Blackfeet, the nearly deadly winter they had passed together the year before. And so much more of both. Finally, he could no longer stand there overwhelmed by sadness. It was time, he decided to let the rage at her capture, abuse, and death drive him. It was time for revenge.

He suddenly spun on his heel, saddled his horse, and rode back the way he had come. Except for the mule to pack what few supplies he had, he freed the extra animals. He rode into the forest, stopping along a small stream. He built a fire and once again ate another uninspiring meal, then rolled onto his extra blanket, pulled his capote around him, and drifted—slowly—off to sleep as darkness crept over the land. In the morning, he stoked the fire, heated coffee, and poured a cup into himself, then concerned himself with food. The meal, such as it was, was done quickly.

Sometime that afternoon, the village was in view again. He maneuvered among the trees to where he was less than two hundred yards from the nearest lodges. He sat on a rock, rifle across his thighs, partially hidden by winter-denuded brush, and waited. And watched.

A tall man came out of Yellow Bull's lodge, piquing Cooper's attention. He was not sure, however, that it was Yellow Bull. But he became certain when he noticed the two eagle feathers dangling from his long hair.

Yellow Bull entered another lodge and Cooper sat back to wait some more. Dark was fast approaching but there was a little light left despite the snow falling softly when Yellow Bull came walking back toward his lodge.

Cooper removed the piece of buffalo hide covering his rifle's lock to keep it from moisture and the cold and set it aside. He poured a little priming powder in the pan and snapped the frizzen shut, then knelt, bringing the rifle to his shoulder. It was a long shot, especially in the low light, but he thought he could make it. Still, there was no telling what might happen if he missed. Either way, he really didn't much care. He planned to be gone long before the Crows could mount a search.

With the snow falling, even broken up some by the trees, he did not have long before his powder would dampen. He sucked in a breath and let it out slowly. Then he fired.

There was a heartbeat during which he thought he had missed before the figure crumbled. "Got you, you son of a bitch," Cooper said.

He reloaded his rifle, watching the village. He saw several warriors standing around searching for where the shot had come from. But with the wind and the snow, he did not think they could spot him.

As he mounted his horse, the sounds of wailing rose from the village, and Cooper knew then for sure that he had killed the old warrior, not just wounded him. He smiled in satisfaction. He moved through the trees away from the trail, hoping he would find another trail through the foothills that would lead him past this village and in the direction of the one where the three men that were his prey were, if they had not moved on. If not, he would make one, he vowed.

TWENTY-EIGHT

HAWLEY COOPER MADE his own way until he came to a trail well marked by the passage of horses and men. He stopped and studied the ground and realized because of shod hoofprints that white men had been the last to head this way. That both excited and dismayed him. He would be happy to see more of his kind, but it might delay his search for his quarry. Still, it would be a pleasure to sit with fellow mountain men. It had been a long time since he had talked with men of his own race.

He moved on, and soon saw signs of civilization, such as it was out here in the wilderness. Judging by what he saw from a distance, he figured it was a pretty big camp. Within an hour he was riding into a large, makeshift village near the confluence of the Bighorn and Yellowstone rivers. The camp consisted of rickety cabins, various size tents, tipis, lean-tos and just a couple of buffalo robes and a fire. Horses and mules were being watched by several men to his left. Few other men were out and about, preferring to spend the time inside out of the cold and wind. Those who were out were dealing with animals and butchering meat. There were some Indian women outside, gathering wood.

Cooper stopped, wondering where to go. Judging by the number of tents, shacks, and lodges, he figured there were close to a hundred men in the camp, and he reasoned that the majority of them were with a company brigade or two. He considered just riding on through the camp. But it was getting late in the day and he was hungry, tired, and cold. He saw a spot free of dwellers and horse manure and stopped there. He unsaddled, tended, and hobbled his horse, then unloaded what few supplies he had left off the pack mule. Much of the wood nearby was gone but he found enough to build a small fire. He warmed himself for a bit, then went searching for more wood, having to roam farther afield.

At last, he set a hunk of his fast-dwindling deer meat to cooking and put his coffeepot near the flames. Before long he was eating, again not really tasting but knowing he had to fill his stomach.

Afterward, with his rifle cradled in the crook of his arm, he wandered about, looking for anyone who seemed to have some supplies he could buy. He spotted a man wandering about and approached him. "Who's the booshway of this outfit?"

"Who wants to know?"

"Me."

"Who're you?"

"Don't matter who I am, and I don't give a damn who you are. Just point me to the brigade leader's lodge, whatever kind it is."

"Don't like your attitude either, sonny."

"Your likes and dislikes don't mean mule spit to me, hoss." Cooper didn't know if the man was drunk or just plain ornery. Or maybe both.

The man took a swing at Cooper, who blocked the arm with his rifle, then slammed a forearm into the man's jaw. The man staggered back.

"I got more where that come from," Cooper snapped. "I just asked you a simple question. Don't take much to answer, even for a feller of limited mental capacity as you."

"Mike Sullivan," the man mumbled. He pointed to a large, almost substantial shack.

"Obliged." He turned and walked off. At the cabin, he called for entry, which was given.

Several men sat on the ground, two against willow backrests, in a semicircle around a fire in a makeshift fireplace in the center of one wall. Stacks of trade goods were lined up against the walls, gear and tack of all sorts were scattered around, and piles of buffalo robes lay about.

Four sets of eyes turned to look at Cooper. A burly man turned and stood. "What can I do for you, hoss?"

"Wonderin' if I can buy a few supplies. Not much. A bit of coffee, sugar, salt, a buffalo robe, maybe a few other things."

"You ridin' alone?"

"Yep. Got business a bit east of here."

"Dangerous out that way."

"I know."

The man stared at Cooper for a few moments, then nodded. He held out his hand. "Name's Mike Sullivan, booshway of the outfit with most of the fellers here. I reckon I can let loose a few small things."

"Be obliged."

"Mind tellin' me what your business is?"

Cooper stood in thought for a bit, wondering why the other three men had also stood and were watching, then said, "Lookin' for a few Crows. I heard they're in a village somewhere east along the Yellowstone."

"There's a Crow village about six miles upriver. Why're you lookin' for these fellers, whoever they are?"

"Grabbed my woman and killed her after abusin' her somethin' awful."

"That don't shine. What was she?"

"Shoshoni."

"Good people. But ain't no native woman worth gettin' yourself kilt over. There's plenty other Indian women, Shoshoni or other tribes."

Cooper just shrugged. "That may be, but the Crows have to pay."

"Not now they don't. I can sell you supplies but not now."

"Why not?"

"Because you're not goin' anywhere near that Crow village."

"Why not?" Cooper was surprised and confused.

"We can't have you rilin' up the Crows. That'd be poor doins for all of us here."

"Then I'll do without the supplies." He turned to leave but turned back at Sullivan's voice.

"You take one step toward that village and you'll be made gone beaver, boy."

"You threatenin' me?" Cooper asked, once again surprised.

"Nope. Not threatenin', just tellin' you the way things be."

Silence grew as the two men stared at each other. Cooper was angry at Sullivan. He was so close yet about to be thwarted again. "That don't shine with me, Mr. Sullivan."

"Whether it shines to you or not, hoss, don't matter to me. I need to think of our men and the upcomin' season. I can't let some damn fool pinin' away for a woman jeopardizin' our hunt. The Crows're touchy, and we'll need 'em at some time for trade and such. You're welcome to winter with us, boy. Or leave. I'll even sell you some supplies, long as you move on away from the village."

Cooper stood there thinking. He could easily head downriver along the Bighorn for some miles, then turn east and head back to the Yellowstone and the Crow camp. It would take a little longer, but he had been delayed so much that another couple of days wouldn't make much difference. It did gall him, though, that such a course of action was being dictated. But it was not something to argue about. He nodded. "Reckon I'll take what supplies I can buy and head out."

Sullivan's voice grew harsh. "Let me tell you this, boy, if you try to circumvent my order, you'll regret it. And the men'll keep watch to make certain you don't go disobeyin' me."

Cooper felt a coldness settle into his stomach. There was no denying Sullivan's seriousness. He would have to think of something else, but for now he would acquiesce. "You still have no objection to me winterin' here among you?"

"Like I said, boy, you're welcome to do so." There was no hint of sarcasm in his voice. "Still need those supplies?"

"Reckon so. I'm mostly short on coffee and sugar. It's all I need for now. Oh, and the buffalo robe."

"I'll have one of the camp helpers seek you out and get you the things. You can pay me now."

Cooper handed over some coins, nodded at the four mountain men, and left. With a sinking feeling he headed toward the spot where he had left his horse and mule, hoping they were still there. He didn't think his fellow mountain men would have taken them, but he knew from his experiences with Josiah Weeks as well as Claude Manning and Hiram Bledsoe that not all mountaineers were trustworthy. To his relief, his camp was undisturbed. He stoked the fire and put on the last of the deer meat, as well as coffee. He would have to hunt tomorrow, hoping he would be able to make meat. With this many men, game was likely to be mighty scarce in these parts.

Just as he began eating, two camp helpers arrived. One carried a sack of coffee beans and a smaller one of sugar, and the second with a good buffalo robe. Cooper had been worried that Sullivan had sold him a scraggly, half-hairless hide. But this one was thickly furred and would offer good protection from the weather. He thought that perhaps Sullivan had figured that a good robe would make his enforced stay here a little more bearable. For Cooper it would do so against the elements, but he found no joy in it otherwise. He still hoped to find a way to get free of this camp and move east.

The imposed stay gave him time to think, and that was, it dawned on him, not necessarily a good thing. But it allowed him to consider his options. When he thought about them now, he realized they were few and not very good. He had never considered what he would do when he found the Crow village. He had no easy way of identifying at a distance the three men who were his quarry. Moreover, he had no notion of how to get them alone to kill them. He could not just ride into the village and ask the chief to hand them over. It was possible, he supposed, that he could ride into the village as a visitor. That might be dangerous as a lone mountain man, but the Crows might be kindly disposed to him, especially with this large group nearby. That prospect was not good, however. They might not raise his hair, but there was a better than even chance that they would relieve him of all he possessed, however little it was, and send him on his way much as Weeks had done two years ago. He certainly did not want to face that again.

He ate without much enthusiasm and before much longer, pulled the buffalo robe around him and drifted off to sleep.

In the morning, he saddled and bridled his horse. He tied a horsehair rope to the pack mule and rode out of camp, heading southwest away from the rivers. Within half an hour of leaving, he became aware of being followed. He didn't know who or how many, but he was certain someone was behind him, keeping watch. Another mile farther on, he pulled into a thicket and waited.

Soon after, two men came riding slowly along with one pack mule. They headed right toward him, and he figured they had tracked him, using all the sign he had left. He cursed himself for not being more careful, though if these two men were as skilled at tracking as he thought, it likely would not have made a difference.

"Ho, there, hoss," one said jovially, "how's doins?"

"Damn," Cooper muttered. They had easily spotted him in the thicket. He rode out. "Howdy. Just out tryin' to make meat."

"Same here. Name's Georgie Barnes." He pointed to his companion. "This here's James McDougal."

"Hawley Cooper." He knew he could not rid himself of these two, so he decided to make the best of it. It irked him that Sullivan had had him followed, though he knew it would happen. He had not planned on breaking the loose confinement imposed on him, at least now, but he had hoped Sullivan would give him a little freedom, seeing as he had left what plunder he possessed, other than what he needed for hunting, where it had been.

"Game's been a mite scarce hereabouts of late," McDougal said.

"Figured it would be seein' the size of the camp."

"There's a spot some miles south of here where we might find us a deer or two. Or maybe a couple antelope," Barnes said.

"Sounds as good a spot as any, I reckon. You boys'd know better than me. I'm still new in this country."

"Let's go, then."

It took several hours of riding and a touch of luck, but they jumped two aging deer and brought them down. They split the meat and loaded Cooper's pack mule and the other men's mule, and began the long ride back to camp.

AS HE ATE deer meat and drank coffee that night, Cooper wondered how long Sullivan would have him followed. He was sure now that he would not be able to outfox the skilled trackers the brigade leader had at his disposal. He was afraid he would be stuck here 'til spring, though that likely was only a month away, figuring they would be on the way sometime in March. The prospect was both depressing and infuriating. And there was nothing he could do about it.

TWENTY-NINE

HAWLEY COOPER WAS sick of the snow and the cold. He had faced too much of both in the three years he had been in the mountains, and he was plain tired of it. It was bad enough that game was scarce enough hereabouts with all the mouths to feed, but the weather made it all the more difficult. Traveling through the snow was wearying for him and his animals. And finding forage was getting nigh onto impossible. Hundreds of horses and mules had taken care of whatever grass there was long, and the rare bits of grass that might remain lay buried under a few feet of snow. Even the cottonwood bark for some miles around was near to extinct these days. Wood, too, was mighty scarce and he had to ride a few miles west along the Yellowstone to find enough to keep his small fire going. And he needed a constant fire because he had no shelter under the cottonwood denuded of leaves and reachable branches that could be used for firewood. It offered no protection.

Almost as annoying was the fact that every time he went out to find firewood or make meat, he had a couple of Sullivan's men on his tail. It was enough to make him seriously consider leaving, not toward the Crow village necessarily, but to anywhere away from here. But he kept putting the decision off, not wanting to face more traveling alone in the depths of the winter. He had survived two such times; he was not sure he could or would do so again.

Two weeks after Cooper had stumbled into the camp, Sullivan led his brigade toward another wintering ground about a day's ride west along the Yellowstone, a place that still had a few patches of grass, plenty of cottonwoods for wood and feed for the animals, and some game. Most of the other men, including Cooper, joined in the move. He found himself a decent spot a little away from the others with a cottonwood also standing by itself. He swiftly tied ropes to some law-hanging branches and, with a couple deer hides taken during his hunts, made a makeshift shelter. It wasn't much, but it would keep him out of the weather to some extent, and with a fire right in front of it, he would be warm enough.

He relaxed a little in his mind. He could wait, he thought, until spring. Then would be the time to find his vengeance. Still, he would wander off on occasion, staring at the river, letting his rage simmer, thinking of what a splendid thing it would be when his revenge was complete.

WHEN HE RETURNED TO HIS "LODGE," as he dejectedly thought of it, he froze. The little camp was a shambles. His shelter had been torn down, the hides trampled, as were his two buffalo robes, one still only partially cured. But most of all, his horse and mule were gone.

It took a little while for the shock to ease off, and the anger to rise. He just stood for some time, gritting his teeth so hard he thought they would break. After several weeks, he had never worried about his animals being stolen in a camp of mountain men, but it had happened. He set off to hunt for Barnes and McDougal, whom he found in their own little trapper's cabin.

"Someone stole my animals and wrecked my camp in the doin'," he snarled.

"Wasn't us," Barnes said, eyes flashing with anger.

"Ain't sayin' it was."

"Then why come to us, hoss?" Barnes asked.

"I reckon you can find out who's the son of a bitch who did it a lot easier than I can."

"Don't know why we should concern ourselves with helpin' ye track down some critters who stole your animals."

"You boys might be next, you don't watch out. Maybe even whilst you're traipsin' after me." He sighed. "Reckon I was a damn fool for thinkin' you might not take a likin' to a bastard stealin' his animals from a fellow mountaineer."

"Can't say as you're exactly a feller mountaineer," McDougal said harshly. "Ye ain't with our brigade."

"I ain't part of the goddamned company either." He shrugged. "Well, never thought you boys'd be too goddamned scared to help another mountaineer. I expect to see you wearin' skirts next time you follow me."

"Why you stinkin' son of a bitch," Barnes snapped, then charged Cooper.

The latter was ready for him, he sidestepped the attack and clubbed Barnes on the side of the face with a fist.

Barnes staggered a few more steps, then fell.

Cooper spun toward McDougal, expecting another attack. "You want some, too, hoss?" he asked, anger thick in his voice.

A smile played across McDougal's lips. "Reckon not. This chil' ain't that much of a fool."

"Good. I'm tellin' you and you can tell this skunk-humpin' piece of shit," he added, pointing at Barnes, "keep away from me. You tail me again, and you'll be gone beaver right off. You can tell Sullivan, too, that I ain't runnin' off to the Crow village even though it's some miles off now."

"I'll do so. But the village moved with us. It's only five miles or so upriver." He grinned. "Still gonna stay in camp?"

Cooper's eyes widened in surprise, and his nostrils flared in anger, his mind thinking of the possibilities. Then he regained his sense. "Yep. I ain't a fool. 'Sides, with my animals gone, I'm a mite short on transportation. But more important, I aim to find the pustulant bastard who done it."

Barnes groggily got to his feet, his hand reaching for his knife. "I aim to make wolf bait of ye, boy, for what ye just done," he growled.

"Come ahead, then."

"Sheath your blade, Georgie," McDougal said. "Ain't no need for fightin' among us."

"Like hell. I ain't lettin' this youngster insult me and come agin me."

"Look, Georgie, he knocked ye on your ass once, I reckon he can do it again. It's over. Ye've lost a fight before. Ye weren't really hurt, so let it go."

Angry, Barnes left his knife alone, but he glared at Cooper and then stomped out.

"I got to worry about him?" Cooper asked.

"Reckon not. He's hotheaded sometimes, but once he gets over an insult, he's fine." His eyes suddenly turned hard. "But ye best watch who you're insultin', boy. Many folks ain't as good-natured as Georgie and me."

"I'll insult—and thump—anybody I damn well please 'til I find the stone-less bastard who stole my animals."

"Can't say as I blame ye. Just watch where you're steppin', boy. I reckon I can ask 'round some."

"Obliged."

"Best thing I can suggest, though, is for ye go talk to the booshway. If there's someone in camp stealin' from one of the boys here, he'll want to know about it, and he'll likely be able to do somethin' about it if he finds the hoss who did it."

"I'll do so. I reckon you ain't so bad a feller as I thought," he said with a tight grin and left. He headed straight to Mike Sullivan's log lodge, the first put up when the men arrived at the new camp, and the largest.

"What can I do for you, hoss?" Sullivan asked, standing and leaning gingerly against a wall.

"Stop havin' me tracked."

"I don't..." He stopped and grinned at Cooper's

glare. Then his voice hardened. "I can't let you go wanderin' to the Crow village. I told ye that."

Cooper nodded. "I'll keep away. You have my word."

Sullivan stared at him for a few moments, then nodded. "Now that that's settled, good day."

"There's something else." At Sullivan's questioning look, Cooper said, "While I was off near the river, someone stole my horse and mule. I ain't got much but those animals."

"That's a strong accusation, boy."

"It ain't an accusation. It's a fact. It happened, there's no denyin' that. And I ain't accusin' anyone."

"Why tell me about it?"

"You're the booshway here. You can find out who did it. You let me know and I'll handle it."

"I can't go givin' you one of my men on your say so."

"Won't be my say so. It'll be you who finds the skunk humper and points him out to me."

"Might not be one of my men. We got a fair number of free trappers here, like ye. It's likely one of them."

"Don't matter who they are. You're in charge here and are sufferin' the existence here of independents, like me. If it's one of your men, I'd expect you to see to a fittin' punishment. If it's one of the free trappers, I'll handle him."

"Think you can handle some of these boys?"

"We'll find out when it comes time. I made wolf bait of Josiah Weeks, and he was known as a tough critter."

"So that was ye. Ye did the world a service by riddin' it of that shit-stinkin' old bastard." He paused. "I'll find the culprit for ye."

"Obliged."

The next afternoon, a camp helper arrived at where Cooper was still trying to restore something like a place to ride out the rest of winter.

"Mr. Sullivan says to come see him," the man said.

Within minutes, Cooper was in the bourgeois's cabin, where he and two other men were slurping down some kind of stew. Sullivan put down his wooden bowl and horn spoon and rose.

"You found the son of a bitch," Cooper said without preliminary.

"I did. Two of 'em. Neither's one of mine, so I can't put the whip to them. 'Specially since I can't find one."

"What's that mean?"

"He skedaddled, probably not long after he took 'em."

"Damn. Know which way he went?"

"Southwest."

"Can you lend me a horse?"

"Nope. All the horses we got are company property and I can't go givin' 'em out, less'n they're paid for."

"You know damn well I don't have that kind of specie on me. Or plews."

"Reckon ye're out of luck, then, less'n ye track down the other feller and get a horse from him."

"Then point me in his direction and I'll disabuse him of the notion that it shines takin' a man's animals."

"Most free trappers're too proud to do such a thing, leavin' a man afoot, though it ain't unknown for them to do so. Most travel in small groups, so there's always someone around their camp to keep that from happenin'."

"All that shines with me is getting' the thievin' bastard and takin' care of him."

"I can point ye to him, if that's where your stick floats."

"It is."

"The other feller is a young man, like ye were a couple seasons ago," Sullivan said. "Ain't had the green wore off yet, and mayhap won't do so for some time. A group of free trappers took him on at rendezvous. They just pulled in day afore yesterday. Feller's name is Zeke Potts. Elson Brooks heads up the bunch." He saw Cooper's look of surprise. "Ye know him?"

"Not Potts. Met Brooks a couple times. Thought he was trustworthy."

"He is. Usually has good fellers throw in with him. I don't know this Potts feller, but like I said, he's young and green. I ain't sure, but if Brooks took him on, he's probably a good feller, just needs some manners and sense taught to him."

"And I'm just the feller to do the teachin'."

THIRTY

COOPER STOPPED in front of the skin lodge that he had been told belonged to the leader of the small group of free trappers. "Brooks," he snapped. "It's Hawley Cooper."

"Come ahead."

When Cooper did, Elson Brooks stood and held out his hand. Three other men sat around the fire and several women worked in the shadows. Cooper ignored the hand.

"Something on your mind, hoss?" Brooks asked, face clouding in annoyance.

"Where's some feller named Potts?" He saw a young man flinch. "That you, boy?"

Before the young man could say anything, Brooks asked, "What's this about, Hawley?"

"Son of a bitch stole my animals," Cooper said angrily.

"What? Stole your animals?" Brooks was only a little surprised considering the way Cooper had acted so far.

"I just said so, didn't I? Now hand him over so's I can teach him that such doins don't shine with this chil'. Then I'll take his horse and go after the feller he conspired with."

"Just hold on, Hawley." Brooks spun. "He tellin' true, Zeke?"

Potts stared at the ground and mumbled, "Yes."

"What in hell ary possessed ye to do such a thing, boy?"

"I...Well, I thought I was helpin' a friend."

"Hell of a friend. Why'd ye go and help this feller?"

"He said this feller," Potts pointed at Cooper, "owed him some money he stole and since this feller didn't have any plews, his horse and mule would do to make good on what was owed."

"Lyin' sack of shit," Cooper growled, anger not lessened a bit.

"What were ye gonna get out of this devilishness?" Brooks asked.

"Some cash. Enough to help out with..."

"When were ye gonna get this money? He didn't give it to ye now, did he?"

"At rendezvous."

"And you believed him?" Cooper demanded.

"Yes." Another mumble.

"Lordy if you ain't as dumb as a sack of horseshoes." Cooper shook his head. "Sullivan says the son of a bitch rode out. You know where he was headed?"

"Ain't sure. Said he knew a small Crow village off to the west where he was welcome."

"Who is this son of a bitch?"

"Feller named Claude Manning."

Cooper's eyes popped wide in recognition.

"Ain't he one of those fellers you had a run-in with back to rendezvous?" Brooks asked.

Cooper nodded tightly. "Him and his partner followed me after rendezvous plannin' to attack me. I caught on to 'em. Killed Bledsoe, but Manning got away."

"Son of a bitch."

"Yep. Now, Mr. Potts, you'll give me your horse and saddle."

"But..."

"Now! I intend to ride out as soon as it's saddled."

"Ye need help, Hawley?" Brooks asked.

"No, I..."

"I'd like to go with you, Mr. Cooper," Potts said.

"So you can steal my animals again soon's I get 'em back? No, boy, that don't shine a'tall."

"I'm plumb sorry for what I done, and I'd like to make it up to you."

"Just go and saddle your horse for me. I'm ridin' out alone. I'll deal with you later."

Brooks said, "Ye got anything needs watchin' over at your camp? Your woman? She's a looker and seemed a fine woman." He grinned. "She toss your possibles out of the lodge and tell ye to be on your way?"

His grin dropped like a stone when Cooper said, "She's gone under. Damned Crows took her and a baby we'd found. Would've raised my hair if I hadn't gotten knocked down into a ravine makin' 'em think I was wolf bait."

"I'm sorry, hoss, I didn't..."

"'Course you didn't. I cached my plews after I run those red devils off before they could take 'em, then headed out on foot. I didn't have a horse or mule," he looked accusingly at Potts, who winced in shame. "But I had my gun and a few things in my possible bag, so I tracked 'em for a spell. Couldn't catch up to 'em, of course. I made it to Cheyenne Killer's village to see if they'd send out a war party after 'em, but they weren't interested in doin' so at the time." His rage at Black Moon's fate was beginning to boil in him again. "I got some animals from the Shoshonis and set out after 'em again."

"There's a heap of Crows about, even a village near here."

"I know. I think the warriors who took Black Moon are there, but I gave Sullivan my word that I'd not go stirrin' up trouble there. And I'm a man who keeps his word."

"You goin' out after 'em again?"

"Yep. But first I got to take care of this business. So, Mr. Potts, do as I said."

Potts walked out, moving warily past Cooper.

"I'll have Bill and Two-Faces here get whatever possibles at your camp and bring 'em here. They'll be safe. Ye have my word."

Cooper thought it over a moment, then nodded.

"Two-Faces, tell your woman to put up some food in a sack for Hawley to take." A few minutes later, a pleasant-looking Flathead woman handed Cooper a sack. "Jerky, pemmican, gourd with elk stew."

"Thanks."

Potts came in. "Horse is ready."

Without another word, Cooper headed outside, mounted the beast, and rode off, moving fast. Cooper knew his own animals' hoofprints and once he found them, they were easy to follow. From the tracks,

Manning was not moving fast. With more than a day's head start, it would take some effort for Cooper to catch him. Cooper hoped he could track the man down before he reached that Crow village. If he was as friendly with that band, those Crows might not be kindly disposed toward Cooper.

He stopped after dark, had jerky and water, slept, ate the same for breakfast, and was on the trail before daylight. Late in the afternoon, he spotted a rider he thought was Manning riding over a small, snow-covered hump in the land. Cooper smiled grimly and kicked his horse into a gallop. He crested the ridge and spotted Manning—he was certain it was the thief now—not more than a hundred yards away.

Cooper slid off his mount, swiftly wrapped the reins around one of the animal's legs and tightened it in a makeshift hobble. He knelt, checked his priming, settled himself, and fired. Manning did not fall, but Cooper knew he had hit the mountain man. He reloaded, watching Manning, who was starting to weave in the saddle.

Cooper undid the emergency hobble and trotted on. He caught up with Manning within minutes, riding alongside him. He grabbed the other mountain man by the hair and jerked his head around. "I should've done this the last time. I won't be that foolish again." He released the hair, pulled a pistol, and blew a large hole in Manning's forehead. Dismounting, Cooper went through Manning's possibles sack, tossing away things but found nothing usable. He took Manning's Leman rifle and accoutrements as being the only things worth appropriating other than the dead man's horse.

Before noon two days later, Cooper rode back into

the sprawling camp along the Yellowstone River. He tied the horse and mule to a rope picket near Brooks's lodges and called for entry to the tipi, then went in.

"You get your animals back?" Brooks asked.

Cooper nodded and addressed Potts. "Time for your lesson, boy."

"I can't let ye manhandle that boy, Hawley."

"Sure you can."

"Well, reckon I can, but I won't."

"Just get out of my way, Elson. I'm in no humor to argue it with you."

"Hold up, there, Hawley," Brooks interjected. "Mayhap we can make things right without makin' wolf bait out of this here young feller."

"Ain't likely."

"Just hear me out. He can mayhap pay you some recompense for your inconvenience."

"Inconvenience!" Cooper exploded. "Son of a bitch left me afoot, here in Crow and Blackfoot country. If I didn't have my rifle and such with me, he would've left me with nothin'. That happened once before, and I faced starvin' times. Nearly went under. I ain't about to let some chil' who nearly did it get off without payin' dear for it."

"I ain't sayin' you shouldn't make him pay. But thrashin' him won't do much good."

"It'll teach him to not do such a thing again."

"Reckon that's true. Then he'd be of no use to the other boys here and we'd have to leave him behind."

"Don't matter to me, hoss. It's what would've happened to me."

"But..."

Potts stood. "That's enough, El," he said nervously.

"You want to thump me, Mr. Cooper, you go right ahead. I'll let you get in the first lick, but then you'll have your hands full."

Cooper almost smiled. "I take the first shot, there won't need to be more."

"Have at it, then." Potts put on a brave face, but his voice quavered.

Cooper turned a little and leaned his rifle against the hide wall, then turned back and took a step forward. The two remaining men—the same ones who had been there the other day—rose and took positions one to each side of Brooks, between Cooper and Potts.

"Can't let ye do it, Hawley," Brooks said. "I know what he did don't shine with ye. Doesn't with me either. But while we're all free trappers here, these boys've made me cap'n, and so I'm responsible."

"Then, I'll take you on too, El."

"'E is not alone, m'sieur," Two-Faces Beaubien said.

"Then I'll take on all of you. It's mighty close quarters in here but I reckon I can whup you."

"There really ain't no need for such doins, Hawley," Brooks said. "We can find a way for Zeke to make amends without inflictin' damages on any of us."

"What've you got in mind?" Cooper was still flaming angry but was beginning to reconsider a brawl with four hardened mountaineers.

"Payment of some kind. Maybe some plews or such."

Cooper thought that over. "Might work, but the cost'll be dear. How many plews does he have?"

"Two packs."

"I want all of 'em, the horse I was usin', all his coffee and sugar."

"That is mighty dear," Brooks said with a whistle.

"That'll leave me with nothin'," Potts said almost plaintively.

"I expect you'll still have one horse besides the one I'm takin', your traps, powder and lead," Cooper said. "A lot more than some folks. You'll still be able to make the spring hunt to get yourself some plews for tradin', and you can always make meat long as you have your Galena and DuPont."

"But..."

"How's about one pack of plews and the rest of what ye ask for?"

"Nope. All of 'em."

After some thought, Brooks nodded. "They're yours, Hawley."

"You can't do that, El! They ain't yours to give away. I'm a free trapper just like the others, and them plews are mine, not yours to give away."

"Close your trap, Zeke. You're lucky he didn't take your personal plunder too." He held out his hand again.

Cooper hesitated for a few moments, before shaking. "I expect everything delivered to my camp this afternoon." He reached for his rifle.

"It will be, but, well maybe this is a queersome time to make such a proposal, but ye might want to throw in with us, at least for a place to stay for the winter."

"That is a damn fool suggestion right now."

"Well, Zeke won't be botherin' your things, and the rest of us'll be around to make sure no one else does. Livin' in one of our lodges might be a little close, but it's a heap more comfortin' than livin' outside." Seeing the expected hesitation on Cooper's part, he said, "Let sit and smoke on it. 'Sides, with ye comin' in here like an angry bear the other day, and today, we never did have a chance to offer hospitality."

Cooper shrugged and took a place at the fire as the other men sat. The two women put down their work and served up bowls of stew and mugs of coffee. He was still angry, but it was beginning to fade. He saw in Potts some of himself just a couple years ago, a young man who knew nothing about life out here and was susceptible to poor influences, much like he had been with Weeks.

"Hawley, ye know Zeke now," Brooks said with a grin. "That dark feller there is Bill White, and the half frog is Two-Faces Beaubien."

Cooper returned the two men's nods. They all ate silently for a bit, then Cooper finally took a deep breath, let it out slowly, and looked at Potts. "What'n hell ever possessed you to help that brigand steal my animals, boy?"

"Well, I...I...well..."

The other three men laughed. "Seems young Zeke here has an itchy pizzle that needs scratchin' regular. He has his eyes set on some Nez Perce squaw he saw at rendezvous whose pa wants a heap of a bride price for her. I talked to him while ye were gone. He said he figured with the money Manning was supposed to pay him, and the plews, he might do well enough to win her pa over and let him marry the girl."

"Stealin' a man's animals to buy a woman who likely won't even be at rendezvous, or at least not married yet, makes you a damn nitwit, boy," Cooper growled. "I don't know if I can excuse that, nor do I find any humor in it." He sighed. "I reckon I'll have to turn you down, El, about winterin' up with you fellers. I don't think Zeke'd be safe long as I was around him."

"Ye might want to reconsider, Hawley," Brooks said. "Ye..."

"Stop, El," Potts said. "The man's right." He looked at Cooper. "You got every right to put me under, Mr. Cooper. What I did was the worst thing, I reckon, and I purely regret it. I don't expect you to believe that, but it's true. And if you throw in with us, you'll never have cause to fear more wrongdoin' from me. Don't expect you to believe that either, but it's also true. My word may not mean much to you right now, but when I give it, I keep it."

It took some time before Cooper was willing to say anything, and when he did it was to question Brooks. "This young feller speakin' true?"

"He is. He's a rambunctious chil', and mighty head-strong most times. Damn foolish at times too. But he ain't ever said he'd do somethin' and not did it. Be truthful myself, I was plumb shocked when ye told me what he'd done."

"Did ye plan on doin' anything for his perfidy?"

"Considered for a time disinvitin' him to our group. But he swore to me, too, that he'd not pull some thievery again, lest it was from Indians. That's what we were discussin' when ye came a callin' again."

"So, you're keepin' him on?"

"I am."

Cooper again sat for a while in thought. He could use some companionship for a spell, even if it was just through the winter. And livin' in a tipi would, indeed, be a heap better than livin' in that makeshift shelter he had made. It would be a relief, too, to not have to worry about his possibles if Potts was telling the truth. He had instinctively liked Elson Brooks since the fellow mountain man had asked him two years ago to join his little group, and he tended toward believing him now.

Finally, Cooper asked, "What'd be my duties?"

"Same as everyone else's here. Help make meat, help bring in wood, maybe help tend the horses at times. Like I said, the boys've made me cap'n, so I make some decisions, but mostly I ain't any better than the rest of the boys." He grinned. "Well, I'm a better trapper and shot and tracker and..." He and the others, except Cooper, laughed, but he quickly regained his solemnity. "Like I told at rendezvous a couple years ago, we share the work and the hardships, but your work is your own. If you stay with us after winter camp breaks up, we'll still share the work, but any plews are yours. Same with buffler robes. Sell 'em to whoever ye want to for whatever ye can get."

"You gave me Zeke's plews."

"True. They weren't mine to give, but as cap'n I had to make a decision about something that affected the whole group. Thought that was best. Zeke don't like it, he can leave and take his plews with him. Be damned difficult carryin' 'em, though, seein' as he's in hock to me for the animals he's been usin'. And of course, he'd have to face ye over him takin' 'em."

Cooper managed to crack a grin. "Where would I be stayin'?"

"Any of the lodges—there's four of 'em—but likely with me," Brooks said. "All the other boys've got squaws with 'em, 'cept me and Zeke. Like I said, he's itchy, but since he can't afford a decent squaw, he makes do with whatever one who'll spread her legs for a handful of beads. Most of which he also owes me for."

"Just as long as he don't try to scratch that itch with me," Cooper said.

"I won't, dammit." Potts sounded angry and embarrassed.

There was another long pause before Cooper said, "I reckon I'm a damn fool to put my trust in you boys after what's been done, but I reckon I'll settle in here just 'til the weather breaks and the spring hunt starts."

"Glad to have ye," Brooks said.

They all brought out their small pipes, filled them, and lit them. It was their version of an Indian's sanctifying smoke.

THIRTY-ONE

HAWLEY COOPER and Elson Brooks slogged through the mud toward Mike Sullivan's cabin, wanting to see what the commotion was about. The weather had warmed up to above freezing, making for a pleasant day. They pushed their way through the gathered mountain men to see several Crow warriors just dismounting as they were greeted by Sullivan. Suddenly Cooper stiffened, and he reached for one of his pistols.

"What's doins, hoss?" Brooks asked. A glance told him he did not like the look on Cooper's face and that it would portend nothing good. He grabbed his companion's arm. "Whatever you're thinkin' of doin', hoss, don't."

Cooper moved his hand away from his pistol, but remained rigid, his teeth clenched.

Suddenly Brooks realized what had enraged Cooper. "You see one of 'em, don't you?"

Cooper nodded once, stiffly.

"Well, just look, don't you go doin' anything foolish.

You gave your word to not cause trouble with the Crows. You best keep it or your word won't mean donkey piss in the mountains forever after—even if you even live more than two minutes after whatever doins you're ponderin'."

"I said I wouldn't cause a stir in the village," Cooper said, rage thick in his voice. "I didn't say nothin' about not killin' some Crows who were foolish enough to come struttin' into camp here."

"You kill one of them Crows here, you'll be gone beaver before that warrior hits the ground."

"That don't matter none."

"You see all three of the bastards over there?"

"Just one."

"Well, you go and get yourself kilt, the others'll not have vengeance brought on them. You want to avenge your woman, you need to raise hair on all three. At least you know now that at least one of them red devils is in that village."

Again, Cooper nodded just once. Then he turned and splashed off. At the lodge he shared with Brooks and Potts, he grabbed his saddle and rifle. Fifteen minutes later, with a pack mule trailing behind him, he was riding out of the camp, heading southwest. It was almost dark when he returned with more than a hundred pounds of elk meat, which he silently handed off to Two-Faces Beaubien. Before long he was gnawing unenthusiastically on some buffalo that Brooks had cooked—well, hung over the fire on a green stick. Finished, he smoked a pipe, then rolled into his robes. But it took a long time for sleep to pay him a visit.

Cooper was in little better humor in the morning.

"Word is that more Crows'll be showin' up today or tomorrow. You plannin' to see 'em?"

"No," Cooper said in a strangled voice.

"Good thing, I reckon. Why don't you tell me what the other fellers look like? If I catch sight of 'em, at least you'll know they in the village too."

"One of 'em's got mighty short hair for one of those goat-humpin' bastards. The other wears a leather gorget."

"The one ye saw?"

"Scar on his face."

"I'll keep my eyes peeled. What're you gonna be doin'?"

"Huntin', I reckon."

"Want some company?" Potts asked.

"No." It was said sharply and flatly.

Cooper did not see that the young man looked upset at the rejection. He would not have cared had he known.

Over the next several days, Cooper let the anger cool until it was just a simmer inside him. He became almost polite to the others, but he kept his distance, preferring to be on his own as he cared for his gear though he would help with the chores. He found that the other men in the group besides Brooks, Two-Faces, White, and Potts—Duncan MacTavish, Luis Gamez, Daniel Anderson, and Jacques Bissonette were decent men.

Cooper rather enjoyed being with the other men. They were, for the most part, good hunters, hard workers, mostly personable, and full of fabulous tales, the majority of them pretty far-fetched, which Cooper thought made them all the better.

After a few days, Cooper realized that no matter what he was doing around camp, Potts always seemed to be hovering nearby. He found it irritating. So one day, he slipped behind a willow, then dodged around a couple of lodges and came up behind Potts. He kicked the younger man's feet out from under him. Then bent and yanked Potts up. "You're startin' to annoy me, boy, by follerin' me around everywhere. Just leave me be."

"I'm just tryin' to make amends. I really do feel poorly about what I did."

"It's over and done, hoss. With the plews, the horse, and other possibles, you've paid your debt."

"But, dammit, I want to earn back your respect."

"You can't." He almost smiled at the look of hurt on Potts's face. "You never had it, boy. I never met you before you run off with my animals."

"Then I want to earn it now. Start afresh. Show you I ain't really the idiot who," he gulped, "stole your animals."

"You really are a goddamn fool, ain't you, boy?"

"Yes, sir." He hung his head. Then he looked up and smiled crookedly. "It's something I'm damned good at."

Cooper stood there just staring at Potts for some seconds, then he laughed. "You are some, boy, you sure are. I can't have you underfoot every damned minute, but you can come with me tomorrow when I head out to make meat."

"Yes, sir."

As Potts hurried off, Cooper shook his head in wonder. For the first time he realized that while he had been looking at Potts as young, the new mountain man was only a year or two younger than Cooper himself.

"Shows you what fightin' a few mountain winters'll do for you," he muttered.

As they rode out the next morning, Cooper asked, "You know how to use that fusee, boy?"

"I'd be a good shot if I had a rifle like yours or Elson's or any of the other fellers."

"It's a poor man who blames his tools for his shortcomins."

"You try usin' this for huntin' and see how you do. Hell, I got to get close enough to damn near shake hands with a buffler before this thing'll take it down."

"Put a bigger charge in it. Any fool knows that."

"And this fool knows that if I did that, the damn thing'll blow up and take my hand off. Or maybe my face."

Cooper couldn't help but smile. "Probably be an improvement, hoss."

"It'd disappoint the squaws somethin' awful."

"Think mighty high of yourself, do you, when it comes to squaws."

"Yep. Better than most, includin'..." Potts clamped his mouth shut when he saw Cooper's face darken as his anger rose. "I'm sorry, Mr. Cooper," he stammered. "I didn't mean...I was just funnin' about me likin' women so much, and I never realized..."

"It's all right, boy," Cooper said quietly, his voice and stare far away to a happier time.

"It ain't right, maybe, of me to ask, but if you're of a mind to talk a little, maybe you could tell me about your woman. She must've been a hell of a fine woman to catch your heart so."

It took a while for him for answer, but Cooper finally said, "That she was, boy. That she was. Shoshoni she was. Finest lookin' woman you ever could see. Except maybe for my sister, Black Moon's best friend, Pony Woman."

"You're a half breed?" Potts was surprised.

"What makes you say that?"

"A gal named Pony Woman is your sister. She can't be a white woman."

"No, she's Shoshoni." He explained how he had come to Cheyenne Killer's village and how he had become a Shoshoni who was a chief's son, thus making Pony Woman his sister. "Feller named Cuts Throat wanted to marry Moon, but I challenged him over her. Damn fool thing to do. I won, but it wasn't easy. So me and Moon got married. Cuts Throat ended up marryin' Pony Woman. He's my best friend among the people."

"Sounds like a tall tale almost," Potts said, hurriedly adding, "though I know it ain't so. Just hard to see how a man could go through all that and come out all in one piece, hale and hearty."

"Well, mostly hale and hearty." He held up his hand with part of the pinkie missing. "And there's plenty of closed over holes where there shouldn't be."

"Closed over holes?"

"Wounds. Wolves, Crow arrows. Some bones don't want to seem to work right after bein' thumped with war clubs by Blackfeet and other Indians."

"Damn. And you've only been out here three years?"

"Yep."

"And that was just your first year in the mountains?"

"Yep."

"What've you done since? Can't have had more times like that."

"Reckon you'd be wrong about that. Fought the weather the past winter. Me and Moon got caught up in one damn storm after another. We were lucky to make it back to her village with our skin."

"A lot of adventures for one feller."

"I reckon you could say, but adventures are a lot more livable in tall tales than they are in real life."

Potts chuckled nervously. "I ain't so sure I want to stay out here. I don't think I'm up to so many such doins." Then he grinned. "Though I aim to have me plenty of adventures with the squaws."

Cooper managed a laugh despite his dark reminisces. "Just watch where you dip your wick, boy. Might get you more adventure than you'd like."

"Yes, sir. So what're you gonna do now?"

"Try'n find us an elk or some unlucky buffler."

"I meant with your life after all that's gone on."

"That ain't none of your concern, boy."

"Yes, sir."

There was silence for a while until Cooper asked, "So how'd you come to be out here? Thinkin' this would be a big adventure when you were still back in the States?"

"Hardly an adventure. I was a troublemakin' little snot. Caused Pa no end of troubles. He finally got fed up when I kept skippin' out on work, both for him and for some of the fur companies loadin' and unloadin' their boats and carin' for furs in the warehouses. He knew some of the fur men and suppliers. He signed me on to one of the supply trains headin' out here. Next thing I know I'm gettin' off a steamer at Westport and gettin' on a nag headin' across the plains."

"Sounds fittin'."

"Yep. I weren't happy at first, of course, but I found it wasn't so bad. When we got to rendezvous, I used my pay to get some supplies. I asked around to see if anyone was fool enough to take me on. Elson hired me as a pork eater with the promise he'd teach me trappin'."

"Taught you well considerin' the packs of plews you gave me." He grinned again.

Potts returned it ruefully.

They eventually spotted a solitary buffalo bull and stopped about a hundred and fifty yards from it. "Reckon his meat's stringier than a torn up old rug, but it's buffler meat, and the hide'll be good for mocs or something."

"Can you hit it from here?" Potts asked.

"Yep. Can you?"

"Not with this damn thing," Potts said holding up the fusil.

"Think you're a good shot?"

"Yep."

Cooper held out his Dickert. "Prove it, boy."

"You certain?" When Cooper nodded, the younger man slipped his rifle through the loop on his saddle and took the rifle Cooper handed him. He dismounted, knelt, and quickly fired. The bull dropped and lay kicking for a few moments. He handed the weapon back to Cooper.

The latter grinned. "Reckon you ain't as full of air as I was thinkin'."

Potts's grin came close to splitting his face.

"Well, you shot him, you can butcher that ol' feller."

"What're you gonna be doin'?"

"Keepin' watch out for hostile Injuns."

With a grimace, Potts began the unenviable task, but Cooper soon joined him, making the work go much quicker. It took a while, but they then were on their way, slowly riding toward camp with the pack mules laden with meat and a large hide.

THIRTY-TWO

"I'LL BE PULLIN' out at first light, El," Cooper said. "The Crows moved out a week ago. I figure that's enough time to wait before I head after 'em."

Though snow continued now and again, it was obvious that spring was in the air. Sullivan was preparing his brigade for the spring hunt, and the other men were eager to be on the move. And Cooper decided it was time to return to the vengeance trail. He would keep his promise to Sullivan about not causing trouble in the village; he would even refrain from stirring things up 'til the Crows and the trappers had parted ways. In the meantime, Cooper intended to dog the Crows' trail at a distance, looking for the men he sought. All three were in the Crow village. Cooper had seen them at times over the past month when some warriors would show up in camp. Though it had been difficult, he had decided after seeing Black Dog that it would be wise to keep a watch on the Crows' comings and goings with an eye toward finding his quarry. He was not disappointed.

"You sure you don't want to hunt with us, maybe ride on down to rendezvous?"

"Reckon not."

"Well, if that's where your stick floats, so be it. But are you plannin' to drag around all those plews?"

"Reckon I got no choice."

"I could haul 'em along with us and sell 'em for you at rendezvous, if you don't make it there yourself. We'll meet up again one day, maybe even rendezvous next year."

"We've become pretty good friends since I threw in with you boys for the winter. But leavin' all my plews with you on your promise to sell 'em gives me pause."

"Reasonable, considerin' how you come to join us." He thought for a minute. "You know how to read?"

"Enough. Why?"

"Got a solution, maybe. You go on about your business and we'll have us a parley later."

Cooper gave Brooks a questioning look, then shrugged and headed outside to make one last check on his horses. While he was doing so, Potts wandered up.

"I'd like to go with you, Hawl," the young mountain man said.

"Reckon not, Zeke. That'd be a damn fool thing for you to do. With me takin' all your plews, you'll need to be trappin' so's you'll have some money to outfit for next year's hunt."

"I'll make out all right. Always do."

"You'll get your hair raised is what you'll do if you come with me."

"What the hell, I'll likely lose it anyway. Like as not some warrior'll be ready to lift my topknot after I've had my way with his woman."

Cooper couldn't help but laugh. "From what I heard from El and some of the others, I wouldn't wager against such a thing." He grew serious. "Why're you so fired up to tag along with me considerin' what I aim to be doin'?"

"I still owe you for what I done."

"You've paid me back in full, Zeke. I've told you that several times."

"I've paid you back in goods, maybe. But *things* ain't that important. What's important is respect, and I'm still mighty shy of it in your eyes I figure."

"I respect you, hoss. I've told you that, too, more times than I can remember."

"That's true, I reckon. But I don't think it's enough that you give me respect, Hawl. I need to do somethin' to *earn* it, and I ain't so sure I've done that despite what you've said."

"Ain't no Indian gonna harm you, hoss. You're touched, and they don't deal with crazy folk." He paused. "You know we might be dealin' with a heap of angry Crows, don't you?"

"I've faced Injuns before. Had a run-in with the Blackfeet last fall."

Cooper stared at his companion, who fidgeted but held Cooper's stare. "I'm likely to regret this but you can ride along."

Potts started to celebrate until Cooper said, "I'm in charge. You do something to spook them Crows and I'll have your hair. You do just as I say, and we'll get along fine. You got a second horse?"

"Just the one after you took my other."

Cooper thought for a moment. "You can have

Manning's. We can use it to pack supplies. I need my other animals to carry my plews." He grinned.

"Damn, you are one aggravatin' critter."

"I come by it naturally, like you bein' a damn fool. Now, go on and talk to El."

Once he finished checking his animals, Cooper wandered over to Sullivan's cabin. The booshway was busy but deigned to give him a few minutes, which Cooper used to purchase some supplies from Sullivan's stores. Back in the lodge he was still sharing with Brooks and Potts, he knelt at his buffalo sleeping robes and took something from inside. He rose, turned, and handed Potts the Leman rifle he had taken from Manning. "If you're ridin' with me, I need somebody who's got him a rifle he—and I—can rely on." He tossed the younger man a shooting pouch. "You got enough powder and lead?"

"Should have if I watch it some."

"Well, now that that's taken care of," Brooks said, a touch of sarcasm in his voice, "I got something for you, Hawl." He handed Cooper a piece of paper.

"What's that?" Potts asked.

"A paper sayin' El will take my plews to rendezvous and sell 'em for the best price he can get but no less than four dollars a pound. He guarantees that he'll do right by me."

"You can believe him, Hawl."

"I know, Zeke." He held out his hand and shook with Brooks.

UNENCUMBERED BY PACKS OF FURS, Cooper and Potts could move swiftly, though there was no reason to push it. The Crows would be out of the mountains and on the prairie, ready for the big spring buffalo hunt. Cooper did not want to wander into their midst during that. He and Potts would wait and make their move as the Crows plodded along to rendezvous.

A week and a half later, Cooper and Potts watched from a wooded mountainside as the Crows made their slow way along an ages-old trail that paralleled the Bighorn River. As the days passed, the two mountain men kept watch from the cover of the woods when they could. If there was no protection of trees, they hung back, giving the tribe a day or so to move ahead. Twice, Cooper and Potts swung far west, then south, then east, and then north, coming onto the trail well ahead of the Crows. They secreted themselves, hoping to catch Lame Weasel, Black Dog, or Falling Stone away from the rest of the travelers, even if alone. They made small fires when they thought they were safe and made cold camps when they spent the night closer to the village. Every few days, the two would pull away to the east or west, whichever was more convenient at the time, to hunt. With a wooded strip along the river or a tributary or a series of grass-covered ridges and several miles between them and the Crows, they could hunt in relative safety.

A few times when overlooking the travelers, Cooper spotted Falling Stone, who could be identified by his short hair. Black Dog and Lame Weasel had no distinguishable features from a distance, though was sure he had spotted them at times since he had become familiar with the feathers and decorated shirts they wore. The mountain man was tempted several times to try to drop the Crows from where he was, but he knew it would be foolish. He was a great marksman, but at three hundred yards or more trying to hit a moving target would be impossible. So he waited and watched.

Cooper was grateful that Potts was not a bother as he feared the young man might be. Potts was still new to the mountains and as such might be prone to jabbering when danger lurked or making foolish mistakes. But the younger mountain man was quiet, listened well, traveled lightly, and shared the chores, including their nightly watch, without complaint.

Though Cooper's rage had not ebbed much, he made every effort to make sure it was not directed in any way toward Potts. Indeed, he found himself talking about his desire for revenge with his companion. It helped keep his fury in check yet still alive. As did the amusement he got from listening to Potts's pining over the fact that he did not have a woman. It did not seem to distract Potts much, though it was always on his mind —or at least on the tip of his tongue. Despite the amusement, such talk reminded Cooper of how much he missed Black Moon, and it kept his anger simmering just below the surface, ready to boil over when the time was right.

Their patience was finally rewarded when Falling Stone, along with six other warriors, including, Cooper was sure, Black Dog and Lame Weasel, rode west, deeper into the mountains.

"Dammit," Cooper snapped. He and Potts were north of the slow-moving village so they would have to move slowly until they got to the trail the Crow warriors had taken, letting the stragglers from the larger group move along.

"Don't fret, Hawl," Potts said. We got them sons a bitches now."

It took a few hours but they finally moved into the mountains on the hunt for the Crows, hurrying along a nonexistent trail through the trees.

Suddenly as they moved past one more tree, one to each side, they stumbled on the seven warriors, two of whom were butchering an elk, while the others rested against trees or looked to their ponies.

Shrugging off the surprise, Cooper and Potts jerked their rifles up and fired, killing the two men carving up the elk, one of them Lame Weasel. Cooper kicked his horse into movement, trampling the two bodies as he headed for the ponies amid the trees ahead of him. Two warriors, Falling Stone and the other whom Cooper was sure was Black Dog, swung onto their horses and charged off through the trees. The other ponies scattered into the forest.

Cooper jerked to a stop, grabbed a pistol, and shot one of the other warriors to his left, throwing off the arrow the Crow had just fired. He glanced over at Potts. The young mountain man had blasted a Crow with a pistol and was facing another, each with a tomahawk in hand.

Potts gave a swift look to Cooper, saw he was all right and noticed the last two Crows fleeing. "Go!" he yelled as he and the Crow closed in on each other.

Without hesitation, Cooper spurred his horse after the escaping warriors. The two split, and Cooper turned toward Falling Stone. He charged ahead, ducking branches, relying on his mount to miss trees and brush. The Indian was managing to keep twenty yards ahead of Cooper.

"Damn," Cooper spat, knowing he would not catch the Crow. The mountain man pulled his second pistol and fired. He didn't think he'd hit the warrior, but he hoped it might give the Indian's pony a scare, enough to knock it off its stride a bit. Instead, the lead ball hit one of the horse's back legs. The animal screamed in pain and went down, flinging Falling Stone over his head.

Cooper jerked his horse to a halt and was out of the saddle before the animal had fully stopped. He surged toward Falling Stone, drawing his tomahawk as he did.

The Indian was groggy and trying to stand. "You pus-eatin' son of a bitch," Cooper roared and he slammed the blade into one the of Crow's arms, nearly severing it. "Take my woman and that chil', you skunk-humpin' shit pile." He hacked the other arm. "Time for you to die, damn you." He chopped the side of the Crow's neck, and the Indian sank back. Not caring whether the warrior was dead yet, Cooper lifted his scalp and tossed it away, then took a couple of minutes to reload all three of his guns.

Then he was back in the saddle, racing after where he had seen the other Crow running. Suddenly an arrow tore through his shirt, barely scraping his side. He jammed to a stop, slid out of the saddle, rifle in hand, and ducked behind a tree. He fired when he saw the Indian's head for a second but succeeded only in throwing a bunch of bark into the air. He darted for another tree and caught an arrow in his side for his trouble, but it had hit a rib and did not penetrate his innards. He yanked it free and tossed it away.

Cooper squatted behind the tree, sweating and

pondering his next move. He did not see any movement from the trunk behind which the Crow was hiding, and he began to wonder a little. Then he heard a twig snap behind him, and he swung around in time to barely block the Crow's knife as it headed for his chest. The blade bit deep into his left forearm.

"Shit!" He jerked his arm, sending the knife flying. With his right hand he punched the Crow—whom he now saw was indeed Black Dog—on the side of the knee. The Indian fell. The mountain man surged to his feet and stomped the Crow's stomach. "Why didn't you just shoot me, you damn walkin' pile of buffler shit?"

"No arrows left," Black Dog croaked.

"That's some misfortune for you, boy." Cooper pulled a pistol and put a lead ball in the warrior's forehead. He lifted Black Dog's scalp, too, and threw it into the bushes. "You and Fallin' Stone ain't makin' it to the happy huntin' ground. Lame Weasel will be joinin' you in hell soon's I get back to him."

He reloaded his rifle and pistol, mounted his horse, got the rope rein to the Crow's pony, and rode back to where it had started.

Potts had a small fire going and some elk meat sizzling over the flames. He saw the blood on Cooper's sleeve. "You all right?"

Cooper nodded. "You're mighty cocky sittin' here with food goin'. What if I'd been those Crows?"

"I would've taken their scalps, too, just like I did with the rest of the ones here—except Lame Weasel's. I figured you'd want his yourself."

Another nod from Cooper. "Don't intend to keep it, though. Like the others, I'll toss it away like the garbage they were."

"That shines. But maybe you should piss on it. Or worse, make extra sure."

"Now that's a shinin' thought."

Potts nodded. "Now, sit. I'll bandage that arm up and we'll eat. Then you can relieve yourself on Lame Weasel's scalp."

"That shines, it purely does."

"Don't take long about it, though" Potts said with a grin. When Cooper looked at him in question, he added, "We best be on the move before long. I've fought enough Crows for one day."

"Me too, Zeke. Me too." He plunked himself down, tired and with a hollow feeling inside that he was not sure would go away anytime soon.

IN THE UNFORGIVING DEPTHS OF A MOUNTAIN WINTER, ONE MAN FACES AN UNYIELDING CHALLENGE FROM THE BLACKFEET TRIBE.

Following numerous battles, Hawley Cooper has grown weary of his confrontations with the Blackfeet. But with seemingly dozens of them swarming the valley and more arriving every day, he has no choice but to brace for another battle.

When a situation appears dire—an outnumbered contingent of mountain men pitted against a formidable horde of relentless Blackfeet warriors—Cooper clings to a single lifeline that involves confronting his adversaries head-on.

With the odds stacked against them, Cooper—accompanied by his trusted friend and frequent trapping partner, Zeke Potts, and an unlikely ally, Nez Perce—embark on a desperate mission amidst the unforgiving snow and biting cold of the Rocky Mountain winter. And should they emerge from this crucible of conflict, another, more personal mission awaits them.

Follow along as one man embarks on an epic journey of survival and redemption and discovers the unyielding strength of the human spirit.

AVAILABLE NOW

ALSO BY JOHN LEGG

Blood Trail Series

The Buckskin Series

Rocky Mountain Lawmen Series

The Arizona Territory Series

ABOUT THE AUTHOR

Though it might sound strange for someone who has published more than 60 Westerns, John Legg was born and raised in New Jersey. An Air Force veteran, he has traveled much of the West, having been a newspaper copy editor for more then 27 years in Phoenix. He works for a major newspaper's editing center in Florida. He has a BA from William Paterson College (now university) in Wayne, N.J., and an MSJ from the Medill School of Journalism at Northwestern University. He has two grown children and two young grandsons.

Made in the USA
Las Vegas, NV
22 May 2024

90242929R00173